If We Never Met

Whisper Lake #5

BARBARA FREETHY

BARBARA
FREETHY
—BOOKS—

Fog City Publishing

PRAISE FOR BARBARA FREETHY

"ALWAYS WITH ME is a heartwarming second chance romance, with a captivating mystery, that keeps you reading and wondering what happens next." Doni - Goodreads

"A beautiful second chance love story with a bit of drama and mystery. I loved it!" Peggy - Goodreads on ALWAYS WITH ME

"Tragedy haunts her, regrets shadow him and passion lures them into a mystery as dangerous as their feelings for each other. Freethy captivates with a sensuous game of tainted hearts and tempting romance. My Wildest Dream is a hotbed of intriguing storytelling. Brodie and Chelsea are sure to get under your skin." Isha C – Goodreads

"My Wildest Dream has just the right mix of romance and suspense to keep the reader interested from the first chapter to the final page. I loved everything about this book. Visiting Whisper Lake is like coming home and reuniting with old friends. You won't be disappointed. Norma – Bookbub

"I have just finished CAN'T FIGHT THE MOONLIGHT and WOW such an emotional book. The characters of Justin and Lizzie were so well written, with so much depth. There were scenes in this book that gave me a lump in my throat. Absolutely loved this book...and can't wait for the next one!" Booklovers Anonymous

"I love the Callaways! Heartwarming romance, intriguing suspense and sexy alpha heroes. What more could you want?" — *NYT Bestselling Author Bella Andre*

PRAISE FOR BARBARA FREETHY

"I adore the Callaways, a family we'd all love to have. Each new book is a deft combination of emotion, suspense and family dynamics." — *Bestselling Author Barbara O'Neal*

"Freethy is at the top of her form. Fans of Nora Roberts will find a similar tone here, framed in Freethy's own spare, elegant style." — *Contra Costa Times on Summer Secrets*

"Freethy hits the ground running as she kicks off another winning romantic suspense series...Freethy is at her prime with a superb combo of engaging characters and gripping plot." — *Publishers' Weekly on Silent Run*

"A fabulous, page-turning combination of romance and intrigue. Fans of Nora Roberts and Elizabeth Lowell will love this book." — *NYT Bestselling Author Kristin Hannah on Golden Lies*

"PERILOUS TRUST is a non-stop thriller that seamlessly melds jaw-dropping suspense with sizzling romance. Readers will be breathless in anticipation as this fast-paced and enthralling love story evolves and goes in unforeseeable directions." — *USA Today HEA Blog*

"Barbara Freethy is a master storyteller with a gift for spinning tales about ordinary people in extraordinary situations and drawing readers into their lives." — *Romance Reviews Today*

"Freethy has a gift for creating complex, appealing characters and emotionally involving, often suspenseful, sometimes magical stories." — *Library Journal on Suddenly One Summer*

IF WE NEVER MET

CHAPTER ONE

DANTE DEANGELIS SIGHED as the never-ending questions came
once more: *How are you feeling? What does the doctor say about
your shoulder? Will you be ready to pitch again before the end of
the season?* Or the worst question: *Will you be able to pitch the
way you once did?*

He didn't have answers for any of those questions, but that
didn't stop his friends, his teammates, the media, or his family
from asking them. Today's questions were coming from his
younger brother, Micah, whose call he should not have answered.

He shifted his phone to his other ear as Micah's voice pierced
through his reverie.

"What's the deal?" Micah demanded. "Nikki says you haven't
been talking to anyone, including her."

"I texted her last night. And I can't answer your questions,
Micah. It's too soon. I have my first rehab assessment tomorrow
morning, with my official therapy sessions starting on Monday."

"And you're going to stay in Colorado to do that?"

"Yes. There's a new rehab center in Whisper Lake, and my
orthopedic surgeon highly recommended it. Plus, I like being far
away. It makes it…easier."

It felt absurd to say easier because nothing about his possible career-ending shoulder injury was easy. Whether he'd be back this season or never was the big question. But right now, he could only focus on what was right in front of him, and that was three weeks of intense rehab at a state-of-the-art facility. The fact that the rehab center was in a mountain resort town was a bonus. He'd been sitting in Micky's Bar and Grill for the past twenty minutes, and not one person had come up to ask him for an autograph. That felt both shocking and amazing.

"Dante!"

"Sorry, what did you say?"

"I'm worried about you. Why don't you come home? You don't have to stay with Dad. You can hang at my apartment. We have rehab centers in San Francisco."

"This one is the best. It's brand new. It's going to be part of a new Olympic Training Center in Whisper Lake, and they have therapists who are specifically skilled in dealing with professional athletes. I will be getting the best care, and I like being away from a big city."

He looked up as a loud group of guys entered the bar. They appeared to be a softball team with the bar's name scrawled across their jerseys, just the kind of men who might know exactly who he was. Luckily, they were too caught up in conversation to notice him. So far, he'd managed to stay under the radar, but that wouldn't last forever.

"Where are you?" Micah asked. "It sounds loud."

"A bar."

"Well, that's good. I was thinking you were sitting in some hotel room alone on a Friday night. Where are you staying?"

"An inn owned by my doctor's sister. I would have preferred a more impersonal hotel, but Grayson insisted that Lizzie would give me privacy. We'll see. She does make awesome chocolate chip cookies every afternoon."

"Is she single?"

"Engaged. And I'm here to heal, not find myself a date."

"All right. Well, I gotta go. Call me if you get bored. Or if you want company…"

"Thanks. But you're busy with your food truck. You don't need to babysit me."

"Not so busy. The truck has some problems."

"What's going on?"

"I can't get into it now. We'll talk soon."

"All right." He set his phone on the table and picked up his beer. He was thinking about getting some food to go with it when a very attractive brunette approached his table with an uncertain look. Apparently, he wasn't as unrecognizable as he'd hoped. She had on a short, silky floral dress that clung to her curves and showed off her tanned legs. Her dark-brown hair fell past her shoulders in thick waves. His gut tightened, but it wasn't because he wanted her to go away.

"You're Danny, right?" she said.

It wasn't the first time his name had been skewed. "Yes."

"Oh, good." Relief ran through her wide-set, big brown eyes. She pulled out the chair across from him and sat down. "I'm Keira, but you probably figured that out, since you've been waiting for me. I'm sorry I'm late. I had a customer come into the shop right at closing." She paused. "And now I'm talking too much."

He was a little bemused by not only how much she was talking but also how pretty she was, with a bright, self-deprecating smile curving her very kissable mouth.

"Can I get you a drink, Keira?" the waitress asked as she stopped by the table.

"Hi, Joanne. I'd love a glass of Merlot," Keira replied.

"You got it," Joanne said, glancing back at him.

"I'm fine," he said at her unspoken question.

"So, your turn to talk," Keira said.

He honestly had no idea what to say. It was becoming clear that she had no idea who he was. She hadn't confused Dante with Danny. She'd taken him for someone else entirely.

"I'd love to hear what you think of Whisper Lake," she added. "You said you recently got to town?"

"I did." He had finally gotten a question he could answer. "I like the town. I haven't seen a lot yet, but the mountains and the lake are spectacular."

She nodded, pride in her eyes. "It's one of the prettiest spots in the country. But I'm prejudiced—I was born here."

"Have you always lived here?"

"No. I went to New York for college and stayed there for my dream job. I was going to be a fashion designer." Shadows entered her eyes. "But my mom got into an accident and needed not only care but someone to help with her real-estate business, so I came home. That was six years ago."

"That's very generous. It sounds like you gave up a lot."

"I'm not sure it was that much. I was just getting started in the business, and I was mostly doing grunt work at a fashion house. When I came home, I got my real-estate license and took over my mom's business."

"Wait a second. I thought you said you worked at a store."

"I do. I opened a clothing boutique two years ago. I've been juggling both careers since then." She tilted her head to the right as she gave him a thoughtful look. "Didn't I mention that when we were texting?"

Before he had to answer that question, the waitress set down Keira's wine as well as crackers and dip. He really should tell Keira that she was at the wrong table with the wrong guy, but it was actually nice to talk to someone who had no idea who he was or what he'd just been through.

"Micky sent his famous artichoke and crab dip over—on the house," the waitress said. "He said he owes you, Keira, for finding a rental for his cousin."

Keira waved a dismissive hand. "That was no big deal but tell him thanks." As the waitress left, Keira picked up a cracker. "Have you had Micky's special dip?"

"No."

"Then prepare to be amazed."

"Amazed, huh?"

"I am not exaggerating." She popped the cracker in her mouth and then gave him such a look of intense satisfaction, his whole body tightened. "Give it a try."

He took a cracker and lathered it with dip. The bite was absolutely perfect—hot, spicy, and creamy.

"Well?"

"I'm amazed," he admitted.

"Told you. If you want to continue to be impressed, you should order the fish tacos. They are out of this world."

"I'll keep that in mind. So, you have two careers going, huh? How do you find the time?"

"I have help. And it's not really two careers, more like three. I also design for friends and family. Still thinking about how to get the custom design business off the ground."

"Busy woman. How do you juggle it all?"

"Sometimes not very well. It's super busy right now. I have a wedding coming up on July seventh for one of my best friends, Hannah Stark. I'm doing her gown and the bridesmaids' dresses. I'm also in the wedding party, so I have to make sure everything is perfect."

"And yet you find time to date," he mused.

"Actually, I don't date very often, but my friends have been pressuring me to get out there. Hannah, in particular, would love for me to have a plus one at her wedding," she said candidly. "That's why I got on the app last week and then you popped up." She frowned. "You don't look exactly like your photo, though."

"Better or worse?" he asked curiously.

"Better."

"That's good."

"Tell me about yourself. You haven't said too much. I know you're changing careers and you're giving up being an attorney to become a writer. I think that's great. I admire people who go after their dreams."

"I admire that, too," he said soberly. Talking about dreams just reminded him how close he was to losing his.

"Danny?" she queried with concern. "You suddenly look serious."

"Sorry. Just thinking about dreams."

"It's something I think about, too. Sometimes they can come true and sometimes they just stay dreams."

Now she was the one who looked solemn. "You mentioned your mother was in an accident, and that's why you came back from New York. How is she doing now?"

"She's much better. She had a head injury, and it was a long road back, but she's been improving every year. I'm starting to feel like she's going to be okay."

"I'm glad to hear that."

"Me, too. The days after her accident were the scariest days of my life, and that is an understatement."

He was surprised at how easily they'd fallen into a personal conversation with so much depth. It certainly wasn't his usual first-date conversation, but he was enjoying it. "Was your father able to help?"

"No. My dad died before I was a year old. I don't even remember him. We lived with my grandmother during most of my childhood. Unfortunately, she passed away when I was fourteen, and then it was just my mother and me." She sipped her wine. "I'm talking too much. What about you? Are you an only child or do you have siblings?"

"I have three brothers."

She arched a brow in surprise. "That's a lot of testosterone in one family."

"You could say that."

"Where are you in the line-up?"

"I'm the second oldest."

"So, a middle child."

"Yes."

"Did your parents keep trying for a girl?"

"My mom always wanted a daughter, but she never got one."

"Are your parents alive and well?"

"No. Like you, I grew up with mostly one parent and some grandparents. My mom died when I was twelve."

"I'm sorry. How did she die?"

He was actually surprised by the question. Most people stopped talking when he brought up an uncomfortable subject like his mother's death. But Keira was gazing at him with genuine, compassionate interest.

"She had cancer. It was aggressive and fast. One minute she was baking cookies and volunteering at school, the next minute she was in a hospital bed in our living room. I hated coming home and seeing her there. It felt so wrong. Even after she passed away, I went into the house through the back door for at least another year, so I wouldn't have to remember..." He shook his head and cleared his throat. "That was too much information." He couldn't believe he'd shared such a personal story with her.

"We're getting to know each other. There's never too much information. I didn't realize we'd both lost parents. Although, your situation is much different. I never knew my father, so while I felt the loss of not having two parents, I didn't know my dad. I didn't have good or bad memories of him."

"It sounds like you have a good relationship with your mother."

"We've always been tight."

"It says a lot about you that you gave up your career to come home and take care of her."

"I never had a second thought about it. She would have done it for me." Keira took a breath. "I don't talk this much normally. I guess I'm a little out of practice when it comes to dating. What about you? Do you do this a lot?"

"This? I almost never do this," he said with a dry smile. "Online dating has always felt awkward to me."

"Me, too, but it's one way to meet someone."

"It is one way," he agreed.

She sipped her wine, then set her glass down. "Tell me about your novel. You said it's going to be a thriller. How far along are you?"

He took a long sip of beer, knowing he had to tell her the truth. But as soon as he did, she'd probably be embarrassed. Or she might be angry that he'd been stringing her along when her real date was probably waiting for her somewhere in the bar. In fact, he was starting to feel like an ass for not having told her before now.

As he opened his mouth to say something, the waitress interrupted them once more. She gave them an odd look. "Uh, Keira, there's a guy who says he's waiting for you, that he's your date. He asked me if I'd seen you."

"What are you talking about? This is my date," Keira said, tipping her head in his direction.

"Well, he's over there." The waitress pointed toward a brown-haired guy sitting alone at a table for two near the front door. "He said his name is Danny."

As the waitress moved away, Keira gave him a wary look. "Your name is Danny, too?"

"Actually, it's Dante. I thought you got it wrong when you first sat down, but I wasn't sure."

"Wait. So, you're not my date?"

"No, I'm not."

"Why didn't you say something?"

"I don't know. You started talking, and you're really pretty, and uh, yeah, I don't have a good excuse."

She flushed. "Well, I'll have to add tonight to one of my more embarrassing moments."

"Don't feel that way. I enjoyed talking to you."

"I'm an idiot. I thought you were a great listener, but you had no idea what to say, because you're not Danny."

"You're not an idiot. I should have corrected you. I was about to, if that helps."

"Not really. You shouldn't have waited so long. We talked about our dead parents."

"I know. That was weird. I haven't actually talked about that with anyone outside my family."

"Why did you tell me?"

"I honestly have no idea."

She stared back at him with a mix of confusion and embarrassment. "Are you meeting a date tonight?"

"No. I just came in for dinner. The innkeeper where I'm staying recommended this place."

"Are you staying at the Firefly Inn?"

"I am."

"Lizzie, the owner, is one of my best friends. You'll love it there."

"It's very nice."

"How long have you been in town?"

"I just got in last night."

"Oh." She drew in a breath and let it out. "I should go and talk to the real Danny."

"Probably. I hope he's fun and plus-one material."

"Me, too." She got up, then hesitated. "Are you even single?"

His pause was a second too long.

She shook her head, anger entering her brown eyes. "Really? You're married?"

"No, I'm not married or engaged," he said quickly.

"But…"

"I am seeing someone. It's not serious." He didn't know why he'd said that. It wasn't like he was going to date Keira. He was in town for three weeks. And most of that time would be spent in rehab.

"I wonder if she knows that," Keira said dryly. Then she walked away.

He watched her greet Danny and take a seat. She had her back to him, and he couldn't see her expression as she spoke to her date, but it didn't feel like she had the same energy with this guy that she'd had with him.

He felt somewhat happy about that.

Danny was nowhere near as attractive as Dante. He had similar features and his hair was the same shade of brown. But Danny didn't have Dante's sharp blue eyes or full, sexy mouth, or deliciously appealing stubble on a strong, masculine jaw.

However, Danny was nice. And he did talk more than Dante. In fact, he spoke endlessly about himself, his former career in law, and now his new writing project, which seemed to be based on some of the cases he'd worked on.

Danny was a Colorado native, who had grown up in Denver and moved to the lake to find more solitude and time for writing. He was an only child like her, so they had that in common. But he didn't ask her much about herself, except to wonder if her mom required a lot of medical care and her full-time attention. She didn't know if he was digging to see how busy she was, although she could have told him it wasn't her mom who put a lot of demands on her time, it was her businesses.

As he spoke more about his book plot, her mind wandered to Dante. She'd deliberately sat with her back to him, but over the past several minutes, she'd been inching her chair sideways, as if to stretch out her legs, but it was really just to get another look at him.

She had to admit when she'd sat down at his table and caught his gaze, she'd felt butterflies in her chest. Her breath had sped up and her palms felt sweaty. She hadn't met anyone who'd made her feel like that in a very long time.

She finally managed to turn her head and take another quick peek at him. He was talking to Joanne, and he had a burger in front of him now. It looked good. *He* looked good. She inwardly sighed and then turned away, forcing herself to give Danny a smile.

Dante had a girlfriend, or at least someone he was seeing. And aside from the fact that she knew he had three brothers and had lost his mother at a young age, she didn't really know anything else about him. Since he was staying at the inn, he was probably just passing through town. Lizzie would know. But she wasn't going to ask her friend. There was no point to that.

"Do you want to order food?" Danny asked, his question interrupting her thoughts.

She should say yes. She should give him a chance, but she wasn't feeling him at all. And even if she wasn't caught up in the blue-eyed Dante, she had a lot of work waiting for her. But wasn't that always her excuse for not dating? "Sure," she said finally.

"Great. What's good here?"

"The fish tacos are excellent."

"Not a fish fan."

"Well, everything is tasty. We could share a pizza."

He glanced down at the menu. "Why don't we each get our own thing?"

"Then I'll get the tacos." She already wished she could change her answer about having a meal. But it was just dinner. She'd survive.

While Danny took several more minutes to study the menu, she glanced at Dante. He'd finished his burger and was sipping the last of his beer. He gave her a nod and a small smile. She kind of wished he'd throw her a life raft, because she could really use one.

She turned her attention back to Danny. "What are you going to go with?"

"Still thinking. I'm torn between the Thai noodles and the Cobb salad."

"Very different choices."

"What to do, what to do…" He drummed his fingernails on the table as he debated.

Five minutes later, she was still waiting for him to decide. If it took him this long to make a menu decision, she couldn't imagine how long it had taken him to decide to quit being an attorney. In fact, she was kind of shocked he'd actually done it.

"What made you change careers?" she asked. "Was it a quick decision or did you think about it for a long time?"

For a moment, she thought he might pick up on the irony of her question, but instead he set his menu aside. "It was a decision that was years in the making. I went into law to follow in my father's footsteps. I didn't like being a lawyer, but I just hung in there, thinking it was what I should do. After my dad died, I went into work one day, and I realized I couldn't do it anymore. I had to do something I was interested in."

"Then your dad's death was the impetus."

"It's not like he forced me to be a lawyer; I just didn't want to let him down."

"That makes sense. At least now you're doing what you want."

"I think so. My mom is a great writer, so I have it in my genes."

"I didn't realize your mother was also a writer." His father died, so he quit the job that he'd done to follow in his father's footsteps and now he was following in his mother's footsteps. It seemed like he was better at following than forging his own path.

"She writes historical fiction, so we're in different genres." He glanced back at the menu. "Maybe I'll get those fish tacos."

"You said you don't like fish," she reminded him.

"But you said they were good."

"They are, but not if you don't like seafood."

He shrugged. "I like it if it's done well."

He liked it because he couldn't make a decision on his own. She tapped her fingers restlessly on her thighs, sending another look in Dante's direction. He had just paid the check. He was leaving. It was just going to be her and Danny now.

"Maybe I won't do the fish tacos," Danny said. "Salad might be better. It's warm tonight."

She bit back a frustrated groan. At this rate, they'd be here until midnight.

As a shadow fell over the table, she looked up, surprised to see Dante standing next to her.

"I'm sorry to interrupt," he said. "But there's a problem at your shop, Keira."

"What?" she asked in confusion.

"The burglar alarm is going off. You need to take care of it."

She looked at him in astonishment. She didn't have an alarm, so she knew it wasn't going off. "Okay. Thanks for letting me know." She looked at Danny. "I'm sorry. I need to check on my store."

"Someone else can't do that?"

"I'm the owner." She grabbed her purse and stood up. "It was nice to meet you."

"I'll text you."

"Great," she said, as she followed Dante out of the restaurant.

When they got outside, she turned and shook her head. "I can't believe you made that up."

"You sent me an SOS, I answered. At least, I thought it was an SOS. Was I wrong?" he queried.

"No, you weren't wrong." Now that they were standing, she suddenly realized how tall and athletically built he was, with broad shoulders and long, lean legs. More butterflies danced through her stomach. "Thank you. I was feeling a little desperate."

"Are you also feeling a little hungry?" He held up the bag in his hand.

"Is that what's left of your burger?"

"Fish tacos. I ordered them for you."

She was shocked. "No way. Why?"

He tipped his head. "I felt bad for not telling you that you had the wrong guy."

She had a feeling she'd actually had the right guy, but he was taken.

"Forgive me? You did say the tacos are out of this world."

"And yet you ordered a burger," she couldn't help pointing out.

"Next time I'll get the tacos. I was craving some red meat tonight." He handed her the bag.

"Thank you for the food and for the save. He was a nice guy, but I think it was going to take him another hour to decide what he wanted to eat."

"I hate people who take forever to read a menu," he said lightly.

"Me, too. And I gave him recommendations. I even suggested we share something, but I don't think he's a guy who shares his food."

"Very telling."

"I think so," she said. "If you share, you get to eat two things instead of one."

"You don't have to convince me. I love to share."

She licked her lips, wanting to keep Dante talking, even though she shouldn't. "Do you want to walk down to the park, keep me company while I eat my tacos? There's a nice view of the lake from there."

"That sounds good." He suddenly swore, his gaze darting across the street. "Dammit. Sorry. I gotta go."

Her jaw dropped as he took off running across the parking lot. A van came to a squealing stop not far from her, and a photographer jumped out, racing after Dante, but he had already disappeared around the corner of the building.

What was going on? Who the hell was Dante?

CHAPTER TWO

KEIRA REALLY SHOULDN'T BE CHASING down a man who had acted in a shady manner, not just once but twice, but she couldn't stop herself. She'd eaten her tacos in the car, hoping that Dante would come back. When he hadn't, she'd decided to drive across town to the Firefly Inn and talk to her friend Lizzie Cole.

But she was having second thoughts as she entered the inn. It really wasn't her business who he was. Dante had a girlfriend. And she had enough distractions in her life; she didn't need anymore. But she couldn't get him out of her head, and she knew she wasn't going to until she figured out who he was.

"Keira, what are you doing here?" Lizzie asked in surprise. Lizzie was an attractive woman with blonde hair, blue eyes, and a smile that warmed up a room. "I thought you had a big date tonight."

"That news traveled fast. I only decided to go this afternoon."

"I ran into Hannah earlier. She told me she'd finally convinced you to accept a date."

"Yes. She wants me to work on getting a plus one for her wedding."

"How was he? I'm guessing not so good, since it's…" Lizzie looked at the grandfather clock in the hallway. "Seven forty-five."

"He was very, very boring."

"Then you need some wine. Come into the living room."

"Do you have time?"

"Yes. Most of the guests are out for the evening and those who are in seem to be happy in their rooms. I could use a glass of wine, too. It's been a long week."

"Problems?" she asked, as she followed Lizzie into the living room of the inn, which had two seating areas, one with three couches in front of a large bay window and the other with two couches and two large chairs in front of a fireplace with tall bookshelves on either side. The inn had originally been a private estate and while it had been remodeled extensively over the years by several different owners, it still had a lot of old-fashioned charm.

"No big problems, just a million little ones," Lizzie replied, stepping behind a bar. "Red or white?"

"Red."

"Perfect. Because I still have almost a full bottle from our earlier cocktail hour." Lizzie poured them two glasses of wine, and then they sat down on a couch by the window. "Tell me about your date."

"There's not much to say. Danny seemed interesting enough when we were texting. He was a lawyer, but now he's writing a novel, which is why he moved to Whisper Lake."

"Not the first lawyer turned writer we've met."

"No, it's almost becoming a cliché. I like creative people who make things, so I thought I'd give it a shot. He was nice enough. A big talker, though."

"One of those who never asks you a question about yourself?"

"Exactly. He chatted on and on about himself. And he was so indecisive. We looked at the menu for like fifteen minutes and he could not make a decision. It's not rocket science. But maybe I was just being too impatient."

"You just didn't click."

"We definitely did not click."

"Well, just because he didn't work out doesn't mean someone else won't."

Dante's image ran through her head. "Actually, I did meet someone that I found myself clicking with right away."

"Now that sounds interesting," Lizzie said, with a gleam in her eyes. "Who and where? Give me the details."

"It happened at Micky's. When I first got there, I mistook another guy for my date. He had brown hair, and he was sitting alone. I was a little late, so I was rushing. I asked him if he was Danny, and he said yes, so I sat down and just started rambling like a crazy person. I thought he was a really good listener, because he didn't say much. But he was so attractive he made me nervous, and I couldn't shut up."

"What happened?"

"Joanne came over to the table and told me that my date was waiting for me by the door. I was so embarrassed. Then the guy told me his name was Dante, not Danny, and that he probably should have told me earlier."

"Wait a second. Dante? Dante DeAngelis?"

"He didn't say his last name, but he did say he was staying here."

"He arrived last night. I actually suggested he try Micky's for dinner."

"That's what he said. So, what's his deal, Lizzie?"

Lizzie hesitated, her body stiffening. "What do you mean?"

Her gaze narrowed at Lizzie's reaction. "Who is he? And why is someone with a camera chasing him?"

"There was someone with a camera chasing him?"

"Yes, we walked out of Micky's together, and this guy jumped out of a van with a camera, and Dante took off."

"Oh, that's too bad."

"Why is it too bad?"

"Because he came to Whisper Lake hoping for privacy."

"Why? Is he an actor? A reality TV star? A billionaire? What?"

"I'm sorry, Keira, I can't tell you. He's a guest, and my inn was recommended to him by my brother, Grayson, who said I could guarantee him privacy."

She needed to respect Lizzie's decision, but now she was even more insanely curious about him.

"I'm sure if you take out your phone, you can figure out who he is pretty quickly," Lizzie added. "I'm surprised you didn't already try that."

"I didn't have his last name."

"Oh, good point."

"He was really nice to me. He actually rescued me from the real Danny. He saw the boring time I was having, and he came over to the table and made up an excuse for me to leave, saying the alarm on my store was going off."

Lizzie raised an eyebrow. "Seriously?"

"Yes. And the story gets better. He ordered me fish tacos to go. I'd actually been raving about them when we were talking, and he remembered. It's so rare that someone would do something like that. He said he felt bad for not having told me he wasn't Danny as soon as he realized my mistake."

"I wonder why he didn't tell you."

"I don't think I gave him a chance. I couldn't stop talking. We just had this instant connection." She paused, licking her lips. "I think he felt it, too. That's why he didn't cut me off."

Concern moved across Lizzie's now serious expression.

"What?" Keira asked.

"You need to leave Dante alone, Keira."

"Why?"

"He has a girlfriend."

"He did mention he'd been seeing someone, but he didn't call her his girlfriend."

"Well, the media calls her that. There are a lot of pictures of them together online. That's all I can say."

"Fine. I'll either look him up, or I'll just forget about him."

"Somehow, I don't think you're going to forget about him," Lizzie said dryly. "I haven't seen you this excited about a guy in forever. I'm sorry he's taken. I'm also sorry that he's not someone who's going to be in town for more than a few weeks."

"I figured he was just passing through." She felt a wave of

depression at Lizzie's words. It was stupid to feel such disappointment over a guy she'd spoken to for about fifteen minutes. She
needed to change the subject. "What's new with you? Where's
Justin tonight?"

"He and Zach are going over plans for Justin's new office
building. I'm glad you stopped by, even if it was just to get dirt on
Dante. Or maybe you thought you'd run into him?"

"He did leave me in an abrupt and mysterious way. If he'd just
said goodbye and walked away, I wouldn't have thought twice
about it. But he literally bolted out of sight. It made me curious.
Not that I have time to be curious. I should be in the shop, working
on Hannah's dress."

"I thought that was done, and you were down to the bridesmaids' dresses."

"No. Hannah's dress is not quite perfect yet. It needs something
and I haven't been able to figure out what."

"Are you sure it's not perfect? Hannah said last week she loved
it. Maybe you're being too hard on yourself."

"I just can't let her walk down the aisle in something that isn't
the best it can be."

Lizzie gave her a thoughtful look. "You don't usually get stuck
or blocked on design. You did Chelsea's wedding dress in a few
weeks and her gown for the awards show in less than a week."

"I know. I'm not sure what's wrong with me."

"Maybe because it's Hannah. You two have been friends since
you were kids."

"That might be part of it."

"Or you're burning out, trying to do too many things: selling
real estate, running your shop, designing clothes... It's a lot, Keira."

"Says the woman who always does too many things."

"True. But I'm learning to delegate, mostly because Justin
screams that word into my ear several times a day."

"How romantic."

Lizzie grinned. "He says other things, too. But seriously, he
showed me how to prioritize the things that really matter. It may
not always make the most practical business sense, but if it's part

of my vision, my dream, then I just have to decide what else I can give up, because I can't do everything. And you can't, either."

"I know, but I can't let go of anything, at least not yet. It's not the right time."

"I get it. I wish I could help. You suddenly look exhausted. I'm tempted to tell you about Dante just to put the light back in your eyes."

She gave her a tired smile. "That was a fun distraction while it lasted. I should go."

"Why don't you just give yourself a night off? See how the dress looks in the morning."

"That's not the worst idea. I also need to go through the real-estate listings for a new client, an old friend of my mother's, although I had never heard of him until he showed up at our house last night. He said he's staying here at the inn, too. Mark Langley."

"Yes, he is. I didn't realize he knew your mother. He's moving here for his new job at the rehab center. He seems very nice."

"Does he? I thought it was weird that he dropped by our house without warning. I don't know how he got my mom's address. He didn't ask you for it?"

"No. If he had, I wouldn't have given it out. But he probably could have asked just about anyone in town." Lizzie paused. "What are you worried about? Do you think he's lying about their past? Did your mom recognize him? What does she have to say?"

"He's not lying. He came with a high school yearbook. My mom did not recognize him at first, but when he said his name, I could see the recognition run through her eyes. And then she smiled and gave him a big hug. She invited him in, and they talked for about a half hour. I didn't catch all of it, because I was on the phone with Brenda, walking her through some contract issues. But at the end of their conversation, my mom asked me to help him find a house."

"Surely you can pass that off to Brenda."

"I suggested it, but my mom was insistent I take care of it, since Mark is a personal friend. If he hadn't had the yearbook with him, I would have been more suspicious, but it was hard to argue when I saw them dressed up as a cowboy and a cowgirl at a high school Halloween dance. And when they started talking, they did seem to share the same memories."

"I thought your mom had trouble with her memory."

"She does, but she has been improving the last year. She has fewer and fewer lapses."

"Maybe Mark will be good for her. Remind her of things she has forgotten. He can fill in some blanks that no one else here in Whisper Lake can."

"That's true."

"But?"

"I don't know, Lizzie. My gut tells me there's something off about him."

"Well, I'm not going to argue with your gut."

As Lizzie finished speaking, the front door opened, and Keira heard voices. A moment later, she was shocked when her mom, Ruth Blake, walked into the room with the man she'd just been talking about. Mark Langley was a tall, silver-haired man wearing dark slacks and a button-down shirt. He was handsome, for an older man. Her mother looked unusually good, too. She had put on a floral shift dress that she had definitely not been wearing earlier in the day.

She got to her feet as her mother gave her a somewhat guilty smile.

"Keira, I thought you were on a date," her mom said.

"And I thought you were at home watching a movie."

"I was, but then Mark called. He said he'd pick me up and we could have some wine here at the inn. I just thought how lovely that would be. I haven't been here in so long. How are you, Lizzie?" Her mom gave Lizzie a warm smile.

"I'm good, Mrs. Blake."

"Oh, please call me Ruth."

"What kind of wine would you like?" Lizzie asked.

"What do you have open?"

"I have a nice pinot."

"That's perfect."

"That will be fine for me, too," Mark said. "And Lizzie, I'm happy to pay you for the bottle. I just thought we could talk better here than in a bar with all the young people."

"Sometimes it's hard for me to concentrate when there is a lot of noise," Ruth said.

"I hope you'll both join us," Mark added.

She wanted to join them, because she did not like anything that was going on. This Mark Langley seemed to be rather aggressive in his desire to get to know her mother again, and she didn't know what to think about that. In fact, the idea of her mother even having a drink with a man seemed completely foreign. Even before her accident, she'd rarely gone out on a date. She'd always said she was happy with her business, her friends, and her daughter.

But lately her mom had seemed at loose ends. She was well enough to feel bored, to want to do more than she'd been capable of doing even a year ago. That was a good thing. But Mark Langley didn't seem like a good thing. He seemed like a man with an agenda, and she needed to find out what that agenda was.

CHAPTER THREE

DANTE MADE his way back to the Firefly Inn around nine o'clock, having successfully evaded the photographer chasing him. He knew he'd stunned Keira by his sudden departure, but he hadn't had time to explain. Nor had he wanted her to get caught by the camera. Her image would have been splashed across multiple sites, and she'd be pegged as his mystery woman. That wouldn't be good for either of them.

It also wouldn't be good for Nikki. She would have to answer questions about a mythical affair between Keira and him. He knew how fast an innocent moment could blow up into something ridiculous and crazy and yet still be believed by hundreds of thousands of people.

Avoiding that problem had been the best decision he'd made tonight.

The worst decision had been talking to Keira for as long as he had and then buying her fish tacos and rescuing her from her date. Although, he still wished they could have taken a walk down to the lake and gotten to know each other better, because he'd enjoyed talking to her. But that would have been stupid. It wasn't just that he was seeing someone; it was also because what he'd enjoyed most in their short conversation was that she hadn't had any idea who he was, and they'd been able to talk without the shadow of his big life hanging over them. She'd probably figured out who he was by now.

It was just as well. He'd come to Whisper Lake to rehab his shoulder and get his life back. Nothing could get in the way of that goal.

As he neared the inn, he saw lights on throughout the building and several cars in the lot. While he appreciated the charming, homey feeling of the inn, he probably should have stayed in a hotel where he didn't have to greet whoever was at reception or say hello to the other guests. But it was too late now.

When he walked into the lobby, there was no one at reception, but there were voices in the living room, and one of those spun his head around. Keira was sitting on a couch next to Lizzie Cole, the manager of the inn. Across from them was an older couple.

Had Keira come to the inn to track him down? Maybe she'd always intended to come to the inn after her date, but it seemed somewhat coincidental. On the other hand, this wouldn't be the first time a woman had showed up at his hotel. It had happened more times than he could count.

"Dante," Lizzie called, as she saw him standing there.

He silently cursed himself for not having immediately gone upstairs.

Lizzie got to her feet and walked into the foyer to greet him. "Would you like some wine? I also have cookies if you haven't had dessert."

"No, thanks. I don't want to interrupt. I'm just going to go to my room."

"You wouldn't be interrupting, and in case you're wondering, I didn't tell Keira anything about you."

"Did she ask?"

Lizzie met his questioning gaze. "Yes. She told me about the mix-up at Micky's. I told her that I would respect your privacy. But she does know your name now, so…"

"So she'll figure it out."

"At some point."

"I appreciate your discretion."

"You should, because Keira is one of my best friends. And we usually share everything, but she respected our proprietor-guest confidentiality agreement."

He smiled. "Is that a thing?"

She grinned back at him. "It is at my inn. But why don't you join us for a drink?"

He was still debating his answer when Keira joined them. She gave him an uncertain look. "Hi, Dante."

"Keira."

As they stared at each other, Lizzie cleared her throat, then moved back into the living room.

"Is everything all right?" Keira asked. "You were being chased by a photographer the last time I saw you."

"I managed to get away. I'm sure he snapped some pics of my back, but they won't sell without the money shot."

"Your face?"

"Yes."

She gave him a long look. "Should I recognize you? Clearly, you're some sort of celebrity. But I don't know who you are, and Lizzie won't tell me."

"You didn't look me up?"

"I don't automatically go online when I meet someone to figure out who they are."

"You just came here instead."

She gave him a sheepish smile. "Okay, you got me. I was curious after the way you left. Want to save me the trouble of looking you up online?"

"I'm a baseball player."

"Really? What team?"

"Miami."

"What are you doing here?"

"Rehabbing my shoulder at the Whisper Lake Rehabilitation Center."

"I didn't realize you were injured."

"You wouldn't know it until I tried to throw a curve ball. But I had surgery six weeks ago in Denver, and Dr. Grayson Cole prescribed rehab here in Whisper Lake."

Her eyes filled with understanding. "That makes sense. Grayson is Lizzie's older brother. I've never met him, but I've heard he's a brilliant doctor."

"Hopefully his brilliance will allow me to return to my career."

She gave him a sympathetic smile. "You must be itching to do that. It's the middle of the season, isn't it?"

"Yes. I'm trying to get back on the mound before the season is over."

"I'm guessing if you have paparazzi chasing you, that you must be really good."

He tipped his head in acknowledgment. "My team won the World Series last year, and I was the winning pitcher. I take it you're not a baseball fan."

"I've been to a few games in Denver to watch the Rockies play, but I don't really follow the sport, or any sport for that matter. Sorry."

"No need to apologize. I came to Whisper Lake hoping for privacy, but it doesn't look like that will happen. Someone tipped off the press."

"Does it really matter if they get a photo of you?"

He smiled at her question. "It's not the photo, it's how it's manipulated, the narrative it suddenly tells, a story that might be completely far from the truth. In a photo of us together, you would be my mystery woman. You would be the reason why I'm in Whisper Lake and not rehabbing in Miami. Your life would be invaded by press. You'd find yourself answering questions about a man you just happened to be standing next to when the camera clicked. But no one would care, because they'd already been told a story that was far more interesting and completely made up."

Her eyes had widened with his every word—her big, beautiful brown eyes that were so expressive, he could read her every emotion. She really was exceptionally pretty, but in a different way than most women he met these days. There was something very real and natural about her. If she had makeup on, he couldn't see it. Not that she needed it.

"I guess a picture of us together would be difficult for the woman you're seeing," she said slowly. "Is that what you're really worried about?"

"That's part of it."

"Wouldn't she believe you if you told her the truth?"

"That I'd bought fish tacos for a woman after pretending to be her date and then rescued her from her real date?"

"Good point. That story does sound…fishy."

He grinned at her words. "Exactly."

"Has she dealt with this kind of thing before, photos of you with another woman?"

"No. We haven't been seeing each other that long."

"How long is long?"

"Two months before I got injured. Since then, we haven't seen much of each other." *Was that relief that entered her gaze?*

"I guess that isn't long enough to build complete trust in each other," Keira said. "But if you have a good relationship, I'm sure she'd believe you."

"Nikki knows how the media can spin a picture, so she'd probably believe me. I just didn't want to deal with all that. So, I ran."

"You were fast. I didn't even see where you went."

"I ducked around the bar, went in and out of a few other places, and then ended up at a coffeehouse for the last hour where I got to hear bad guitar and even worse poems."

Her smile blossomed across her face once more. "It's open mic night at the Java Blast."

"There was one guy who played the sax who was good, but everyone else should have saved their performance for the shower or their living room."

"I think it's brave when people take the stage and put themselves out there."

"Have you ever done it?"

"No way. I am good at a lot of things, but not music or poetry."

She gave him a speculative look. "Do you have more talents than being able to throw a baseball?"

Before he could answer, a loud burst of laughter drew their attention to the living room. "I'm keeping you from your friends," he said.

She frowned as the older woman continued to laugh and the man sitting next to her on the couch put his hand on her shoulder.

"No way. No touching," Keira muttered.

"Excuse me?"

"Sorry. I need to interrupt that."

"Interrupt what?"

"Whatever that man is attempting to do with my mother." She stomped into the living room.

Her comment intrigued him, so once again he opted to follow her rather than go to his room. Keira had told him that her mom was ill, but this woman looked vibrant and happy. Keira, on the other hand, looked like a storm cloud about to burst.

"Mom," Keira said. "Can I talk to you for a minute?"

"What about, dear?" her mother asked.

"Why don't we go to the other room?"

"That would be rude. Why don't you introduce me to this handsome man you've been talking to?"

Keira followed her mother's gaze to him. "Oh, this is Dante."

"Hello, Dante, I'm Ruth," the woman said. "Keira's mother."

"You two look like sisters."

"And you're quite charming. This is my friend, Mark Langley."

When he looked more closely at the older man, he realized the man was staying in the room next to his. "Dante DeAngelis," he said, extending his hand. "I think we're neighbors."

"Yes, I saw you this morning," Mark replied with a friendly nod.

"Mark is the administrator of the new rehab center," Lizzie put in.

"Then I'll probably see you again. I'm rehabbing my arm and shoulder there for a few weeks."

"That's excellent. We'll take good care of you."

"Why don't you both sit down?" Lizzie suggested. "Can I get you some wine, Dante?"

"Actually, I'm going to head upstairs."

"Oh, don't run off," Ruth protested. "Tell us about yourself. How long will you be staying in Whisper Lake?"

"A few weeks, depending on my rehab progress," he answered.

"And then you'll be going where?"

"Miami. I play baseball there."

"Oh, that's interesting," her mom said. "Are you sure you don't want to join us?"

"He already said no, Mom," Keira interjected. "In fact, we should go, too. I can drive you home and save Mr. Langley a trip across town."

"No. I'm going to stay and chat with Mark. I'll meet you at home," Ruth said firmly.

Keira blew out a frustrated breath.

He didn't know why Keira was acting so crazy about her mom being out with Mark Langley, but clearly there was something going on he didn't understand.

"I'll make sure she's not out too late," Mark said quietly, giving Keira a reassuring look, but she didn't look at all reassured.

"You go on, dear," Ruth said, waving Keira toward the door.

"All right. I'll see you at home," Keira said.

As she left the room, he followed her into the entry. "What's wrong?" he asked quietly.

"That man is wrong."

"Why?"

"Because I don't trust him," she said in an angry, hushed voice.

He opened the front door for her, then waved her onto the wide front porch that held a half-dozen Adirondack chairs. But neither one of them sat down.

"Why don't you trust him?" he asked curiously.

"He showed up at our front door yesterday, completely out of the blue. He had a high school yearbook with him and told me that he and my mom had gone through high school together in Denver. Before I could ask him more questions, my mother appeared. She didn't recognize him at first, but when he showed her the photo of the two of them together at a dance, it started coming back to her."

"I'm not hearing the problem."

"He's being super-aggressive. He stayed for a half hour last night. He only left because my mom had a friend coming over. And then tonight he apparently went to our house, picked her up and brought her to the inn for drinks."

"That's horrible," he said dryly.

She made a face at him. "You don't understand. My mom had a traumatic head injury six years ago. She's had to relearn how to walk and talk and she still has problems with her memory. She's vulnerable. I don't like that this guy has shown up out of nowhere and is so eager to get to know her again when it's been forty-five years since they were in high school."

He was beginning to understand the problem. Keira was clearly protective of her mother, and who could blame her after the health issues her mom had been through?

"I'm sorry. I don't know why I'm telling you all this," Keira said, tucking her hair behind her ears. "It's not your problem."

"Maybe it's not a problem at all," he suggested. "Mark Langley could be a decent guy. He has a good job. I'm sure he was vetted for that."

"That's true. My gut just tells me there's something off about him, and I need to protect my mother. She might look like she's normal now, but she is still fragile." Keira blinked back tears of emotion. "Sorry again." She dabbed at her eyes. "It's just been a long road with her, and I'm tired. I'm going to go before I talk your ears off."

She was down the steps before he could say he wanted to hear more, because he did. But he shouldn't want to hear more. He didn't need to get involved in Keira's life. He needed to focus on his own, so he let her go.

He walked into the inn and jogged up the stairs to his room. When he was inside with the door closed, he sat down on the bed and let out a breath. He wanted to feel the peace of the room, but instead he felt wired and restless. And that was because of a woman who'd sat down at the wrong table and flashed him a smile that he couldn't seem to forget.

He got up from the bed and walked over to the desk, turning on his computer. He opened one of the dozen or so pitching videos he had on his computer, avoiding the one from the last game he'd pitched.

He could remember the exact moment when he'd realized something had torn in his shoulder. The pain had been intense. It had shot down his arm to his fingers and the ball that had left his grip missed the plate by three feet. He'd somehow ended up on his knees. He'd been pitching a no-hitter. He'd been having the game of his life.

Now, he was terrified that it might have been the last game of his life.

To distract himself, he watched an older video of his younger self. That cocky and determined kid would have never believed he'd end up here. But he wasn't here forever. This was just the next stop on his road to recovery.

And that's what he was going to do in Whisper Lake—recover. He would get past this obstacle the way he'd gotten past everything else he'd faced: with grit and a stubborn refusal to accept anything less than a complete recovery. There was no time in his healing process for a beautiful brunette with a brilliant smile.

CHAPTER FOUR

KEIRA WOKE up Saturday morning with a pounding headache. She took a quick shower, threw on skinny white jeans and a tank top, and then headed downstairs. She'd tossed and turned all night, thinking about the two very different men who had suddenly come into her life this week—Mark Langley and Dante DeAngelis.

She was still suspicious of Mark, and she needed to find out more about him as soon as possible since her mother seemed to be getting more involved with him by the minute.

And then there was the hotter-than-hot Dante, who had stirred all her senses in a very significant way. But he was taken. And even if he wasn't taken, he probably thought she was crazy after she'd sat down at his table at Micky's, then tracked him down at the inn, capping off the night by unloading her personal problems on him. She inwardly groaned at the embarrassing memories. She needed coffee and a fresh start.

When she entered the kitchen, she saw her mom standing at the counter, cutting up strawberries and bananas. She wore tan slacks and a sleeveless top, and her short brown hair curled around her face as she hummed a happy tune under her breath.

"Good morning," her mother said, looking up with a smile. "Coffee is ready."

"Great." She poured herself a cup of coffee. "You're up early for a Saturday. Are you going somewhere?"

"No. It's so lovely out. I thought I'd work in the garden before it gets too hot. Are you working at the store today, or do I even need to ask?"

"I'm working." She sipped her coffee, then added, "Did you have fun last night?"

"I did." Her mom set down her knife and gave her a pointed look. "Even though you tried to stop that from happening. What got into you, Keira? Why were you so rude to Mark?"

"I was surprised to see you at the inn. You didn't tell me you were going out last night."

"Mark called late in the day on the off chance I might be free, and I was. You were on a date. I didn't want to bother you."

"But if I'd come home, and you weren't here, I would have been worried."

"I left you a note on the fridge. It's still there." She tipped her head to the refrigerator, where they often left notes for each other.

She had actually seen the note when she'd gotten home. "I did see it," she muttered. "But I still think you should have texted me."

"Keira, what is wrong with me seeing an old friend?"

"This man came out of nowhere. He seems to be very pushy. I think you should be careful."

"Careful…that's a funny word. I was being careful when a car ran a red light and smashed into me. I wasn't even moving. I wasn't going over the speed limit. I had my seat belt on, and I still almost died. But I didn't die, and it has taken me a long time to feel even marginally like myself again." She paused. "You are the reason I'm doing as well as I am. I can never thank you enough for taking care of me the way you have."

"The way I always will. It's been the two of us against the world forever."

"I know. And I love you so much, honey, but I am doing better. You don't have to watch me every second. I may not feel comfortable driving, and I don't always remember every little thing, but I feel like I have most of my wits about me."

"You didn't remember Mark until he showed you the picture in the yearbook."

"Well, goodness, it's been forty-five years. And his hair was brown when I knew him. But the memories came back quickly when we started talking."

"So, what do you know about him? Give me some details."

"Let's see. He was married for thirteen years. He and his wife, Valerie, had a son, Richard. They got divorced when Richard was nine. He's twenty-four now, so Mark has been single for about fifteen years. His son lives in Los Angeles. Mark has moved around for his job. He was most recently in Las Vegas working for a hospital when he decided to trade the desert for the mountains." Her mom smiled. "He's not a criminal, Keira. He's just a man I used to know…I used to like, actually."

Her stomach curled at the new light in her mother's eyes. Her mother had dated a few men over the years, but not a lot. She didn't have a great track record when it came to relationships. The men she had picked to date had never seemed that great to Keira. In fact, the one she'd been seeing when she got in the accident had vanished before she was out of the hospital.

"Did you date Mark in high school?" she asked.

"Yes. We went out for about four months my senior year."

"What happened?"

"Oh, nothing really." She waved a dismissive hand in the air. "Just kid stuff. I think I saw him at a party with another girl and jumped to conclusions."

"He cheated on you?"

"We weren't serious, Keira. We were teenagers."

"And you haven't seen him since high school?"

"Actually, I saw him at our ten-year reunion. I had forgotten about that until he reminded me. That was the last reunion I went to." Shadows filled her eyes. "I was upset that weekend. I wanted your father to go with me, but he refused. He didn't want to stand around while I caught up with my friends. It really bothered me, because we spent most of our life with his friends. Anyway, Mark was very nice to me that night. He made me feel a lot better."

She frowned, wondering if anything else had happened that night when Mark was being so *nice*, but there were some things she didn't discuss with her mother and one of those things was sex.

"Once you get to know Mark, you'll like him," her mom added. "Will you have a chance to look at some listings today, or should we get Brenda involved? I know Mark is eager to find a more permanent place to live."

"I'll do it. In fact, I'll talk to Mark today and find out exactly what he's looking for."

Her mother gave her a sharp look. "All right, but be polite, Keira. I don't have that many friends. I don't want to lose a new one."

"You have lots of friends."

"Not from my high school years. Just give him a chance. Now, let's change the subject. Let's talk about that very attractive man you were speaking to at the inn last night."

"There's nothing to say about him."

"There must be something."

"Fine. I'll say this. He has a girlfriend."

Her mother frowned. "Well, that's disappointing."

"I don't even know him. We had a brief conversation. That's it." She refused to admit that she was also disappointed.

"What about your date last night? How was that?"

"Not worth talking about. I need to get to work."

"Can I make you some breakfast?"

"I'm not hungry." She finished her coffee, then put her mug in the sink. "I'll take a look at the listings and get in touch with Mr. Langley today. I assume you have his number."

"Yes, I'll text it to you. I know he's working at the rehab center today. He's setting up his office and getting up to speed on his job, but I'm sure he'll make time for you."

"Okay."

"And you can call him Mark."

"Mark," she repeated, even though his name still left a bad taste in her mouth. She couldn't say her gut was always right, but sometimes it was. She would have to figure out if Mark was after more than friendship with her mother. Her mom had already bought whatever he was selling, so she would have to protect her mom without her knowing. "I'll see you later."

She was almost at the kitchen door when her mother called her name.

"Keira?"

"What?" she asked, seeing a thoughtful look in her mom's eyes.

"As much as I love it being the two of us against the world, I wouldn't mind if you found a man to share your life with. I don't want you to miss out on anything because of me."

"I'm not missing out."

"I hope not. Maybe you should find out how serious Dante is about his girlfriend."

"I'm not going there. So, get that idea out of your head." She left the kitchen, knowing she needed to take the advice she'd just given her mom.

Dante spent time Saturday morning with the two therapists who would be overseeing his treatment plan. When they'd finished with their initial assessment at noon, he felt both tired and frustrated. He'd believed he was doing better than he actually was, and the simple exercises that he could not accomplish pushed a dark reality in front of him, one that he couldn't ignore. The therapists had assured him that improvement could come quickly, so he needed to focus on the positive, not the negative.

On his way out of the building, he decided to stop at the smoothie bar in the lobby, which was located in a wide-open and spacious atrium, with skylights and large windows overlooking the lake and the mountains. In addition to the smoothie bar, there was also a café and a lounge area with tables, sofas, and couches. There were only a few people around today, as the rehab center was not yet fully open. In another month, it would probably be packed.

His phone vibrated as he took his acai and strawberry smoothie to a nearby table. The Denver number was familiar—it belonged to his orthopedic surgeon, Dr. Grayson Cole. They were only a few years apart in age and over the past seven weeks, they'd become more than doctor/patient; they'd also become friends. Grayson had played baseball through college and understood his love of the sport and how much he needed to get back to doing what he did best.

"Checking up on me?" he asked. "Or did Rita and Marian call you to tell you that I'm their worst patient?"

"I haven't spoken to your therapists yet. I wanted to hear from you first," Grayson replied. "How was the assessment?"

"I thought it would be easier than it was. I don't have pain anymore doing normal things, but I guess I haven't been pressing my arm that much. It was a bit of a shock to realize how far I still have to go."

"You'll make good progress. You're in excellent physical shape, and you have a work ethic and a determination that will take you a long way."

"My dad used to say I was a stubborn ass, so maybe that will help me now."

"It will. What do you think of Whisper Lake?"

"It's charming. It feels like everyone is on vacation. And your sister has been very welcoming."

"That's Lizzie. Every one of her guests is treated like family."

"She probably treats me better than my family," he said lightly. "Your sister is always inviting me to have wine or cookies. I may be ten pounds heavier by the end of this."

"Well, try to have some fun while you're there. I have to run now. I will be checking in with your therapists over the next week, and I'll be in Whisper Lake in about ten days to check on you in person." Grayson paused. "By the way, Chuck Walters has been calling me, asking me for updates. I told him he'd have to get those from you."

He sighed at the mention of his general manager. He was a huge supporter, but Chuck wanted answers that he didn't have. "I know. I've been avoiding him. But I will get back to him at some point." He didn't want to talk to Chuck until he'd been through at least the first week of rehab and could see what kind of progress he was making.

"Sounds good," Grayson said.

"Thanks for checking in." As he set down his phone and sipped his smoothie, he saw Keira come through the front doors, and his gut tightened. She wore a navy sleeveless top, white jeans and wedge heels, her long hair falling loose around her shoulders in messy waves, held back only by the pair of sunglasses she'd pushed up on her head. When she saw him, she stopped abruptly, then changed direction and headed to his table.

"We meet again," he drawled. "Are you looking for another date here at the rehab center?"

"Funny, no. I'm meeting Mr. Langley."

"Research?"

"Yes. I also need to find him a house, so two birds—one stone."

"I never liked that saying. I had a friend who threw a stone at a bird, and it was not pretty."

"Ugh. Now I will never use that saying again." She licked her lips. "Did you just finish a therapy session?"

"I did."

"How did it go?"

"It went."

"You really are a man of few words."

"Or perhaps you're just a woman of many words."

"That's true. I'm sorry I unloaded on you last night."

"It wasn't a problem." As she hovered, he added, "Do you want to sit?"

"Maybe for a minute. I'm a little early. Did you speak to Mr. Langley today?"

"No. I haven't seen him. What did your mother have to say about her date?"

"Not much, beyond the fact that she was having fun getting to know an old friend and I should butt out."

"And yet here you are."

"Because of the house. I'm supposed to find him one."

"But that's not your real reason; it's just what you told your mom."

She made a little face at him. "True. It's possible I'm being overly suspicious, but I have a feeling in my gut that I cannot ignore."

"If the feeling is there, you need to figure out why."

"That's what I'm going to do. If he's a legit nice guy, then maybe I won't worry about my mother. Although, she has never had the best record with men."

"Are you counting your dad?"

"No. Although, I don't actually know what their relationship was like. She doesn't talk about him much. I think they might have gotten married because she got pregnant. I was born eight months after their wedding. My mother claims I came early."

"Maybe you did. Or do you just see secrets everywhere?"

"Not everywhere, but I can be a suspicious person. However, I have had good reason to be wary when it comes to my mother's male friends. One man moved into our house for six months and ended up stealing two thousand dollars out of my mom's checking account. That was when I was fourteen. Another man was charming her with his smile and good looks, and it turned out he had a wife in another state. That was when I was sixteen. So, you tell me if I'm too paranoid."

"Your concern makes more sense now."

"My mom is a very trusting person. Someone has to make sure she isn't putting her trust in the wrong person."

"I get it. What about you? Have you run into losers like that in your own personal dating life?"

Before she could answer, his phone began to vibrate. As Nikki's name flashed across the screen, he felt a twinge of guilt, not just because he didn't want to answer the phone, but also because he hadn't returned her last two calls or texts.

"Do you have to get that?" Keira asked.

He silenced the call. "I'll call her back."

"Was that your girlfriend?"

"I told you, she isn't exactly a girlfriend."

"Sounds like a guy who doesn't like to commit."

"You have no idea what kind of guy I am."

"That's true. I've been doing all the talking—again. I should go find Mr. Langley." She got to her feet. "I hope you don't think I came here to find you. This was purely coincidence."

He smiled. "I believe you have another reason for being here."

"Good, because I don't poach men who have girlfriends or girls they're just seeing. Not that you'd want me to, but if you did, I wouldn't…" She ran her fingers through her hair. "I don't know what it is about you that flusters me, Dante. Anyway, in the interest of full disclosure, I will be at the Firefly Inn tomorrow night for a party that Lizzie is throwing. Her sister, Chelsea, is a nominee for a country music award, and Lizzie is hosting a viewing party. I'll be there, because not only am I friends with Lizzie and Chelsea, but I also designed the dress Chelsea will be wearing."

"I got an invitation for the party under my door this morning. Apparently, Lizzie wants all of her guests to attend."

"You should come. Lizzie throws a great party, and I promise not to talk incessantly to you."

He stood up. "Keira…" There were things he wanted to say, but as she stared back at him, he couldn't seem to find the right words. Clearing his throat, he said, "If this was another time, another place, another moment in my life, I'd be interested."

"Me, too," she said softly, meeting his gaze. "But it's not. So, we'll be friends, or not…"

"I'm good with friends."

"Then maybe I'll see you tomorrow night."

"If not before," he joked.

Her eyes sparkled with humor. "There is a good chance we'll run into each other again. Whisper Lake is a small town, but if we do, I'll try not to give you another chapter in my life story."

"I like the chapters I've heard so far."

"Maybe one of these days, you'll give me one of your chapters."

"I've talked about myself in news articles over the years. I'm sure you can find the info online."

"I'd rather get the information from you. But…" She glanced at her watch. "I need to meet Mr. Langley. So, next time."

"Next time," he murmured, having a hard time dragging his gaze away from her beautiful face.

She gave him another somewhat nervous smile and then walked away. He couldn't help but watch her until she stepped into the elevator. Then he sat back down, feeling somewhat deflated and even more tired than he'd been before.

His phone rang again, and this time he picked it up. Maybe he needed to talk to Nikki as much as she needed to talk to him.

CHAPTER FIVE

"Finally," Nikki said, a mix of relief and anger in her tone. "Why haven't you called or texted me back, Dante? I've been worried about you."

"I'm sorry." He figured she'd rather have an apology than an explanation. "How are you?"

"I'm—I don't know how I am. I feel like we're so far apart."

He'd been feeling that way, too, not just because they'd been physically apart for the last six weeks, but because they didn't seem to have much to talk about anymore. That was probably his fault. He was so caught up in his injuries and his health that he just hadn't been able to be interested in anything or anyone else. "I just need to get through the next three weeks," he said. "Then I'll have a better idea where I stand."

"I know it's been difficult for you, but you'll be back to normal soon. Life will be even better than it was before."

Her optimism should have been reassuring, but instead it grated on his nerves. "We'll see."

"One silver lining in all of this is that you'll have some time off this summer. Linc Adams has invited us to come on a five-day cruise on a super yacht in the Bahamas the first weekend in August. It will be amazing."

Linc Adams was a popular actor who'd recently starred in a series of action-adventure films. Nikki had had a walk-on part in his newest film, playing her supermodel self. He'd met Linc once and they'd gotten along, mostly because Linc was a big baseball fan.

"I can't make any plans right now," he said.

"Why not? You're not going to be playing until at least September, right? Isn't that the earliest date?"

"I don't know. I have no dates. I have to see how rehab goes, but even if I can't play, I'll still need to join my team at some point."

"Just to sit in the dugout? I'm sure the coach would give you time off." The irritation in her voice rose with every word. "Why not take advantage of this opportunity to spend more time with me this summer?"

"I can't decide anything at this moment," he repeated, feeling his own frustration level rising.

"Well, our relationship can't just be about you."

"I know that. Let me just get through the next three weeks."

"Fine. But I'm going to tell Linc that we're tentatively in, just so we don't lose our spot. What about JT's birthday party next weekend? Can you come down to LA?"

"No, I'm in the rehab center six days a week."

"He's one of my best friends. And the party will be over the top at a Malibu mansion."

"I'm sorry. I know I'm not giving you the answers you want, but I can't take time off rehab for a party. Let's talk about you," he added, hoping to change the subject. "How are you doing? Do you have any travel coming up?"

"I'm staying in LA until mid-July. I want to be in town for the movie premiere. Of course, I'd love you to be there for that, too."

Nikki had so many plans, none of which he wanted to commit to. And he knew she would quickly tire of him saying no. Nikki was a tall, gorgeous blonde. Whenever she walked into a room, she got everyone's attention.

He'd been happy to get hers when they'd met in February.

While he'd dated models before, Nikki was probably the most famous. She had a huge social media following and was on everyone's VIP guest list. She'd told him the first time they'd met that they would look good together, and he hadn't argued.

But while they might photograph well, they didn't have a lot in common. Nikki had been born into money and into a world where she was always celebrated. She needed that from the man in her life, too. And his injury had been a huge inconvenience for her. He'd been irritated with her for weeks, but he hadn't wanted to deal with their relationship in the middle of everything else. It had been easy to avoid having a difficult conversation, because they hadn't been together, but that time was coming soon. He just didn't want to get into it all now, when he needed to focus on rehab.

"Dante?"

Her sharp voice pierced his reverie. "Sorry, what?"

"Even when you're talking to me, you seem distant."

"I'm tired. Why don't we talk another time?"

"All right. But it's difficult to find a day when you aren't tired."

"I can't argue with you on that. Maybe we should think about taking a break," he said shortly.

"No, no," she said quickly. "We don't need a break. Everything will be fine when you're done with rehab. We'll talk later, when you're not exhausted. Bye, Dante."

She disconnected the call before he could get another word in. He blew out a breath, knowing the hard conversation still needed to be had, but he was fine to leave it for another day.

Keira had to wait ten minutes for Mark Langley to finish up a meeting, and every one of those minutes increased her dislike and distrust of him. He'd set this time to meet. It irked her that he thought she had ten minutes to just waste away in his outer office. She could be at the store right now or looking at a contract that Brenda had sent through for a rental property they were managing.

Or she could be designing Hannah's wedding dress. But instead, she was waiting, and she'd never been particularly patient.

Finally, his office door opened, and he gave her an apologetic smile. "I'm so sorry," he said. "We had a minor emergency with some equipment that seems to have gone missing between Denver and Whisper Lake."

She got to her feet. "That doesn't sound good."

"We managed to find it. Please come in."

"I don't have a lot of time, but I would like to go over some properties you might be interested in."

"Perfect." He turned to his assistant, a woman named Andrea, who had been nice enough to make her some tea while she was waiting. "Will you hold my calls, Andrea? And thanks again for coming in on a Saturday. If you can stay until one, that would be helpful."

"Of course, Mr. Langley," Andrea replied.

Mark waved Keira into his office, which was a luxurious executive suite with large windows overlooking the lake, an enormous oak desk with a brown leather chair, as well as a seating area with a small table and four chairs. He showed her to the table.

She was happy to be joining him there rather than sitting across from him at his desk, where he would be in the power position.

"I've found several properties that I think you might be interested in," she said, pushing a file folder across the table. "Two of the properties are two-bedroom single-family homes. I also found a three-bedroom house and a luxury one-bedroom condo with a loft near the heart of downtown. You can walk to everything." It was also the farthest one from her mother.

"I'm not sure how big of a place I need, but I would think two bedrooms at the least, maybe three. I can turn one into an office."

"Of course. Do you anticipate having a lot of guests? Perhaps family and friends will be coming to visit? My mother said you have a son."

"Yes, I do," he said, his tone somewhat heavy. "But I don't think he'll be visiting. We don't see much of each other."

"That's too bad."

"He has his own life. He's studying to be a veterinarian. I'm very proud of him, although, sometimes, I have a difficult time accepting that he's grown up."

"My mother has the same trouble. Where does your son live?"

"Los Angeles."

"I know you went to high school in Denver with my mom. Do you still have family there?"

"No. My parents have passed away, and my sister moved to New York a long time ago. Perhaps I don't need more than two bedrooms, although this one looks nice." He tapped his finger on the photo of the three-bedroom home. "It's in your neighborhood, isn't it?"

"About three blocks away, but I think it's overpriced for the square footage."

Mark gave her a thoughtful look. "Is that it? Or do you also think it's too close to your mother?"

She hadn't been expecting such a direct question. "Uh, no. You can live wherever you want."

"You seemed bothered by the fact that I was with your mom last night."

"I was surprised. I thought she was at home watching a movie. She doesn't go out much and never with people I don't know."

"But she knows me."

"She didn't recognize you when she first saw you," she countered.

"I took her by surprise, and I've changed a bit. I used to have dark-brown hair."

"That's what she said." She paused. "I don't know how much my mom told you about her life—"

"She told me she was in an accident and that she had a brain injury. It sounds like you have done an amazing job getting her back to health."

"It has been a long road. I'm protective of her."

"As you should be." He met her gaze. "I hope as you get to know me, you'll be able to trust me."

"I hope so, too." He seemed like he was being direct and

honest. *Was that just part of his game? Or was she being ridiculously suspicious?*

A knock came at the door, and then Andrea popped her head into the office. "I'm sorry, Mr. Langley, but you have a call, and she won't take no for an answer. She wouldn't give me her name, but she said it was urgent. She seemed quite upset, almost hysterical."

"All right. I'll pick it up." He got to his feet, an apology in his gaze. "I'll take a look at these and get back to you, Keira."

"Sure, take your time. If you're interested in seeing any of them, I'll set up a showing," she said as she stood up.

"I will do that. I wish we could talk more, but I have to get this."

"Please, go ahead." She headed to the door as he answered his phone.

She lingered just long enough to hear him say, "Mandy, why on earth are you calling me here?" He paused, then said, "No, you listen. This stops now." The anger in his voice was unmistakable.

She wished she could hear more, but Andrea was giving her a speculative look, so she pulled the door shut behind her and left the office suite.

Mark had definitely gone from friendly and sincere to extremely pissed off with the woman on the phone.

Why? Who was Mandy?

Mark had almost persuaded her that her suspicions were unnecessary, but now alarm bells were going off again. She needed to find out more about Mark.

As she moved through the lobby, she couldn't help noticing that Dante was gone, which was just as well, or she might have been tempted to tell him about her latest encounter with Mark, and she didn't need to do that. She'd already gotten him more involved in her life than he needed to be.

CHAPTER SIX

KEIRA DIDN'T GET a chance to dig into Mark Langley's life until Sunday afternoon. But after helping her mom in the garden until one, she took her computer and a tall glass of iced tea out to the pool patio. She sat down at a table under an umbrella to keep the hot summer sun off her face and then opened up her search engine. Twenty minutes later, she was frowning at her lack of success.

Mark wasn't on social media. However, she was able to come up with a business profile. He'd started out in pharmaceutical sales and then worked his way into healthcare administration, working at a number of small clinics and hospitals before moving to Whisper Lake.

But the information she wanted was much more personal. She thought about what she did know. Her mom had said his first wife's name was Valerie. And he had a son, Richard, who lived in Los Angeles and was studying to be a veterinarian.

Tapping those details into the search engine didn't yield better results. She couldn't find a Valerie Langley online. It was possible she was using her maiden name or perhaps she'd remarried. There were a dozen or more results for Richard Langley, but none that seemed to be the right age.

She thought about what to do next. There were sites she could pay to do research for her. *Was she ready to go that far?* Not quite yet.

She opened a new search window and put in Mark and Valerie Langley, as well as the city of Los Angeles. She flipped through several screens, nothing popping out until her gaze settled on a news article about a house fire in the Los Feliz area. A twenty-six-year-old woman named Gretchen Yates had died in the fire. The house was owned by Mark and Valerie Langley, who were not at home at the time. Nor was their nine-year-old son, Richard. Gretchen Yates had been their nanny.

Her heart sped up as she thought about what she'd just read. *Did it mean anything?* Her mother had told her that Mark and his wife divorced when their son was nine. *Was it a coincidence that the two events had happened the same year? Or was she trying to make something out of nothing?*

She thought for a moment and then entered the name Gretchen Yates. She had to add in several more keywords before finally locating the obituary. Gretchen had been survived by her parents, Rena and Stan, her brother, Donald, and her sister, Amanda. Her pulse jumped again.

Was Amanda—Mandy—the woman who'd called Mark? Why would they have a connection now, fifteen years after Gretchen's death?

Her imagination started working overtime, coming up with all kinds of implausible theories. She tried to rein herself in. She really didn't know anything except there had been a fire in Mark's house, a woman had died, and that woman's sister might still be in touch with him. Maybe he'd simply been taking care of Gretchen's family since then. He could be the amazing man her mother wanted him to be.

As a series of texts popped up on her screen about the party at Lizzie's inn, she realized she needed to put Mark Langley aside for the moment. Lizzie needed someone to pick up a special cake she'd ordered while she waited for someone to fix the cable TV at the inn. She was freaking out that they wouldn't be able to get reception for the awards show.

Chloe, who was supposed to be bringing a case of wine and a lasagna, said that her almost-three-year-old son, Leo, had just come down with a fever, so she wasn't going to be able to come at all, and if someone could pick up the wine and lasagna, that would be amazing.

Gianna texted that she was leaving for Denver, so she and Zach might be late. And Hannah said she was stuck at work until five and the bakery would be closed by the time she got off.

She volunteered to pick up the wine, lasagna, and the cake. Her friends had always been there for her, and she'd always be there for them.

She took her computer back into the house. Her mom was washing her hands in the kitchen. "I need to help Lizzie for tonight's party," she said. "Do you need anything?"

"No, I'm fine. I'm just going to read this afternoon. I have a new novel I'm itching to start."

"That's good. Have you heard from Mr. Langley again?"

Her mother smiled. "I told you to call him Mark. And, yes, he texted me earlier. He asked me to go to dinner at the Lakeshore Bistro tonight."

"And you agreed." She didn't even bother to make it a question.

"Of course. I love the Lakeshore Bistro. And you're busy tonight, anyway."

"What time are you going?"

"Six. I'll be home by eight. You really don't have to worry, Keira."

She didn't have to, but she still would. However, she couldn't skip the party, nor could she talk her mother out of going to dinner, not without some solid ammunition. Right now, all she had was a lot of speculation.

"Is that handsome man going to be at the party?" her mother asked.

She'd been trying not to think about Dante, but her mom's question put his very attractive face back in her head. "Lizzie invited everyone at the inn, so there's a chance he'll be there. But I told you, he has a girlfriend."

"When I first met your dad, he had a girlfriend. Until someone is married, anything can happen."

"Not if I don't let it. Besides the fact that he's involved with someone, he's just passing through, Mom. A few weeks, and he'll be gone."

Her mom sighed. "That's too bad."

She couldn't agree more. She also couldn't help but hope he'd show up at the party.

Dante tried to read. He'd picked up a book downstairs from Lizzie's extensive library, but it didn't hold his attention. Putting it down, he picked up the remote and turned the TV on, surprised and happy when it worked. He'd seen Lizzie running frantically around the inn with two guys from the cable company, panicked that the cable wouldn't be back before her party, but it was fixed with an hour to spare. He flipped through the channels, not really interested in anything. He didn't feel like starting a movie, and he was staying away from sports, especially baseball games.

It sometimes killed him not to know what was happening with his team, but he thought it would frustrate him even more if he did know. If they were doing great without him, he'd be happy, but it would make him wonder how valuable he really was. If they were bombing, he'd want to get back so he could help his team. Keeping that information out of his head seemed like the best idea.

He turned off the TV, got off the bed, and walked to the window. His room overlooked the patio, and he could see several guests sitting at a table, sipping cocktails. He recognized two of the older women as being guests at the inn, but the two other younger couples he didn't know. Probably Lizzie's friends.

He still didn't know what to do about the party. He had nothing else going on, and he was hungry. He also wouldn't mind having a drink. But he'd have to talk to people, some of whom might recognize him and ask him questions he didn't want to answer. Of course, none of that concerned him as much as seeing Keira again.

They'd agreed to be friends, which was the best decision for a lot of reasons. Unfortunately, the idea of just being her friend wasn't appealing. He was attracted to her. He'd felt it since the first second she'd sat down at his table, and he felt it even more now that he'd gotten to know her. She was outgoing and friendly and had a dry, self-deprecating sense of humor. She didn't seem to take herself too seriously, and he liked that. He also liked how protective she was of her mom.

He wondered if she'd discovered anything new when she'd met with Langley yesterday. The guy seemed nice enough. He'd passed him in the hall earlier and exchanged greetings. They were the only two rooms on the third floor, so he had a feeling they'd be seeing each other a lot.

Turning away from the window, he knew he had two options. He could go into town and find a restaurant and eat alone, or he could join the crowd downstairs. One good thing about staying in was the opportunity to avoid the press. He hadn't seen anyone since Friday night, so it was possible they didn't know where he was staying yet. He had used a credit card attached to a corporation, so his name wasn't on the register, but this was a small town. He doubted his anonymity would last long. Maybe he'd at least check out the party, get the vibe. If it was uncomfortable, he could always leave.

He grabbed his keycard and phone, slipped them into the pocket of his jeans and headed downstairs. The laughter and chatter hit him as soon as he reached the foyer. When he walked into the living room, he saw that Lizzie had rearranged the room so that all the couches and chairs faced a large-screen TV. The bar in the corner was quite busy with Lizzie's fiancé, Justin Blackwood, pouring margaritas. In the adjacent dining room, two long tables had been set for a buffet while another six round tables were covered with linen cloths with flower centerpieces.

There were probably two dozen people mingling between the rooms, but while a few he recognized as being guests at the inn, he didn't see Mark Langley. Nor did he see Keira.

He headed to the bar. When he reached the front of the line, Justin gave him a smile.

"Margarita, wine, beer? What's your pleasure?" Justin asked.

"I'll take a margarita. It looks like that's the drink of the day."

"It is, and I make a good one. Don't tell Lizzie how strong they are," Justin added with a laugh.

Justin was a tall, good-looking guy with a dark-blue gaze that sparkled with amusement. From what Lizzie had told him about her fiancé, he knew Justin ran a huge company, specializing in robotics. Apparently, after falling in love with Lizzie, he'd decided to set up a field office in town so that Lizzie could continue managing her inn. The sacrifice was impressive. He didn't know a lot of guys who would move for a woman, although he certainly knew a lot of women who had moved to follow their men all over the country, from the minor leagues to the majors, and city to city.

Justin handed him a margarita. "Let me know what you think."

He got a strong taste of tequila. "Very good. I like your pour."

Justin leaned in, lowering his voice. "It will make watching an awards show a lot more fun."

He smiled. "Sounds like we're on the same page."

"Most of the guys here are on that page, not that we don't love Chelsea. Lizzie's sister is a sweetheart and so talented. Her voice can give you chills. I love watching her perform, and I really hope she wins the award she's up for. It would show that she's officially made her comeback."

"Comeback?" he queried.

"She quit music for several years. It's a long story. But she's back, and her talent is more impressive than ever."

"I'll have to listen to one of her songs."

"She sings a mix of country and pop. She's on all the platforms."

"I'll check her out."

"Check who out?" Lizzie asked, interrupting their conversation. "Hello, Dante. I'm so glad you decided to join us."

"I could smell the food upstairs."

"That's how I lure people down," she said with a laugh. "So, who are you checking out?"

"Your sister. Justin said I should listen to one of her songs."

"Oh, you should. She's amazing."

"Do you sing as well?"

"Only in the shower. How are the margaritas? They're not too strong, are they?"

"Perfect," he said, catching Justin's small smile.

"Great," Lizzie returned. "We're going to open the buffet in a few minutes. And I hope you'll stay for the show, too. I haven't had a chance to show you much hospitality yet."

"Not true."

"I promised Grayson you would be well taken care of, so while I know you're in town for serious reasons, I want to make sure you also have some fun."

"Don't fight it," Justin told him, as Lizzie moved away to speak to another group of guests. "Lizzie is a force of nature. If she wants to entertain you, then you will be entertained."

"I'm beginning to realize that."

"She thinks of every guest as family. When I first came here, I thought she was over the top when it came to events, but I soon realized that what she does is what makes this place special."

"I have to admit I've never stayed at an inn before."

"It wasn't my thing, either. But my grandparents held their fifty-seventh wedding anniversary vow renewal here. I came and met Lizzie, and the rest is history. I never expected my life to go this way, but I'm thankful it did." Justin paused as another couple stepped up to the bar. "What can I get you?"

As Justin poured more margaritas, Dante moved away from the bar, thinking that he'd never expected his life to go this way, either, but he didn't feel thankful. He was frustrated and restless to get back to normal. But normal seemed very far away.

As he headed into the dining room, he saw Keira set down a large sheet cake at the end of the buffet table, and his heart jumped. She looked beautiful in dark jeans, and a gauzy top that fell off her shoulders. Her face was a little flushed when she stepped back to admire the cake. When she looked up, she caught his gaze, and her eyes sparkled as a smile spread across her lips.

His gut clenched. *Damn!* He hadn't reacted like this to a woman in a long time. And she wasn't even trying to get his attention. In fact, she'd made it clear she wouldn't try, because he was attached.

And he was still attached. His tentative suggestion that he and Nikki take a break had gone nowhere. Now he wished he pushed the issue, because Nikki was turning into a shadowy figure he could barely remember while Keira was a bright light that he couldn't see past.

Keira came over to join him. "Hi," she said softly.

"Hi," he echoed, as they exchanged a long look that sent blood racing through his body.

She licked her lips. "What did you do today? More rehab?"

"No, I walked around town. I went through the park and down to the lake. The beach was fairly crowded."

"Wait another week and you'll barely be able to put a towel down. Fourth of July is a big holiday. You'll still be here then, won't you?"

"I think so. We'll see how things go."

"It's a good time to be at the lake. The weather is great. The water is getting warmer every day. And there are lots of activities going on all over town."

"It sounds like people do nothing but party around here."

"The vacationers do nothing but party. As for the locals, we still work a lot. However, it was a long, cold winter, and now that it's summer, everyone wants to be outside, celebrating."

Summer had always been his favorite time of the year, but that's when he'd been playing baseball. There had been nothing better than a Saturday or Sunday day game, except maybe a double-header. But he didn't want to think about that right now. "What did you do today?"

"A little digging and not only in the garden. I finally got online and looked up Mr. Langley."

He saw the gleam in her eyes. "Did you find something?"

"Yes. I'm not sure what it means or if it changes anything, but it was a little odd." She looked around, but no one was paying them any attention.

"If you're looking for Langley, I haven't seen him," he told her.

"He's probably on his way to my house. He's taking my mother out for dinner."

"If you found some dirt on him, why is your mother still going out with him?"

"I didn't tell her yet. It's not solid. She'd tell me to butt out, and I can't do that."

He had to admit he was a little curious. "Okay, so what did you find out?"

"There was an article in an LA newspaper where Langley used to live. Fifteen years ago, his house burned down, and his nanny died in the fire."

He stared at her, surprised by her words. He didn't know what he'd been expecting, but it wasn't that. "That's sad."

"It is. Langley's son was nine at the time. My mom told me that Mark divorced his wife when his son was nine. It happened the same year."

"Okay. What does it mean?"

"I'm not sure. There's something else. When I was talking to Mark in his office yesterday, he asked his assistant to hold his calls. But his assistant came in a few minutes later with an urgent call from a woman, who she claimed was hysterical. As I left the room, I heard Mark say, 'Mandy, why are you calling me here?' He paused to hear something she said, and then he replied, 'This stops now.' He was definitely angry."

"Okay, but we don't know who this Mandy is."

"Here's something else that's odd. The woman who died in the fire was survived by her sister, Amanda. I'm thinking Mandy could be this Amanda. What do you think?"

He couldn't help but smile. "You have a big imagination, don't you?"

"Maybe, but I'm not imagining what I just told you."

"No, but you're taking a lot of small clues and putting them together in a way that sounds sinister. Mandy might not be the same woman. And the fire… Was Mark there? Did he set it?"

"The article said Mark, his wife, and child were out of town when it happened."

"Then he was a victim."

"That's true. I know I could be putting the puzzle together incorrectly, but there's something odd about the story and about his phone call. Even putting the fire aside, I'd like to know who Mandy is and what kind of relationship she has with Mark, because he was definitely angry that she called him. I need to do more research."

"You do," he agreed. "Try not to look at everything through suspicious eyes."

"I can't promise that." She gave a helpless shrug. "I feel how I feel, and that won't change until Mark proves himself in some way or I find information that leads me to believe he's a perfectly harmless old high school boyfriend who just happened to end up in the same town as my mom."

While a part of him thought that Keira was making something out of nothing, he was also impressed with how much she cared, how far she was willing to go to protect someone she cared about. He liked the fierceness of her loyalty and her love. It was kind of strange, but in some ways, she reminded him a little of his mom. His mother had always been on top of everything that they were doing, what was happening in school, who their friends were, what they were thinking. He'd hated her constant questions when she was alive, but after she'd died, he'd missed that, especially when his father's interest in his thoughts or whereabouts was basically nonexistent.

"Dante?" she questioned. "What are you thinking?"

Before he could answer, they were interrupted by an attractive woman with hair the color of a dark-red flame. With her was a tall, athletically built guy with brown hair.

"Hello," the woman said, giving him a speculative look, before extending her hand. "I'm Hannah, one of Keira's best friends. And you are?"

"Dante," he said, shaking her hand.

"And this is my fiancé, Jake," Hannah added. "I have to confess that we know who you are. Your presence is all over town. There were reporters in the Blue Sky Café this morning asking where you were staying."

"Great," he muttered.

"I don't think anyone said you were staying here. Actually, I didn't even know you were staying here. Lizzie didn't share that."

"She has been very discreet."

"I didn't really recognize your name," Hannah added, "but Jake practically had a heart attack."

"Uh, I wasn't that bad," Jake said. "She's exaggerating."

"He's lying," Hannah said with a laugh. "Jake knows a lot about your stats. He bored me with quite a few on the way over here."

"But I won't bore you with what you already know," Jake said, shaking hands with him. "Sorry about your injury. That's rough."

"Thanks." The word came out short and sharp. He knew he'd been too abrupt, but he didn't know what to say next. He'd let down his guard while he'd been talking to Keira, and now he was caught between his past and his present.

"We should eat," Keira said, jumping into the awkward silence. "We can talk more over dinner." Keira grabbed his hand and pulled him toward the buffet table.

He was surprised by the sudden heat of her fingers wrapping around his. She was clearly an affectionate person. He hadn't grown up in a family where people held hands or hugged when they saw each other. Maybe his parents had been like that before his mom died, but since then, he and his brothers and his dad had more of a slap-you-on-the-back kind of relationship, and even that was a rare occurrence.

She let go of his hand when she handed him a plate. As she met his gaze, a warm flush crept up her cheeks. "Sorry. I shouldn't have grabbed you like that."

"You got us to the front of the line; I'm good with that," he said lightly, as he spooned some salad onto a plate.

"You looked like a deer in the headlights when Hannah and Jake recognized you. I'm surprised you're not more used to it."

"I am used to it, but it was a lot easier when I…" He didn't know how to explain it to her.

"When you were on top," she said softly.

He met her gaze. "When I knew who I was." He regretted his words almost immediately. They were too personal. They were too honest. He'd revealed too much. But there was something about Keira's warm gaze that broke down his defenses.

"I understand."

"How could you?"

"Because I can," she said simply. "You don't have to worry. I won't tell anyone your secret."

He wanted to believe she understood. He wanted to believe she'd keep his secrets. But he'd been let down many times in the past. Trusting someone wasn't a risk he could afford.

However, he didn't need to trust her. He just needed to keep his mouth shut.

CHAPTER SEVEN

AFTER FILLING THEIR PLATES, they made their way to a nearby table. Hannah and Jake followed shortly thereafter, with Jake sliding into the seat next to him.

"Hey, I'm sorry," Jake said, giving him an apologetic look. "I shouldn't have mentioned the injury."

He shook his head, angry at himself for making Jake feel awkward. "It's not a secret. Don't worry about it."

"I told Jake to be cool," Hannah put in. "He is not usually a fan-boy, but he makes an exception for baseball."

"I'm not a fan-boy," Jake told Hannah. "I just like the game."

"I know. I watched you play a lot of games in high school. You were obsessed." Hannah looked at him. "Jake was really good."

"I was average," Jake corrected.

"You two went to high school together?" He wanted to move the conversation away from baseball.

"Yes. We loved each other and then we hated each other," Hannah said. "That's the short version. It took us about twelve years to get back to the love part."

He saw a hint of that love in the glance they now exchanged.

"Which I was really happy to see," Keira interjected. "I had a front-row seat to their love-hate relationship in high school, as well as the past year. I was tremendously relieved when they decided to stop fighting each other."

"What turned it all around?" he asked curiously.

"I did a lot of groveling," Jake joked.

"Not any more than you needed to do," Hannah said pointedly. "The truth is, Dante, we both had to grow up and realize we weren't the people we used to be. We also had some family baggage to deal with. When we finally got honest with each other, we were able to see past the hurt and the anger." She held up her left hand, a sparkling diamond on her third finger. "Now, we're engaged, and I'm getting married in less than two weeks." Hannah smiled at Keira. "And I'll be wearing a Keira Blake original."

"I hope you'll be wearing it. I still need to finish your dress," Keira grumbled.

"It's already done. You just won't let it go."

"It's not perfect yet, and for you, it has to be perfect."

Hannah shook her head in bemusement. "I honestly don't know what's wrong with it, but I will trust you, because you're the designer." She turned back to him. "Did you know that Keira designed the dress Chelsea will be wearing on the awards show tonight?"

"I heard something about that."

"I'm sure you're going to get a lot of calls for work after Chelsea walks down the red carpet," Hannah added to Keira. "This could be a big starter for you."

"We'll see. Let's talk about something else," Keira said. "Did you work today, Hannah?"

"Unfortunately, yes. I had to cover Rose's shift." Hannah looked at him. "I'm a nurse. The hospital is getting busy as the tourists arrive in town, although summer is never as bad as winter. The snowboarders and skiers break a lot of bones and pull a lot of muscles."

"I'll bet."

"Are you a winter sports guy?" Hannah asked.

"No. I've been snowboarding a few times, but I've never gotten past the medium hills. I bet you're all very good at winter sports, considering where you live."

"Keira is the best."

He turned to Keira. "You're a pro, huh?"

"I wouldn't go that far, but I grew up on these mountains. And I like speed. I was always a very responsible kid, but when I skied, I let myself go. I even did some downhill racing, but I had a bad fall when I was a teenager, and my mom was so freaked out about how I could have killed myself that I backed off the circuit."

He wondered how many other sacrifices Keira had made for her mom. It certainly seemed like more than a few. He was a little surprised she liked speed and racing, although maybe he shouldn't be. Keira clearly had a zest and an energy to participate in life. She wasn't a spectator. She was definitely a doer. She had multiple businesses, she was the family caretaker, and she was very involved with her friends.

The conversation shifted as Lizzie and Justin joined them for dinner, and there was an easy comfort among everyone in the group. Lizzie talked about the inn. Justin mentioned his new office center that was apparently being designed by an architect, who was also a friend. Jake spoke about his adventure sports business while Hannah threw shade at just about everyone.

He liked all of them, more than he would have imagined, and he found himself being drawn into their conversation but in subtle ways. No one asked him about his stats or his injury or anything to do with baseball. That might be because he'd made Jake and Hannah uncomfortable, but he found himself sharing information about his family, growing up in San Francisco, even his old dog, Rosie, who had shagged baseballs for him.

Apparently, Keira had also had a golden retriever named Dusty, and they bonded even more over stories about their dogs. She mentioned that she and her mom still occasionally thought about getting another puppy, but that was just one more job that she probably didn't have time for. He, of course, had never considered getting a pet, because he was on the road too much, but talking about Rosie made him realize that having a dog was something he'd missed. Having a laser focus on baseball had made him tremendously successful, but in some ways, it had kept his world very narrow.

As they finished their meal, they headed back to the buffet table to admire the cake. It featured a stage and a woman in a beautiful dress holding an award. Apparently, the woman was Chelsea, and the dress was a copy of what Keira had designed. Several photos were taken of the cake before it was cut, and it struck him that it was the first time he'd seen anyone take a picture of food since he'd arrived in Whisper Lake. Whereas when he was in his real life, and especially when he was with Nikki, there were more photographs taken of the food they ordered than actual bites.

Of course, Nikki had to stay thin for her job, but she also looked at food as a photo op more than a pleasure or even a necessary sustenance. In fact, most of what they did was designed to provide a good post for one of her social media channels. He couldn't fault her for working her business, but sometimes he felt like a prop.

In fact, hanging out with Keira and her friends reminded him of when he was young, when he hadn't been a celebrity or a superstar, when his friends had felt more real. Back then, his friends weren't with him because he was picking up the tab or because he had connections. They were just friends.

"Okay, it's just about show time," Lizzie announced. "Get your dessert, coffee, whatever you need. The red carpet starts in a few minutes, and we need to see Chelsea in Keira's dress."

They took their cake into the living room. Keira had a seat of honor on the couch in front of the television, and he ended up next to her. As Hannah and Jake squeezed in, he found himself very close to Keira, so close he could smell the scent of her perfume, and every nerve in his body tingled.

"There's Chelsea," Lizzie said, waving her hand toward the TV.

He directed his attention to the screen. A stunning dark-blonde woman showed off a strapless gown, which seemed like a stunning cloud of turquoise and silver, the front shorter than the back, revealing a pair of what looked like diamond-studded boots.

"She looks amazing," Hannah said. "You got her exactly right, Keira."

"You did," Lizzie put in, others murmuring their agreement.

"I wanted her to be her bohemian self but also kind of fancy," Keira said. "But she's so beautiful, she looks good in anything. I just hope she wins."

"Well, her award won't be coming up for at least thirty minutes," Lizzie said. "We'll have to wait on that."

"I'm going to get another margarita," Keira said, getting to her feet.

"I'll join you." He was eager to get off the couch. He couldn't care less about the red carpet. It reminded him of Nikki, and he didn't want to think about her.

They moved to the bar and filled their glasses, and then Keira led him through the dining room and out the door to the patio, where white lights twinkled through the trees surrounding several tables and a fountain. Everyone was inside the inn, so they had the patio to themselves. They took a seat. It was a warm night, perfect to be outside.

Keira took a long sip of her margarita. "I feel so weird being the center of attention, everyone making such a big deal about a dress I designed. It's Chelsea's night, not mine."

"It can be about both of you."

"I guess, but I'm not big on being in the spotlight." She gave him a thoughtful look. "I bet you love the spotlight."

"You'd win that bet. Thirty thousand screaming fans, bottom of the ninth, two outs, one more batter to strike out for the win. That's the moment I live for."

"That sounds incredibly stressful."

"That's the best part of it."

"How do you stay calm enough to throw your best pitch?"

"I breathe deep. I shut out everything else in my head. It's just me and the hitter. It's a battle between the two of us. I want to get him out. He wants to hit a home run. Only one of us will come close to what we want."

"How many of those moments have you had?"

"A lot."

"Does one in particular stand out?"

"Yes. Last year in the final game of the World Series. I was the starting pitcher, and I was pitching a no-hitter, so the coach let me keep going past where he'd normally bring in a reliever. It was going to be the last game of the season. I'd have plenty of time to rest, and I wanted to pitch the whole game. We went into the ninth inning with a one-zero lead. I struck the first two batters out. But the third batter got on base with an error by the second baseman. On the next pitch, he stole a base. I lost my concentration for a split second, and I threw a wild pitch. That moved the runner to third. I had a full count. One more pitch. I could walk him. And it wouldn't be the end of the world. I could get the next guy. But I wanted to end it right there."

"What happened?" she asked, completely caught up in his story.

He could remember the moment so clearly, the feeling of purpose followed by triumph. "I struck him out. We won the World Series. It was the greatest moment of my life. My teammates were jumping on me. Fireworks were going off, or maybe that was just in my head. It was everything I ever dreamed of."

"Wow. That must have been an incredible feeling. I had no idea your team won the World Series, or that you pitched the final game and got the win. You really are a superstar, aren't you?"

"I was. I don't know what I am anymore." A somber feeling ran through him.

She gave him a searching look. "Because of your injury?"

"Yes. I don't know if I'll be able to come back. Even if I can come back, I don't know if I'll be able to regain the form I had."

"That must be scary."

"I don't like to admit that."

"Is that part of being a pitcher? Never let them see you sweat?"

"It is, but I learned to keep my feelings to myself when I was a kid. My dad didn't like whiners."

"Being in pain from an injury is not whining. Being worried about the end of your career doesn't make you weak."

"It would in his book. My dad always told my brothers and me that unless there was a broken bone or blood gushing from a wound, we were expected to pull ourselves together and get over it."

Her lips turned down in a frown, her gaze narrowing. "Okay, I'm not liking the sound of your dad."

"He's not a bad guy." He didn't know why the automatic defense sprang to his lips.

"Then what was he?"

"Distant and unemotional. He didn't know what to do with us after my mom died. She was in charge of the kids. He went to work. That was the way it was divided up. He didn't know how to be a father or a parent without her."

"I'm sorry. I don't think it excuses him, though. You were a kid. You needed a father to support you, not to tell you to toughen up or get over yourself."

He appreciated her fierce words. "I did, but it was what it was. My grandmother stepped in after my mom passed, and she helped balance things out. But my brothers and I basically raised ourselves."

"Are you close in age?"

"Within seven years. Danny is the oldest. He's thirty-three now. He's a builder and works for a construction firm in San Francisco, where I grew up. I'm thirty-two, Micah is thirty. He runs a food truck. Paul is the youngest. He's twenty-seven and works in finance. He's a numbers guy."

"Did any of them play sports like you?"

"Paul did not. Danny was a football player. Micah played some soccer. No one else was that serious about their sport."

"Interesting that you picked different sports."

"My dad was into football. I think Danny wanted to get close to him by playing the same sport."

"Did it work?"

"Not really."

"Are your brothers married?"

"All single and all in San Francisco."

"Is that where you think you'll end up?"

"I have no idea. I go where baseball takes me."

Keira sipped her margarita. "Tell me about your mom. What was she like?"

He couldn't remember the last time anyone had asked him about his mother. "She was…amazing. She always had a lot to say. She was very opinionated, but also kind and nurturing. She was a chef before she married. Micah says she taught him how to cook. I guess I was hitting baseballs during those lessons."

"What does your dad do?"

"He worked for a package delivery service for thirty years. He retired last year."

"He must be proud of you."

"I don't know. Maybe. He doesn't say much. But last year when I won the World Series, he texted me, and he said he was impressed. That was it."

"Well, that's something."

"It was the first time he ever really said anything particularly complimentary. He was usually more ready to point out our mistakes than celebrate our successes. He's basically just a terrible communicator."

"Has he been supportive since your injury?"

"He's texted me. But he's a negative person, and I don't need that energy right now. I'm sure he thinks I'm done."

"I hope your brothers are more positive."

"They are, but I actually haven't talked much to anyone. I went to Colorado for the surgery and stayed in Denver for six weeks. I haven't been around my family, my friends, or my teammates, which is fine. No one knows what to say, and I don't really want them to say anything, because I don't need reassurances from people who have no idea if I will recover or not. I need results. I need my arm to work again, the way it did before." He paused, blowing out a breath. "I don't know how we got on this subject."

"I'm not sure, either, but it's nice to hear about your life, Dante. I feel like this is the first time you've really opened up."

"It must be Justin's very strong margaritas."

She laughed. "They are strong, aren't they?"

"They got me talking. What about you?"

"What about me?"

"Your friends mentioned a couple of times at dinner how you have so many businesses going that they're worried you're not pursuing your real dream."

"Well, they don't understand the big picture."

"Which is what?"

"I don't live in an ideal world; I live in the real world. Money and responsibilities factor into my decisions."

"Desire factors in, too. If you don't have it, you can't force it."

She frowned, giving him an annoyed look. "What does that mean?"

"If you're not going after the design business, maybe it's not really what you want."

"It is what I want," she argued. "It's what I've always wanted. I've been sketching and sewing since I was eight. I love creating clothes. I love dressing someone so that they feel their best, their most confident, their most creative, but it's a difficult business, and it's not easy to succeed. I'm sure you'd say, well, being a Major League Baseball player isn't easy, either. But it's not the same."

"I know it's not the same. I'm not judging you, Keira."

"It feels like you are."

"Or maybe I just said what you were thinking, and you didn't like it. I struck a nerve."

"You don't know me, Dante. You don't know what I want. Don't try to fix me." She got to her feet. "I'm going inside."

He stood up. "Wait. I'm sorry. You're right. It's your business, not mine."

"You just don't know what I've been through, what I'm still going through."

"Can I apologize again?"

She drew in a breath and let it out. "It's all right. I guess you hit a sore spot. I have a lot of balls in the air, and no one understands the pressure I'm under. It's not so easy to just go for what I want. I have to consider other people, too."

"Okay."

"You think I'm making excuses, don't you?"

He hesitated. She was already pissed at him. *Did he want to answer that question?* He couldn't seem to stop himself. "Are you?" he challenged. "In my experience, we make time for the things we really want unless we're afraid to want them, afraid to go for them, or we don't want them as much as we think we do. That's when all the distractions and excuses come in."

"I know what I want. I just haven't figured out the logistics yet."

"Then you're good."

"I am good," she said hotly.

The air between them sizzled. "I know what I want, too," he said.

"To get back to baseball."

"Yes, but I also want something else." His heart was suddenly thudding against his chest.

Sparks lit up her eyes as she read his expression. "Bad idea, Dante."

"You're thinking the same thing. You're wanting the same thing. Aren't you?"

"Maybe you were right. Maybe I don't know what I want."

"Now you're chickening out."

"Because it's…reckless."

"I thought you liked being reckless, going fast, taking chances…"

"I was talking about skiing."

"Were you?" He took a step closer, his arms sliding around her back as his body took over his brain. Bad idea or not, he wanted to kiss her. He gave her one second to pull away, but she didn't, so he covered her mouth with his.

She tasted hot, sweet, and a little salty from the margaritas they'd been drinking. But her lips were incredibly soft and seductive, and he didn't want to stop kissing her. He wanted to lose himself in her. And when she opened her mouth to his, when she kissed him back, the hunger only deepened.

Then a door clattered open, and they jumped apart, turning at the same time to face Hannah's surprised gaze.

"Sorry to interrupt," she said.

"You didn't." Keira stepped away from him as she ran her hand through her hair. "We were just getting some air."

"Sure," Hannah said with a knowing smile. "Chelsea's award is coming up. I didn't want you to miss it."

"We'll be right in," Keira said.

As Hannah left, she gave him a helpless look. "I don't know what that was, but it can't happen again. I need to go inside."

She was gone before he could say a word. It was just as well, because even though he knew it shouldn't happen again, he couldn't promise it wouldn't.

CHAPTER EIGHT

KEIRA SPENT most of Monday and Tuesday in a state of distraction. When she wasn't reliving the unexpected and incredibly good kisses she'd shared with Dante, she was worrying about her mom, whose friendship with Mark Langley continued to grow. Her mom had been giggling on the phone like a teenager. She couldn't remember when her mother had last had so many long phone chats. It was like she was reliving her high school years.

By late Wednesday afternoon, Keira was ready to snap out of her lethargy. She'd been working at the store all afternoon, but she'd barely accomplished anything, and it was almost five. She was tired of her lack of focus and concentration. She needed to get over it.

She hadn't seen Dante since they'd left the patio. Thankfully, he hadn't stayed for the rest of the awards show, and she'd left as soon as she'd seen Chelsea make her acceptance speech. Dante hadn't tried to contact her since then, and she had stayed away from the inn, so it looked like they were back to being strangers. It was for the best. There was an unmistakable attraction between them—not just physical, but also emotional. She'd liked kissing him, but she'd also liked talking to him. It had felt so easy, so natural. But Dante was taken, and that was that.

She was a little surprised that Hannah hadn't been in touch to ask her what was going on. It wasn't like Hannah to butt out; she usually liked to butt in. Maybe that's why she was also distracted; she was waiting for the other shoe to drop.

But no more. She was moving on. She was getting her act together, and that started at six when she would show Mark Langley two houses. That would get her mother off her back and also give her another chance to talk to Mark. She hadn't dug any deeper into the fire at his house or any other part of his past. After telling Dante the story, she'd realized how far out on a limb she was getting. Hopefully, after spending more time with Mark tonight, she could put some of her doubts to rest.

She looked around the small boutique, which was currently empty. The last shopper had left ten minutes ago after trying on six dresses and not buying anything. But it had been a busy day before that and the racks needed straightening and the two dressing rooms needed to be cleared out. She should have had Daphne do it before she left, but Daphne had just gotten home from college and had a family birthday party to get to. She smiled to herself, knowing she was way too easygoing with the four women who helped out in her store, but aside from Daphne, Connie, her assistant manager, was a middle-aged woman who helped take care of her elderly mother, Pamela was a young mom with two kids under six, and Laurel was a high school senior, whose dreams of a career in fashion were being replaced by dreams of the hot guy with the motorcycle who showed up to take her home after work. She'd known them all for years, and it wasn't always easy to separate being their friend from being their boss.

She straightened as the door opened. She should have switched the sign to Closed. But to her surprise, it wasn't a customer; it was Hannah. She wore denim cut-off shorts and a short-sleeve blouse, and her red hair was swept up in a ponytail.

"You look like summer," she said. "No work today?"

"I switched shifts when I worked Sunday. Today, I went to the beach with my sister and her kids. It was fun and not that crowded."

"How is Kelly doing?"

"Great. She's really a good mother, but she has her hands full, that's for sure." Hannah looked around the shop. "No customers? That's unusual."

"It was busy earlier. I was actually just about to close."

"That's good," Hannah said, an oddly hesitant look in her eyes.

As the silence lengthened between them, she said, "What?"

"What do you mean?"

"You know what I mean. You have something to say. I'm actually surprised you waited this long to say it."

"I was hoping you might call and tell me what's going on."

"There's nothing going on."

Hannah tilted her head to the side. "I saw what I saw, Keira."

"Did you tell anyone else?"

"No. I'm your friend. I can keep your secrets. I know you don't want anyone to know you were kissing Dante DeAngelis. But I am curious, and I am tired of waiting for you to spill, so here I am."

"There's nothing going on. We kissed. It was…amazing. But it was an impulsive moment that won't happen again."

"Why not? Seems like you're both interested."

"He has a girlfriend, and he's only in town for a few weeks. Those are two huge strikes against him."

"Oh. Well, the girlfriend is a problem. The couple of weeks could just be fun. It doesn't have to be something serious."

"I can't get involved with someone who isn't free. I did that once before; it did not end well."

"That guy was lying to you," Hannah reminded her. "You didn't know he was hooking up with his ex-girlfriend."

"Maybe I just didn't see what I didn't want to see. Either way, I learned my lesson. If someone is involved with someone else, he is not involved with me. I don't plan to see Dante again."

"Got it. But it may not be that simple or clear-cut."

"Why not?"

"There's another reason I came by. I was just at the inn, and Lizzie said she's been trying to reach you, but you haven't been picking up your phone."

"I don't usually check my phone when I'm working. Is something wrong?"

"A reporter came by the inn, looking for Dante."

"What does that have to do with me?"

"He asked Lizzie if she could identify the mystery woman in a photo he'd taken." Hannah took out her phone and set it on the counter between them. "This is the picture and the article that's running online today."

She stared down at a photo of Dante and herself leaving Micky's the first night they'd met. They were facing each other. He was smiling, and she was laughing as he handed her the bag of fish tacos. But the headline spun the simple interaction into something much more dramatic. "Dante DeAngelis Scores a Beautiful Brunette During Rehab."

"I can't believe this," she muttered. "He handed me a bag of tacos outside the restaurant. It was nothing. I never even saw the photographer take the picture. He must have gotten it before he jumped out of the van. That's why Dante bolted so fast. He said he wanted to keep me out of any photos."

"He wasn't very successful. And that wasn't the only time the photographer caught you together." Hannah swiped the screen to reveal another photo of them sitting together in the glass-walled atrium at the rehab center.

She was shocked. "I ran into Dante when I went to see Mark Langley, my mother's friend. I had a meeting with Langley, not Dante. He just happened to be in the building when I arrived, so I said hello." She paused. "I wonder if Dante has seen these."

"Lizzie said she texted him, but he's been at the rehab center all day. What are you going to do?"

"Nothing. I'm sure it will blow over quickly."

"Maybe not that quickly. It's not just Dante who's famous; it's his girlfriend."

"Really? She's famous, too?" She hadn't asked Dante anything about his girlfriend.

"You don't know who he's dating?"

"I didn't ask him about her. I didn't really want to know."

Hannah picked up her phone and flipped through it. "It's Nikki Voltari, the supermodel. They started dating in February."

"Nikki Voltari?" she echoed. "I met her years ago when I was in New York. She was about seventeen then. She met with the designer I was working for. She was stunningly pretty, blonde, tan, thin, with incredible hazel eyes."

"She's still all that." Hannah turned her phone around once more. "This was taken of them at a red-carpet event in LA last March."

Nikki was as beautiful as she remembered, but Dante was even more handsome in a black tux. "They look good together." A large wave of disappointment ran through her. "Really good."

Hannah gave her a commiserating smile. "I'm sorry, Keira."

She shrugged. "It is what it is. It's not like he didn't tell me he had a girlfriend. Actually, he seemed eager not to call her that. He just said they were seeing each other."

"Maybe it isn't serious."

"Or he was downplaying it because he's in a small town and feeling bored."

"There is that possibility," Hannah admitted. "But he seemed like a nice guy."

"I think he is a nice guy. But he's injured. He's lost. He's not in his real life. I can't just be a distraction."

"No, you can't. But even if you don't want to date him, you're going to have to deal with the fallout from these photos."

She sighed. "I'm going to be painted as the other woman."

"I'm afraid so. How about I buy you a drink, and we can talk about it?"

"That would be nice, but I have to meet my mother's friend to show him a house. Do you know Mark Langley? He's the administrator of the rehab center."

"I met him last night. We had a cocktail party to welcome the new rehab staff members."

"What did you think of him?"

"Handsome for an older man. Seemed smart, articulate. Why?"

"He showed up at our house out of the blue last Thursday.

Apparently, he went to high school with my mom, and he's been taking her out ever since then. They've had dinner. They've gone on walks. They talk for hours on the phone. It's weird."

"Are you saying he's dating your mom?"

"It sure seems that way. She thinks he's wonderful, but I find him to be overly aggressive. My mother disagrees. She says he's just being nice and they're getting reacquainted."

"Wow. This is big news. I never pictured your mom dating again."

"I didn't, either."

"She is a lot better, though. Maybe this is good for her."

"She's still vulnerable. I don't know that her ability to see through someone's motives is that good. I need to protect her."

"I can understand that feeling. I was doubtful of my mother's boyfriend, too, because of her addiction issues. But he seems to respect the fact that she needs to be in a sober environment, so there's nothing else I can do. I just worry that my mom tends to lose herself when men come around. But your mom has never been like that. I hardly remember her seeing anyone when we were growing up."

"There were a few losers, like the one who stole money from her."

"Oh, right. I remember that one. So, what are you going to do besides show him a house?"

"Try to get to know him and see if I can figure out if he has a hidden agenda." She glanced at her watch. "I better lock up. I have to meet him in thirty minutes."

"Okay. If you want to talk later, you know where to find me."

"With Jake?" she teased. "Yes, I know where to find you."

Hannah gave her a big, happy grin. "Even if I'm with Jake, I'm still available to you. You know that."

"I do. And I'm glad you're with Jake. It was a long time coming."

"I just had to get out of my own way. That may be advice you need to take."

"I'm not in my way; there's a girlfriend, a baseball career, and now the paparazzi."

Hannah gave her a regretful smile. "I wish it were different. You and Dante seemed like you really clicked."

"I thought so, too. But it was just a click, nothing more—the end."

"We'll see."

"There's nothing to see. Go back to being cynical Hannah; I'm not used to this optimistic version."

"Sorry. I fell in love, and everything just looks rosier."

She pushed Hannah out the door, then locked it behind her and flipped the sign to Closed.

She not only needed to meet Mark Langley, but she also needed a minute to think about what the photographs might mean and what she needed to say if she ran across that photographer. One thing was clear: if she'd needed another reason to stay away from Dante, she'd just gotten it.

CHAPTER NINE

A HALF HOUR LATER, Keira pulled up in front of a two-bedroom house in a newer development near the outskirts of town. She wanted to show Mark Langley this house first, simply because it was farther away from the home she shared with her mother. She got out of the car and walked up to the front door to open the lock-box. When she entered the house, she turned on the lights. Even though it was still bright outside, she wanted the house to look inviting, and it did. The home had recently been remodeled in neutral colors. Everything was sleek, sophisticated, and well-designed. There weren't many frills, just a clean design, and that seemed perfect for a single, older man.

A car pulled up in front of the house, and she walked out to the porch. Mark Langley got out of the car, wearing brown slacks and a white shirt. He was a handsome older man, she grudgingly admitted. But good looks didn't necessarily make him a fit for her mother.

He gave her a friendly but somewhat wary smile. "Hello, Keira. Thanks for meeting me."

"No problem. The house is ready for you to look at."

She waved him inside, happy that the air conditioning was working well, as it was a warm summer evening. She told him a little about the home as he entered, pointing out a few things before he wandered off on his own. He walked through the house fairly quickly. She wasn't completely surprised, as her male clients were usually focused on only a few key things.

"This house looks good," he said, as he rejoined her in the living room. "I'm just not sure about the location. It's farther from town than the other one."

"By only a couple of miles. Nothing is that far in Whisper Lake. This house is probably the most up to date you'll find in this price range. The roof was recently done as well. It's a house you can move right into and just enjoy."

"I can see that."

"But you're not sold."

"As I said, it's nice, but I'm not convinced this is the location for me."

"All right. We're just starting to look, so that's good to know. I can zero in on better locations."

"I'm not in a hurry. I'd like to find something soon, but I want it to be the right place for me. In the meantime, I'm happy to stay at the inn. Lizzie does a great job taking care of me."

"She's the best."

"Yes." He gave her a thoughtful look. "I feel like we've gotten off on the wrong foot. Have I done something to offend you, Keira?"

She was taken aback by his direct words. "No."

"I know you're concerned about my relationship with your mother, but you really don't have to worry. I care about Ruth, and I would never do anything to hurt her. I know she's had a rough time, and I understand your sense of protectiveness. In fact, I admire the sacrifices you've made for your mother."

"I did what any daughter would do."

"It sounds like you went above and beyond, giving up your life in New York to be here with her and then changing careers to keep her real-estate business afloat so that she would still be able to earn money."

She appreciated his words, or maybe they were her mom's

words, but she still needed to keep her guard up. Mark was very smooth. He knew the right things to say. "My mom is the one who fought her way back to health, but…she's not all the way back. She has trouble with her memories. Sometimes the right word escapes her. She occasionally confuses faces."

"I haven't noticed any of that. She seems very sharp to me."

"Well, you've only been here a few days." She felt compelled to remind him how short their reunion had actually been.

"That's true. I'm looking forward to getting to know everything about her. I feel so lucky to have found her again. When I saw the job opening in Whisper Lake, the town name jumped out at me. I was fairly certain that's where your mom had ended up, but we hadn't been in touch in years. I wasn't sure she was still here. When I arrived, I told one of the therapists at the clinic that I'd gone to school with your mother, and she knew her. She told me where to find her."

"Who was that?"

"Her name is Nancy. Nancy Rodriguez."

She knew Nancy Rodriguez. She'd been one of her mother's therapists after the accident. "Nancy was very helpful in furthering my mother's recovery."

"She's an excellent therapist, from what I've been told. Anyway, that's how I showed up at your door last week. I know I took you by surprise. I guess I wanted to see the look on your mom's face. She didn't recognize me at first, but then she saw the photo, and she looked into my eyes, and it all came back."

She remembered that moment as well as he did, but while it had made him happy, it had made her suspicious. "My mom said you went out in high school."

"Yes. We dated for a couple of months our senior year, but it came to an end at graduation. We were going in different directions. My parents were moving to California, and I had gotten accepted to UC Santa Barbara. She was going to stay in Denver for school."

"But it wasn't just because you were moving. My mom told me you cheated on her."

Surprise filled his gaze. "Really? She said that?"

"She did."

"That's not what happened. She actually kissed someone else and then apologized for it. I was a very proud seventeen-year-old, so I didn't accept her apology. I was an idiot. After that, I started seeing another girl, but your mom was the one who strayed. Looking back, I can see why it happened. We were both late bloomers, and we weren't ready to be exclusive."

"Hmm, I guess she doesn't remember it the same way." It was entirely possible her mother had mixed it up in her mind. Or maybe Mark was just trying to make himself look better. "When did you meet your wife?"

"She's my ex-wife. We've been divorced for fifteen years. We met at a trade show when we were in our early thirties. She was a pharmaceutical rep. I was working in health care as well. We got married very quickly and then spent about six years trying to have a baby. Eventually, we had my son, Richard. He's twenty-four now."

"What broke you up?"

He hesitated. "A lot of things, many of them extremely painful. We needed to split up and move on from each other. It was the best thing for our son and for us."

"I'm sorry." She felt frustrated at his vagueness. But she couldn't really expect him to tell her his life story. Still, she wanted to push a little. "And you never remarried or fell in love again?"

"I've had other relationships, but marriage wasn't something I was eager to rush into a second time. Your mother said it was never something she wanted to do a second time, either."

"That's true."

He gave her a speculative look. "I'm not after anything, Keira. I just wanted to see Ruth again. It has been fun catching up with her, talking about old times, old friends. We have memories in common."

"That's what she said."

"I'm glad she's been enjoying our conversations as much as I am. Now, shall we take a look at the next house?"

"Yes. I'll lock up here. You can follow me, or I can meet you there, whichever you prefer."

"Why don't I meet you there? Your mom told me it's just a few blocks from your house, and she'd like to take a look at it as well, so I'll pick her up on the way."

"I didn't know she was interested in seeing the house. I can get her."

"It's no problem. We'll see you in a few."

He was gone before she could protest. *What could she say, anyway?*

Mark and her mom had already made a plan, and she'd been left out of it. She locked up the house, feeling decidedly out of sorts. When she arrived at the next property, she felt even more annoyed when her mother got out of Mark's car, looking remarkably put together in white pants and a floral top. When she'd left her mom this morning, she'd been in pajamas and an old robe. But she'd put herself together quite nicely: hair, makeup, and stylish sandals.

She told herself it was good. Mark was making her mom happy. That was what was important. She just wished she could stop seeing a potentially catastrophic downfall ahead. She didn't want to see her mother end up in pieces again, even if they were only emotional pieces and not physical. She didn't think she could handle it. She didn't think her mother could, either.

"Hello, Keira," her mom said with a bright smile. "Mark said the first house you showed him was lovely."

"It was, but the location didn't work for him. This house is in a great neighborhood, of course, but it is older."

"Yes, but it's charming," her mom said. "Let's go inside. This will be fun. I haven't looked at houses in a long time. It reminds me of the old days when I spent every Sunday working an open house."

"You're always welcome to come with me," she said, as she unlocked the home. "I didn't realize you felt like you were missing out."

"Well, I didn't feel that way until just now."

As her mother and Mark wandered around the older three-bedroom home, she could hear them chatting and laughing. Her mother seemed to find Mark hilarious. She couldn't fathom why. He had a dry sense of humor, but he wasn't exactly a comedian.

She popped into various rooms to point out good points as well as flaws, but no one was paying her much attention.

Finally, they ended up back in the kitchen, which had been the one room in the house that had been recently remodeled, although it was still on the smaller side.

"This kitchen is beautiful." Her mom ran her hand along the sleek white tile. "It's not huge, but the balance of counter space to appliances and cabinets is excellent."

"I can see myself cooking here," Mark agreed.

"Do you cook a lot?" she asked.

"I do. I didn't start cooking until I was in my forties, but now I love it."

"I told him we need to check out the farmers' market on the weekend," her mom put in.

"I can't wait," Mark said. "And I'd love to make you and Keira dinner next Sunday if that works out, if you don't mind lending me your kitchen."

"I'd love it," her mom exclaimed. "Keira?"

She gave a weak smile. "Sounds good."

"Then we'll count on you being there," Mark said.

"Great. What do you think of the house, Mark?"

"It's perfect," he replied. "I love the neighborhood. It's close to everything."

"It's on the higher end of your price range," she couldn't help noting.

"I think it's worth it."

"Are you ready to make an offer?"

"I need to sleep on it."

"Of course."

"But don't wait too long," her mom said. "Houses go fast in this neighborhood. It would be nice to have you close. We could take walks together."

"I'd love that."

As they exchanged a warm look, she cleared her throat, feeling very much like a third wheel. "Just let me know what you decide. I'll send you the disclosures tonight."

"Excellent."

"We're going to walk down to the lake now. It's so pretty at dusk," her mom said. "I made a curried chicken salad earlier. It's in the fridge if you're hungry before I get back."

"Thanks." She sighed as she locked up the house. It felt like her mom and Mark were on a runaway train. She just hoped that train didn't crash.

When she returned home, she went into the kitchen and opened the fridge, then closed it again. She wasn't hungry. She was restless. She needed a walk, too, or maybe a bike ride, but it would only be light for another hour.

As she was debating her options, her phone buzzed. She reached into her bag, noting the missed calls and texts from Lizzie, but the number lighting up her phone was not familiar to her. She almost didn't answer. *What if it was the media?* Well, she could always hang up.

"Hello?" she said tentatively.

"It's Dante."

Her stomach clenched at his deep, husky male voice. "Hi." Her hand tightened around the phone.

"Lizzie gave me your number. Have you heard about the photos?"

"Yes. Hannah stopped by the shop to show them to me."

"I'm sorry, Keira."

"It's not your fault."

"We need to talk about how to handle this."

"Is there anything to handle? It's done, right?"

"I'm afraid it could just be the beginning," he replied. "Can you meet me somewhere private, somewhere we won't be seen?"

She thought about that. The photographer had already been to the inn. And by now, he might know where she lived, too. But she did have one idea… "There's a cabin that my realty company is getting ready to sell. It's not on the market yet, but I have the key. It's on the east shore of the lake. Do you have a car?"

"Yes."

"Okay. I'll text you the address and then head over there."

"I'll see you soon."

His parting words sent a thrill of anticipation through her. It was stupid. This wasn't a date. They were just going to talk, sort things out, but still, she couldn't help running upstairs to change her clothes and fix her face. It might be the last time they'd see each other, and she was going to look good, give him something to remember. It might be the only satisfaction she would get.

Before Dante could leave his room, his phone rang. It was Nikki. They'd been missing each other for the past few hours. He had to take the call.

"Who is she?" Nikki shrieked in anger.

Dante winced. "It doesn't matter who she is. Nothing is going on. You know how these photos can get twisted. It has happened to you, Nikki."

"You were smiling at her, and I haven't seen you smile like that in a long time."

"I literally met her a few minutes before we walked out of that restaurant together."

"But you saw each other again."

"She had an appointment at the rehab center. We simply ran into each other."

"I don't like this, Dante. I don't like it at all. Everyone is texting me. They all want to know if you're cheating on me."

"I'm not." He felt slightly guilty about kissing Keira, but it hadn't gone any farther than that, and she'd made it clear she didn't want it to go farther.

"Are you sure you don't like this woman? Does she know you have a girlfriend?"

"Yes. Look, I know the photos are upsetting, but the story isn't real. That's all I can say about it. You can believe me or not." His terse tone did not go unnoticed.

"I don't know why you're pissed. I'm the one who looks like a fool."

"I'm angry that we even need to have this conversation. I thought I could get away from the press up here."

"Well, you couldn't, so maybe you should come to LA and rehab here. At least then we'd be together. The only photos would be of the two of us."

"The therapists I'm working with here are excellent. I need to see this rehab through." He glanced at his watch. "And I need to go."

"Go where? We have to talk about this."

"I haven't eaten dinner yet, and it's been a long day. I'm going to get some food. I'll call you later, Nikki."

"You can't just blow me off, Dante. Is this woman the reason you suggested we take a break?"

"No. I suggested that because we haven't been on the same page in a while. We've drifted apart, and maybe we need to reevaluate our relationship."

"We've only drifted apart because of your injury. When you're well, everything will go back to the way it was. Maybe I should come to Whisper Lake."

"No. That's not a good idea. I'm busy all day with rehab and then I'm exhausted."

"I don't want us to just give up. We're so good together, Dante. Everyone says we're the perfect couple."

He had a feeling the *everyone* she was referring to included mostly her social media followers. She'd worked their relationship to increase her presence online, and it had been successful. But maybe he was being too cynical. "No one else is in this relationship but us. What they think doesn't matter."

"Of course it matters. What's her name?"

"Keira," he said tightly.

"What does she do?"

"She runs a clothing boutique, but that's not important. Look, I'll call you later."

"Okay. I…I miss you, Dante."

Her words felt awkward and untrue, but he didn't know what to say except the obvious. "I miss you, too." He was acutely aware of his lie as he slipped his phone into his pocket. He hadn't missed Nikki at all. She seemed very far removed from his current life, and he was having trouble remembering why they'd even gotten together.

But he had missed someone the last few days…

He barely knew Keira, but he couldn't stop thinking about her, and he wanted to see her again, even if it was only to tell her that they needed to stay away from each other, because he didn't want to put her in the middle of his crazy life.

Nikki understood what it meant to be a celebrity, and she had trouble dealing with a faked-up story. *How could Keira possibly handle it, or even want to handle it?*

Not that she would ever have to. He was only in town for a few weeks, but he was here tonight, and that's all he was going to think about for the next few hours.

He jogged out the door, down the stairs, and through the dining room. Lizzie was in the kitchen. She gave him a smile. "Did you eat dinner, Dante?"

"No, but I'm going to meet Keira now, so…"

"That's what I figured." She picked up a shopping bag from the counter and handed it to him. "After you said you wanted to meet with her, I made you dinner to go—for two, just in case."

"You didn't have to do that."

"It was no problem. I was making enchiladas for me and Justin, so I just made extra. There's also a salad."

He was constantly amazed by how thoughtful Lizzie was. "Thanks."

"My car is in the garage. You have the key. Take the road behind the property, and you should be good."

Lizzie had been generous enough to offer him her car so that he could leave without being seen. He'd left his rental car conspicuously parked in front of the inn.

He headed into the adjacent garage and got into the car. On the way off the property, he kept a sharp eye out for the press, but didn't see anyone. As he drove through town, he made enough turns to feel confident he wasn't being followed, and then he headed to the east shore of the lake where the houses were spaced farther apart, and cabins were tucked into forested hills.

When he got to the address, he parked in the driveway, grabbed the shopping bag, and headed up the steps.

Keira opened the door as he hit the porch and waved him inside, closing the door behind him. They stared at each other, and he felt like his heart was beating way too fast. Keira's dark eyes were lit up, and her breathing seemed fast.

He wanted to kiss her more than he wanted to take his next breath. But he hadn't come here for that… *Had he?*

CHAPTER TEN

DANTE WAS GOING to kiss her, and her lips parted in response. She should say no. She should stop him. But she couldn't seem to move. He couldn't seem to move, either. The air between them was charged with tension. She could feel the sizzle. But one of them had to make a move. They couldn't just stand there and stare at each other.

She sucked in a breath and stepped back. "Was the cabin hard for you to find?"

"What?" Confusion entered his eyes.

"I know this street can be tricky to find."

"Oh, no. I didn't have any problem." He cleared his throat. "Lizzie thought we might be hungry. She sent enchiladas and salad. There's a bottle of wine in here, too." He held up the shopping bag in his hand.

"I can't believe she did all that. I guess you told her you were coming to meet me."

"Yes, and she offered her car so I could make a clean escape."

"That was a good idea. I'm glad you were able to leave the inn without anyone realizing it. This all feels a little crazy and surreal to me."

"I'm sure. It's not your life."

"No, but it is yours."

"Unfortunately, yes. It's the least favorite part of my life."

"It was weird to see myself in a photo with a headline that had nothing to do with the truth," she said.

"They don't care about the truth. Fiction always makes more money."

"I guess. Why don't you come into the kitchen? We can open that wine and see what Lizzie packed for us." She led the way down the hall, taking the time to pull her head together. She hadn't expected him to bring dinner, which meant he'd be staying for more than a few minutes. She wanted him to stay, but after the tension that had flared between them, she was also a little worried that keeping him in the friend zone would not be easy.

As they entered the kitchen, he set the bag on the table, while she pulled out some wine glasses and looked for a bottle opener.

"You called this a cabin, but it's a lot nicer than that," he commented.

"The exterior is more cabin-like than the interior. That's the beauty of it. You get the charm of a cabin in the woods with all the modern amenities." She pulled out the opener and took it to the table, along with the glasses.

"And this place is for sale?"

"It will be going on the market next month. We're still waiting for a new stove, some lighting fixtures, and a washer and dryer to arrive. The owner is a friend of mine. She and her husband moved to Dallas a couple of weeks ago. They're staying in corporate housing, so they've left all their furniture here until they find a place to buy. In the meantime, I'm taking care of all the little details that need to happen before we list."

While Dante opened the wine, she unloaded the rest of the shopping bag. There was a delicious-smelling tray of enchiladas, a side of guacamole, and a green salad filled with veggies and tortilla strips. A small container of dressing had also been provided. It was like a picnic date. But she really shouldn't start thinking about it like that. She grabbed plates and utensils and then sat down across from Dante.

He handed her a glass of wine. "Are you showing this house to Mark Langley?"

"No. It's too far from the clinic for him. He's interested in one about three blocks from the house I share with my mom. She's very excited about that idea," she added, rolling her eyes.

He gave her a small smile. "Still on the hunt for dirt?"

"I haven't had a lot of time to do that, and after I told you about the fire, I lost some of my drive."

"Why?"

"Saying it out loud made it seem like I was grasping at straws. I'm not someone who usually jumps to conclusions or makes up conspiracy theories, just so you know."

"I didn't have that impression."

"What impression did you have?"

"That you love your mother and that you can't stop worrying about her just because she's feeling better."

"You're right. My mom says I have to step back. I have to let her be better. I have to trust that she is. But I have a difficult time with that. She's not a hundred percent, and this man came out of nowhere."

"Not really nowhere. He has a job history, a personal history. You didn't find any criminal records, did you?"

"I honestly didn't go that far." She opened the foil covering the enchiladas, pleased to see they were still warm. "We should eat before these get cold."

"Sounds good to me. I'm starving."

She filled their plates, then said, "I know we should talk about the pictures. That's why we're here."

"Let's do that after our meal. I don't want to lose my appetite."

She was fine with delaying that conversation. "Okay. How has your week been going?"

"The rehab is more difficult than I imagined, but the clinic is first-rate, and my therapists are very good. I do a variety of exercises to strengthen and increase my range of motion. They also have me working on my total body: walking, running, and swimming."

"That's interesting. Is that just to keep you in overall good shape?"

"The therapists have talked a lot about how everything in the body works together and that concentrating on just one area can sometimes put other muscle groups at risk. Of course, the main focus is the shoulder and the arm."

"Is this the first time in your career you've been injured?"

"Second time. A line drive fractured my left wrist when I was in college. Luckily, it wasn't my throwing hand, but it took me off the mound for a while."

"That sounds like a scary moment. Are you ever afraid of getting hit in the face?"

"I never think about that. I feel confident in my fielding skills." He took a sip of wine. "The shoulder took me by surprise. But it shouldn't have. I think I'd gotten a little lazy in my training. I was letting other things distract me in the off-season. I wasn't in as good of shape as I could have been."

"You're not easy on yourself, are you?"

"I don't think anyone is harder on me than I am on myself," he admitted. "I've always been that way. I have high expectations."

"Do those expectations encompass everyone around you?"

"No, just me. I don't have a lot of expectations of anyone else. It saves me from feeling disappointment."

Hearing the edge in his voice, she suspected that quite a few people had disappointed him, but probably no one more than his dad. "Your father let you down a lot, didn't he?"

"Too many times to count, and it took me a long time to realize that would always be the result. Finally, I stopped caring or expecting anything."

"Does he let your brothers down as well?"

"He seems to be closer to Danny now. My oldest brother lives near him, and he talks my dad's language. They watch a lot of football together. As for Micah and Paul, I think they have the same relationship with him as I do. But while my dad wasn't there for us, we were there for each other. Sometimes, we were beating each other up, but when it came to the big stuff, I knew I could count on my brothers."

"That's nice. I always wished for a sibling. Although, I did get a lot of attention as an only child, and I didn't have to share."

"Being an only kid does have its perks."

"True. I also had good friends growing up: Hannah, Chloe, and Gianna. We were very tight."

"I like Hannah. She's very direct and seems very loyal."

"As loyal as they come. She's sometimes a little too sarcastic and cynical, but that's just who she is. Gianna and Chloe are great, too. Chloe was married to her high school boyfriend, but they divorced last year, so she's raising their little boy alone. Gianna recently got married to Zach Barrington. He's an architect in town. They're raising his daughter, Hailey."

"Has everyone been in Whisper Lake their entire lives?"

"No. Gianna left for a long time. Hannah was gone for several years, as was I. Chloe has pretty much always been here. She manages the Big Sky Café."

"I stopped in there yesterday to have lunch. They have great food."

"They do."

"What about Lizzie?" he asked. "When did you meet her?"

"A few years ago, when she moved here to open her inn. Her sister Chelsea came shortly thereafter, as well as her brother, Adam. He's a police detective."

Dante nodded. "I think Grayson told me that."

"Lizzie is trying to get her entire family here, and it might happen. She has dogged determination."

"I have seen examples of that. I don't know how she does all she does, like packing us this very delicious dinner."

"I think sometimes she must have a clone, or two or three. I could probably use a couple of clones, too."

"How has your week gone?"

"It's been busy." She was unwilling to admit how much time she'd wasted thinking about him.

"And you like to be busy."

"I do, but maybe not this busy. I'd like to find a happy medium, a good balance."

"I think balance is overrated."

She gave him a thoughtful look. "Why do you say that?"

"Because you can't be all things to all people. Some endeavors require brutal, single-minded focus."

"Like your job."

"Yes. I don't know many successful pro athletes who have a million different things going on. They just can't. And that's not a dig at you," he added quickly. "I know I made you angry the other night. I'm not judging you. I'm talking about myself."

"But you did point that comment at me when I mentioned trying to find a balance."

"Guilty."

She ate for a moment, then said, "You told me the other night that you were terrified your career might be over. What would you do if you couldn't pitch?"

"I don't allow myself to think about it."

"Never?"

"Nope. I have one focus, and that's getting back to the mound. It's not balanced. It's all in."

If he couldn't pitch again, he was headed for a huge fall. "I'm a little scared for you. But I'm also really impressed."

"Why would you be impressed?"

"Because your level of commitment is huge."

"Baseball is all I've ever committed to."

"You've had tremendous success with it, so your commitment worked."

"Until my arm decided to go its own way."

"I really hope you get back to pitching, Dante. I'm rooting for you."

"Thank you. By the way, no one else knows how scared I am about my future."

"Why not?"

"Because I don't share that."

"You told me."

"And for the life of me, I don't know why. But when we talk, I find myself telling you things I don't usually share. Nikki has never even once asked me about my family, my relationship with my father or my brothers."

She was surprised. "Really? It seems so ordinary to talk about family."

He shrugged. "Not in my world."

"Your world sounds a little superficial."

"It can be," he admitted. "I don't think I noticed until I came here."

The look in his eyes was unsettling. She took a long sip of her wine. "Well, if it makes you feel any better, I've shared a lot of personal information with you, too."

"You have, but I am curious about something, since we're going deep tonight."

"What's that?"

"What was it like giving up your design career?"

"It was nothing like what you're going through. I wasn't established. I wasn't at the top of my game, like you are. I was working an entry-level job at a fashion house. I ran a lot of errands, and any designing was done after hours in the hope that one day someone would give me a chance to show my designs. But that didn't happen."

"Still, you were pursuing your dream."

"It was a dream to be living in New York," she agreed. "The long hours, the nothing pay, the crappy apartment that I shared with three other girls didn't matter. I loved the city, the excitement, the energy, and the possibilities. I loved being around the designers, the models, and watching clothes come to life. Fashion Week in New York was my favorite time of the year. But in reality, I was more of a spectator in the fashion world than a participant."

"Do you think you'll go back to New York?"

"It's been on my mind the last year. More so since I started designing for my friends. But I don't know, Dante. I feel like that life has already passed me by."

"Why? You're not that old. Are you thirty? Thirty-one?"

"Thirty-one. And it's not just age; it's about lifestyle. What I was willing to do at twenty-two, twenty-three, I'm not sure I want to do now. Money has become more important to me. I don't want to live in a crowded apartment with three other people. I don't want to get coffee and run errands and go back to what I was doing."

"So, don't do that. Start higher. You have more experience now. A country music star just wore your dress on the red carpet. You don't have to do what you did before."

"It's still such a long shot. And New York is a long way from Whisper Lake. If something happened to my mom because I went off to try for something that's probably impossible to achieve, I don't think I could forgive myself."

"Something could happen to your mom while you're living in her house. You know that, Keira. Get honest. It's about fear that you're not good enough."

"I might not be good enough," she said.

"You won't know if you don't put yourself out there."

"It's more complicated than you understand."

"I get it. You have your mom to worry about. And as you told me before, practical matters, like money, play a role. But you don't want to look back years from now and wish you'd given your dream another shot. Have you talked to your mom about it?"

"No. I don't want her to think she is holding me back. That would hurt her too much."

He gave her a sympathetic smile. "You're a very kind, loving person. That's probably why you can't be as selfish as I can be."

She didn't know if he was selfish, or if he'd become an island of focus after his mom died and his father emotionally abandoned him. Maybe his pursuit of baseball had become the one thing in his life he could control. Now he'd lost that control, and he was desperate to get it back. But she'd probably done enough amateur psychoanalysis for one night. And she didn't want to keep talking about her career choices, either. She cleared her throat. "So, should we talk about the pictures?"

"Not yet."

She didn't ask him why he was stalling, because she didn't want to end the night yet, and it would end as soon as they got around to the real reason they were here.

Instead, she pushed her glass toward him. "In that case, top me off."

―――

Dante needed to get down to the reason they were meeting, but he wasn't ready yet. He refilled both of their glasses and rested his arms on the table as he gazed into Keira's pretty brown eyes. Despite the fact that their conversation had gotten very personal, he felt surprisingly good. "Let's talk more about you," he said.

"I think we've already dissected my career prospects."

"What about your dating life? Have you heard from the real Danny again?"

"No. I think he got the hint when I left the bar so abruptly. We were not a match."

"I wonder how he's doing on his novel."

"Who knows?"

"He might become a famous novelist one day, and then you'll be like, damn, I had a chance to date him," he said with a grin.

She smiled. "That would be just my luck. But fame and money aren't important to me."

Other women had told him that, and he hadn't believed them. But he actually believed Keira. "What do you care about?"

"Being able to talk and laugh with someone. It's so right that it's easy. Every time I'm in a relationship that's too hard, I try to fix it, only to waste weeks of time to finally admit that it just doesn't work."

"If there isn't an immediate connection, it never really happens," he agreed. "How picky are you?"

"Not that picky to meet someone, but after that, I can get critical. I've seen all of my friends fall in love, and I want the best of everything. I want the smoking hot chemistry and the best friend."

"You do want it all."

"Yes, I do. There's a song by Etta James, 'A Sunday Kind of Love'. Have you heard it?"

"No."

"It's not about the guys who are hot, sexy fun on Saturday night. It's about finding a man you want to spend all day Sunday with. That's who I'm looking for—that guy."

He wasn't that guy. He was usually pitching on Sundays. He knew he was taking it too literally, but that helped prevent him from making the ridiculous declaration that maybe he could be that guy, because he couldn't. And it wasn't just because of baseball. He was a Saturday night guy. He was a *gone the next morning* man. At least, he always had been. "I take it you haven't met that guy."

"Nope."

"Ever get close?"

"A couple of times I thought maybe…but none of them worked out. The last few years, dates have been sparse. I've been busy, and I don't exactly live in a big city with a lot of options."

"Is staying in Whisper Lake a deal breaker?"

"Maybe. But I don't have to make that decision now. What about you? Have you been in serious relationships before Nikki?"

"Just to clarify once more, Nikki isn't a serious relationship."

"What about before her?"

"I've had a couple of relationships that lasted a year or so, mostly when I was younger—high school, college. Once I was drafted and started traveling from city to city, my primary relationship was with baseball. I've lived a rather narrow life when I think about it." His words actually surprised him. He hadn't thought of it that way until now.

"Narrow? Your life seems big to me."

"But in just one specific area. Do you want more wine?" he asked, as she finished her glass.

"No. If I drink more wine, I won't be able to drive home. We need to talk about the pictures, Dante."

"I know. I have to say I was surprised by the shots. I didn't think the photographer caught us at Micky's."

"And I never saw anyone outside the rehab center. But you

were right. Once the photographer saw us together twice, he started spinning a story about us that was completely fictional."

"It's possible that it will get worse now. Even if more paparazzi don't show up, people will be taking out their phones and snapping photos wherever I go. You can make good money taking pictures of celebrities."

"I feel like Whisper Lake is pretty good about letting celebrities have their privacy. Chelsea has gone through some of that scrutiny, but most people leave her alone now."

"That might be true if I lived here full-time, but I'm at a moment in my life that's very tenuous, and a lot of sports reporters and fans are eager to know if I'm going to make it back this season. It would be better for you if we didn't get close enough for anyone to take another picture."

"So, we're breaking up," she said. "Even though there's nothing to break up."

He thought about that for a moment. "Isn't there, Keira?"

A sudden uncertain gleam lit up her gaze. "What do you mean?"

"You know what I mean. There's something between us."

"There's also *someone* between us. Has Nikki seen the photos?"

"Yes. I told her there was nothing to them."

"Did she believe you?"

"She knows how the press is. She's a very popular model, and she has dated a lot of high- profile celebrities. She's used to cameras."

"I actually met Nikki a long time ago when I was in New York. I'm sure she wouldn't remember me. She was a young model, and I was an errand girl. She's really beautiful. You're lucky."

He didn't feel lucky. He felt like he'd gotten caught in an unexpected trap.

"We didn't really need to meet for you to tell me to stay away from you," Keira continued. "You could have said that on the phone. Why didn't you?"

"Because I wanted to see you again. I told Nikki that things weren't working out for us, but she cut me off when I suggested we take a break. She said we'd talk about it later."

Surprise moved through her gaze. "Why did you tell her that?"

"Because it's the truth. We haven't been in sync for weeks, long before I met you."

"I don't want to be the reason you break up with her. It's not like we have a future ahead. You'll be leaving in a few weeks."

"I know. If this was another time, another place…"

"But it's not."

"No," he agreed, feeling weighed down by that answer. "So, this is it?"

"I think so." She forced a smile onto her face. "It was fun while it lasted. I don't want things to be awkward between us. This is a small town. You're staying at the inn. It's likely we'll run into each other. Let's not make this into a bigger deal than it is."

She was saying everything she could to make their situation easier, and he should have appreciated that, but he didn't.

Keira stood up. "I'll clean all this up and get the dishes back to Lizzie tomorrow. You can go, Dante."

He got to his feet, not at all happy with the way things were ending. "This isn't what I want."

She stared back at him. "Sometimes you have to accept that you don't always get what you want."

"I never accept that. I just keep fighting until I reach my goal."

"I'm not your goal, Dante. And until you actually break up with Nikki, you probably shouldn't be kissing anyone else."

"You were irresistible," he said with a smile.

Her lips curved upward. "So were you, but it's over. That's the best decision for both of us." She stuck out her hand. "Deal?"

He took her hand, his fingers curling around hers, and he held on for far too long.

"You have to let go now," she said.

"You first," he replied, a challenging note in his voice. "Or we could have a goodbye kiss."

She licked her lips, and his heart thudded against his chest.

"I'm really tempted," she whispered. "But it won't make me

want to say goodbye." She yanked her hand away from his. "Can you please go before I change my mind?"

He really didn't want to leave. He wanted to pull her into his arms and kiss her until she was breathless. And then he wanted to take it even further. But he couldn't do that, not while he was tangled up with Nikki, and maybe not even when he was untangled. Because this woman seemed like someone who could be a distraction for a very long time.

"Dante," she pleaded, an almost desperate note in her voice.

"Okay, I'm going. Just for the record, I don't think this is over." He left before she could respond, letting the front door slam behind him in frustration. He was a man who got what he wanted. But he couldn't have her—not now, probably not ever—and he didn't know how to just accept that. But he was going to have to figure out a way.

CHAPTER ELEVEN

DANTE DIDN'T SLEEP WELL, and his rehab session on Thursday was brutally rough. He was tired. He was in a bad mood, and his patience was thin. By noon, his therapists had seen enough and suggested he either call it a day or take a two-hour break before the afternoon session. He'd opted for the break, not wanting to lose any valuable time in his recovery. He just needed to get his head together and remember why he was in Whisper Lake. It wasn't to romance Keira. He just wished he could stop thinking about ways to see her again, even though they'd both agreed to stay apart, not just for the sake of avoiding a photograph, but also because he was still attached to Nikki, and he was just passing through.

When he walked into the inn, he gave Lizzie a nod.

"Dante," she said with a welcoming gaze. "I'm glad you're back. You have a visitor."

His gut tightened. "Who?"

"Nikki Voltari."

"What?" His gaze swept the entry and adjacent living room. "She's here?"

"Yes. She said she was exhausted from her early flight, so I gave her a room. I didn't feel right putting her in your room. She's on the second floor in room six."

He couldn't believe Nikki had come to Whisper Lake.

"Thanks."

He moved up the stairs, feeling a mix of emotions, none of them good. He knocked on Nikki's door. A moment later, she threw it open. She wore a cropped top and wide-legged pants that did little to hide how thin she was. Her straight blonde hair reached halfway down her back, and when she came toward him, he almost choked on the strong scent of her perfume.

"Dante," she squealed, then threw her arms around his neck and gave him a kiss. "Are you surprised?"

"I am," he admitted, as she pulled him into the room and shut the door. "I just talked to you last night. You didn't say anything about coming."

"I decided after we spoke. Craig let me use his plane this morning. There's a private airfield about twenty minutes away."

"You didn't have to come."

"I did have to come. I need the press to see us together, so I can reframe the story on my social media pages."

"Reframe the story? What does that mean?"

"Don't worry about it." She sat down on the end of the bed and pulled him down next to her. "It's been so long since I've seen you. You look good."

"Thanks. You look as beautiful as always." He wasn't lying, but he also didn't feel any chemistry anymore. She was too much: too made up, too styled, too perfumed. She was right in front of him, but he felt like he was looking at a photograph.

"The innkeeper insisted on giving me my own room," Nikki added with a roll of her eyes. "But I can move my stuff to your room now that you're here."

"Uh, how long are you planning to stay?"

"I'm not sure. Why?" She sat back, giving him a disgruntled look. "You're not happy to see me, are you?"

"I told you that I'm focused on my rehab. I'm on a break now. I have to be back at the center for an afternoon session."

"Can't you take some time off?"

"No, I can't. You shouldn't have come."

Hurt filled her eyes. "Dante, I'm your girlfriend. Why don't you let me help you?"

He would have felt more touched if he thought she actually wanted to help him, but she had not pressed to be with him at any point since his injury. She'd been happy to wait until he was completely back to normal. She'd never wanted to sit in the hospital with him or even hang out in Denver, where he'd done his initial recovery. It was only because of the story the press had made up that she'd felt compelled to come and see him. She was worried about how she was looking, not how he was feeling.

Maybe he was being too cynical, but he didn't think so. "You can help me by going back to LA," he said. "My whole career is riding on this rehab."

"I understand that, and I want you to get better. I want you to go back to doing what you do. I can help you."

"You really can't."

"I can," she said with determination. "I can get the press off your back and stop them from making up nonsensical stories about you and that woman. My being here will put an end to that."

"I think your presence will just draw more photographers."

"Let me worry about that. You focus on your rehab. I'll handle the media."

"I'd rather you just went back to LA."

"Well, I'm not going to do that yet. You may not think you need me, but you do."

He was too tired to argue with her. "Fine. We'll talk about this later."

"Tonight. Let's have drinks and dinner. I'll find a good place and text you the address."

"All right. But I'm tied up until five."

"We'll do it at six." She leaned forward and kissed him. "We can move my things later."

"Nikki—we really need to talk about everything."

"We'll do that at dinner. Go, do your thing. We'll talk later."

He knew he couldn't keep letting her put him off. He just didn't have time to get into a big scene, and with Nikki, big scenes were a fairly common occurrence. "I'll see you later."

As he walked out of the room, he blew out a frustrated breath. Nikki's surprise appearance had done one thing—it had shown him in very clear-cut terms that she was not the woman he wanted.

But the woman he now wanted he couldn't have.

Keira stared at the wedding dress on the sewing table in front of her. After a busy morning in the shop, she'd taken a late lunch break in the back room of her store to work on Hannah's dress, but she'd been staring at it so long, her eyes were blurring. When her manager, Connie, popped her head into the room, it was a relief to be forced to look away.

"I just wanted to remind you that I'm leaving early today," Connie said. "My mother has to go to the doctor, and she needs a ride."

"Right." She looked at her watch. It was almost two. "You better get going."

"Daphne will be in at three, and she'll stay until close."

"That's fine."

"How's the dress going?"

"Not that well. Taking a break from it will be good," she said as she got to her feet.

"It always helps to have fresh eyes. By the way, have you checked your emails today?"

"Not yet. Why? Is there a problem?"

"I was skimming through to see if there was any store business—"

"Of course," she interrupted. "I'm happy to have you keep an eye on emails I need to respond to."

"Well, you do need to respond to these emails, but they're not about the store. You have two emails from Karli Holton, one from a guy name Rafa Delgado, and another from Talia Bee."

"Seriously? Talia Bee and Rafa Delgado are very successful and well-connected stylists."

"I know," Connie said with a gleam in her eyes. "And Karli Holton is an up-and-comer. I looked her up. They all want to talk to you about designing dresses for their clients. They all referenced Chelsea's beautiful gown."

"That's amazing." She'd thought she might get some interest in her work after Chelsea's gown was photographed, but not from top stylists.

"Your side hustle could be turning into a lot more, Keira. So, answer your email."

"I will take a look," she promised, following her manager back into the store. There were no customers at the moment, so after Connie left, she logged into the computer on the counter.

Each email was nicer than the last: compliments about her design, her originality, and the sheer beauty of Chelsea's gown… Her smile grew with each word, and she felt a thrill of excitement and satisfaction.

Talia Bee was looking for a designer for Crystal Jeffers, who was her main client. Crystal was starring in a blockbuster film being released in September and would need a red-carpet dress. Rafa Delgado wanted to know if she had any gowns already done that one of his clients might be interested in, and Karli Holton simply asked for a call to discuss opportunities with her clients, who were primarily country music singers. Designing Chelsea's gown had definitely opened some doors for her. Now she just had to walk through those doors.

Her exhilaration dimmed as she thought about the practical logistics of addressing these requests. She had Hannah's gown and the bridesmaids' dresses to complete, as well as managing the store and keeping an eye on the real-estate business.

Where was she going to find the time to do all of this?

As she pondered that question, the door opened, and a beautiful, tall blonde came through the doors, wearing a very short red dress that showed off the sharp angles of her very lean body. She had on ridiculously high heels and a pair of what appeared to be very expensive sunglasses. As she removed her glasses, Keira stiffened in surprise. She knew this woman. She hadn't changed much at all in the last seven or eight years since they'd met.

"Are you Keira?" the woman asked.

"Yes."

"I'm Nikki Voltari."

"I—I know who you are," she stuttered, swallowing hard as she tried to get her wits about her.

What the hell was Nikki doing in Whisper Lake? And why was she here? This could not be good.

"Then you must know I'm Dante's girlfriend."

She cleared the lump in her throat. "Yes, and I also know that you're a supermodel. In fact, we met several years ago. I'm sure you wouldn't remember."

It was Nikki's turn to be surprised. "We've met? How is that possible? I've never been to this town before."

"I was working in New York for Jacques Bateau. It was years ago. You were a teenager. You came in for a fitting before our Fashion Week runway show. I went out to find you the perfect matcha tea."

Nikki stared back at her. "I don't remember."

"I didn't think you would. I was pretty much an errand girl and not the designer I wanted to be."

"How did you end up here?"

"I'm from here. My mom had an accident. I came back to care for her." She paused. "I want you to know that you don't have anything to worry about. Dante and I barely know each other. Those photos were misconstrued."

"That's what he said."

"I hope you believe him."

Nikki tilted her head, giving her a thoughtful look. "I do, but a lot of women would take advantage of a mistake like that to wedge themselves into his life."

"That's not me."

"Maybe. Maybe not. Here's what we're going to do. You're

going to meet me for drinks on the patio at the Lakeshore Bistro at five thirty."

"Why?"

"Because I want us to talk, and I want us to be seen together. Wear one of those cute dresses in the window."

"Wait—" she began, but Nikki was already gone, the door clanging behind her.

She blew out a breath. She really wished Dante would have given her a heads-up that Nikki was coming her way—unless he didn't know. But Nikki said she'd spoken to Dante, so he had to know. Maybe he was happy to go along with whatever Nikki wanted. She certainly was beautiful. She'd forgotten how striking Nikki was.

Why had Dante been flirting around with her when he had Nikki?

Probably because he'd been bored, she thought, as she worked herself up, anger running through her.

She'd let herself believe that there was something real between them. Dante had said that he wanted to take a break from Nikki. But if he wanted to take a break, then Nikki wouldn't be here. And Nikki certainly hadn't acted like a woman whose boyfriend had just broken up with her.

The last thing she wanted to do was meet Nikki for drinks, but she did feel like she owed her something, because she felt a little guilty that she'd kissed Dante. So, she'd meet Nikki at the Bistro, and hopefully that would be the end of it—the end of everything. She could stop being distracted by Dante, stop thinking *what if…* when she knew there was *no* what-if.

Tonight, maybe she could finally make herself believe that.

───────

"You did much better this afternoon," his therapist, Rita Donohue, told him after they finished their session late Thursday afternoon.

"It didn't feel that way." His shoulder was aching, and his breath was still coming hard.

"Because you want everything in a second, but each day you're getting stronger and your range of motion is improving. You're right where you're supposed to be."

"I'm supposed to be in Miami on the pitcher's mound, throwing strikeouts."

"One day at a time," she said with a smile.

Rita was a kind but firm woman in her early forties. He hated the platitudes she occasionally threw out, but he did appreciate her efforts. She stayed positive while she kicked his ass, and that's what he needed.

"I'll see you tomorrow," Rita said. "You might want to take it easy tonight, get a lot of rest."

That was exactly what he wanted to do, but he had a problematic girlfriend waiting to have drinks with him. He didn't think rest was in the cards.

He headed toward the locker room, took a quick shower, dressed, and then took the elevator down to the parking garage. When he stepped out, he was surprised to hear shouting, and the two people involved in the argument included Mark Langley and a middle-aged red-haired woman. They were having an animated and heated conversation. The woman put her hand on Mark's arm, and Langley shoved it off.

"You'll be sorry," she warned.

"I've been sorry for a long time."

"This isn't over."

"It is over. You just need to accept that." Langley then stormed away from her, jumping into a gray sedan before speeding out of the garage. The woman had her hands on her hips, her glare following his vehicle until it disappeared. Then she got into a white car and drove away. Neither one of them had noticed him at all.

As he got into his vehicle, he wondered what he'd just seen. The woman was not Keira's mother, that was for certain. But they clearly had some sort of relationship. Maybe Keira's instincts about Langley were not as far-fetched as he'd thought. There had been definite anger and dislike between the two of them.

But who was that woman? Was it the Mandy who had called him a few days earlier?

He tapped his fingers on the steering wheel, then took out his phone.

Before he could call Keira, he saw several texts from Nikki. She wanted him to meet her for drinks at the Lakeshore Bistro. Damn. He didn't want to have a public argument with her, but he felt like that's where they were headed. He sent her a quick text asking her to just meet him at the inn, but she replied immediately. *I came all this way. Just meet me for a drink.*

With a sigh, he sent back a thumbs-up. She probably wanted to prove to the world that they were still together. Whatever. He could have a drink and they could talk after that.

He punched in Keira's number. While they'd agreed to stay apart, he needed to tell her what he'd seen. Unfortunately, his call went to voicemail. He didn't know if she was avoiding him, but he left a brief message. "I have some information on Langley," he said. "If you're interested, call me back." He'd leave it to her to decide.

Setting down his phone, he drove out of the garage, keeping an eye out for paparazzi, but there was no one around. He hadn't seen anyone on his trips back and forth to the inn, either. He'd like to believe the photographer had given up and gone back to whatever rock he'd crawled out from under, but that didn't seem likely. Maybe he was following Nikki around. He doubted she'd come into Whisper Lake under any kind of radar. She never went anywhere without announcing it on social media. She wanted people to follow her, especially the press. The more pictures, the better, as far as she was concerned.

It hadn't really bothered him before, but then he hadn't thought much about it. When he'd been on top of the world, the press and the photos had all just seemed part of his life, and he had nothing to hide. But while his injury was no secret and had occurred in real time on national television, his recovery was private and probably felt a little mysterious to a lot of people. Throwing in a hot brunette had given the press a new story to run with. They'd had a void to fill, and they'd found a way to fill it.

He needed to take back control, not just with the press but also with Nikki. He'd let her put him off and stall the hard conversation that she didn't want to have. He'd talk to her tonight and then he'd figure out what to do about the press.

CHAPTER TWELVE

THE LAKESHORE BISTRO was set on a bluff overlooking the lake, with an interior dining room and a spectacular patio with an even more impressive view. He made his way through the dining room and onto the patio. Nikki sat at a table by the railing. In the seat across from her was Keira. His gut twisted. *What the hell?*

He froze, tempted to leave before either one saw him, but then Nikki's gaze swung toward him, and she waved. He had no choice but to walk over to the table.

"Sit here," Nikki said with a smug smile. She waved her hand toward the empty chair between them.

"What's going on?" he asked, looking at Keira.

"Ask Nikki. She set this up," Keira replied tersely.

"Nik?"

"It's all part of my plan to reframe the story," Nikki replied. "I told you to leave it to me. I know exactly how to play this." She slid her chair closer to his. "Now you both need to turn, face that way, and smile like we're the best of friends."

"What?"

"You heard me," she said through lips that were fixed in her trademark smile.

He turned his head toward the right as Keira did the same, only then realizing that there were several photographers standing just off the patio. Their cameras flashed continuously for a good minute.

Nikki put her arm around his shoulders and pressed her lips against his cheek as the shots continued. He tried to smile. But it was a battle. He could see the discomfort in Keira's gaze as she valiantly tried to look like she wasn't a third wheel.

"Keira, slide your chair closer to Dante," Nikki ordered.

"Uh, okay." Keira did as she was told until the three of them were very close together, with himself in the middle.

The cameras flashed again, and then Nikki waved to the photographers. "That's it, guys."

One of the men moved closer. "Are you going to be back this season, Dante?"

"I told you no questions about baseball," Nikki interrupted. "Go send your pics off. Make some money."

"Hope you make it back, man," the photographer said, then he followed the others away as the owner of the restaurant came forward to make sure they were leaving.

Keira moved her chair back to where it had been. "Well, you don't need me anymore."

"You can't leave yet," Nikki said firmly. "The press will be in the parking lot for at least another ten minutes. We don't want this to look fake."

He shifted, too, moving his chair away from Nikki. "What the hell was that?"

"It was the best idea I could have had," Nikki replied. "Now, let's all have some champagne. You two need to smile. Even if the photographers have left, everyone on this patio has a phone, and they're looking at us."

He could see that was true, which made him even more uncomfortable. Since Keira's expression was extremely stressed, he had a feeling she'd been ambushed as well.

Nikki pulled a bottle of champagne out of a nearby ice bucket. "I got a great bottle of bubbly. I'll pour."

"I don't want champagne," he said tersely.

"So just pretend to drink it," she said sharply. "You, too, Keira. I went to a lot of work to solve this problem. The story of your mystery romance is now over. The three of us are friends. In fact, Keira and I are actually old friends. That's the story that will be online tonight. I'll add to it later."

"You should have told me what you were planning."

"You would have said no."

"You're right. I would have said no. Creating a story as fake as the last one only creates more problems."

"It's not completely fake," Nikki replied. "Keira and I did meet years ago."

"I mentioned that to her when she came to the store earlier," Keira interjected. "Nikki didn't tell me you were coming tonight when she invited me for a drink. She also didn't tell me she was setting us up for a photo."

"I figured. I'm sorry."

"Why are you apologizing? You two should be happy," Nikki said. "I've changed the narrative. It's all good."

He didn't feel good, and he didn't think Keira did, either. But there was no denying the smile of satisfaction on Nikki's face. "You just whet their appetite, Nik. They'll hang around to see what other photos they can get."

"But I'll be the focus, and I love the camera." She lifted her glass. "Let's make a toast."

"To what?" Keira asked in bemusement.

"Our threesome," Nikki said with a laugh.

"Nik," he protested. "That's not funny."

"Fine. Let's just drink to the end of a story that didn't benefit any of us. By the way, Keira, I love that dress. Who's the designer?"

"It's actually one of mine."

"What? I thought you just ran a boutique."

"I do run a boutique, but I also design in my spare time. A few things here and there. I do mostly custom-designed gowns, but I've also made some summer dresses like this one."

"Keira designed a dress for Chelsea Cole," he said.

"Really?" Nikki said, surprise in her eyes. "Chelsea Cole is a big star. How did you get her?"

"She lives here." Keira set her glass down and stood up. "I have to go. Hopefully, this is the end of the problem. Goodbye."

Her words felt very final and put a pit in his stomach. He wanted to call her back, but he couldn't, not until he cleaned up the mess he'd made.

Nikki gave him a smile as Keira left. "Don't look so tense, Dante. Everything will be fine. You'll see."

Everything would not be fine. It was time he told her that.

"Nikki," he began.

At his tone, her smile dimmed. "Look, I know you're pissed that I didn't include you in my plan, but it worked. Can't you just appreciate what I did? You don't have to worry about rumors. You can concentrate on your rehab."

"You should have told me and Keira what you were planning. No one likes to be ambushed."

"I was ambushed when those photos appeared. Let's not forget who looked the worst in this whole scene."

He wasn't going to win that argument. "All right. Let's forget about the photos."

"Fine by me. Shall we order food?"

"No. I'm not hungry. Let's go back to the inn."

"Well, I am hungry, and I've been stuck in that inn half the day. So, I want to order some appetizers, at least."

"You can't keep putting me off, Nik."

For the first time since he'd arrived, there was uncertainty in her gaze.

"Just take a breath, Dante. Things are not as bad as you seem to think they are."

"And they're nowhere near as good as you think they are. I've tried to tell you that a few times. You need to hear me." He paused, glancing around the patio. Most people had gone back to their conversations, but he still didn't want to create a new scene. "I really don't want to talk here."

"Well, I'm going to enjoy my champagne, so you can do the

same, or we can have some public and awkward conversation. It's up to you."

She was daring him to do it, because she didn't think he would. But she was wrong. Her challenge just made him more determined to speak.

"All right, we'll do it here," he said. "We don't work anymore, Nikki. We haven't in a long time. You know that as well as I do. I don't want to just take a break; I want to break up."

She sucked in a breath at his blunt words. "That's shitty, Dante. I've been so supportive of you."

"You haven't seen me in six weeks. You couldn't even sit at the hospital when I had my surgery."

"Hospitals make me nauseous, but I texted you all the time, and I sent you fun presents. It's not like I could do anything for you. And besides that, you didn't want me around. You didn't want anyone around."

She had a point. By the time he'd gotten to Denver to see Grayson, he'd been wrapped up in a cocoon of pain and misery. "You're right. I wasn't in the right space to deal with anyone but myself."

"I'm glad you can see that."

"But the surgery was six weeks ago. In all that time, we never got together. We barely texted."

"Again—your choice."

She was rewriting history, but she was very good at that. "I don't want to rehash the past."

"Then stop."

"Nikki, you have to hear me. We had fun for a while, but we need to move on."

"You're just in a weird place right now, Dante, because of your injury. Once you're back on top, it will be like it was before."

"It won't be, because I've changed."

She stared back at him in alarm, as if his words had finally sunk in. "That's not true."

"It is. Having to deal with a possible career-ending injury has made me look at my life differently."

"You're making a huge mistake, Dante. I'm a catch."

He smiled at her proud self-confidence. "Believe me, I know that. The next story in the press will be how big a fool I was to let you go."

"That won't be the story," she said harshly. "It won't be your decision to break up; it will be mine. I will have let you go. In fact, that's the real reason I came to Whisper Lake. I needed to break up with you in person."

He could see the wheels spinning in her head. "Whatever you want to say is fine with me. I don't want to hurt you, Nikki. I do care about you. But we don't want the same things. You love to travel, to party, to be seen, and after traveling with my team for months on end, I want to stay in one place. I don't want to take pictures every second. I don't want to be part of a media story."

"Well, that's part of my career. I had to make sacrifices for you —sit in the stands and watch endless games that you weren't even in some of the time. If you had to pose now and then, what's the big deal?"

"It's just an example of how different we are. You should find someone who wants to be in every picture with you."

"I'm not that superficial, Dante. Our relationship is about more than photos."

"Is it?" he challenged.

Her lips turned down in a pouty frown of annoyance. "Well, it could have been, but you were the one who was always leaving or pulling away. I still think things could get better once you've completely recovered and you're back in your real world. I get along great with your teammates."

"You do. They'll all think I'm nuts."

"They wouldn't be wrong."

He nodded, knowing he was doing the right thing for both of them. He felt like a weight had just slipped from his shoulders, one he'd been carrying too long.

"Well," she said, as the silence lengthened between them. "I guess we should go, but I'd like us to leave together with your arm around my shoulders."

He was beginning to remember just how many public moments she'd directed. "Whatever you want. Let me pay for the champagne." He waved the server over to the table and handed her his credit card.

They sat in an odd, uncomfortable quiet. There should have been more to say, but there wasn't, and that only reinforced his decision to call it quits. Nikki took out her phone. He did the same. A moment later, the server returned, and he signed the receipt with relief, then ushered Nikki out of the restaurant. Since she'd taken a cab to the restaurant, he drove her back to the inn. She spent the ride on her phone.

When he parked at the inn, he said, "Can I help you get a flight home tomorrow?"

"Already done. I'll be heading back to Denver tonight."

"That was fast."

"There's no reason to go slow, is there?" she challenged. "You're not going to change your mind. And I'm not going to waste time crying over you."

"I am sorry, Nikki. We had some good times."

She drew in a breath. "We did. We still could. But, clearly, you're lost in some alternate reality. When you finally wake up, it will be too late. Then you really will be sorry. Because I don't give men second chances."

"I know."

They got out of the car and walked into the inn together. When they hit the second-floor landing, he paused. "Do you want me to help you with your bags?"

"I'm sure the inn can send someone to do that." She paused by her door, her sharp gaze raking his face. "Were you lying before?"

"About what?" he asked warily.

"Keira. Was it as innocent as you both said it was? Or is she a part of this?"

"She's not the reason we're breaking up, and those photos were innocent." Those two answers were the truth, even if they weren't the whole story.

She gave him a long look. "You might be lying to me or you might be lying to yourself."

"Or I'm telling the truth."

"I guess we'll see."

As she moved into her room, he exhaled and then headed up the stairs. He tossed his phone and his keys onto the dresser and then stretched out on the bed, looking at the ceiling. Breaking up with Nikki had been the right thing to do, and it felt good to make one decision about his life, to have something under his control. But the rest of it was still a cloud of confusion.

Would he get his life back? And if he did, would it be the same? How could it be?

The injury had not only derailed his career, but it had also forced him to stop and look at his life, at his relationship with Nikki. *Had it always been so superficial?*

He'd never thought about it before, but their relationship had mostly been a series of one-night stands or weekends together. He'd met Nikki right before the season had started, and after the first three weeks of dating, he'd gone off to spring training. Then the season had started.

Nikki had popped in and out of Miami. Occasionally, they'd meet up on the road somewhere. They'd spent a lot of time in clubs and at parties, but not doing real world stuff. They hadn't had to deal with mundane issues like who needed to take out the trash or who spent too long in the bathroom. It had all been fun and sex and a lot of drinking. They'd certainly never had to deal with one or the other being sick until he'd gotten injured, and that hadn't gone well.

Well, he and Nikki were done, and she was definitely leaving with her pride intact. He didn't know if her bravado was a defense mechanism or if she was even more narcissistic than he'd realized, but she'd turned the breakup into his biggest mistake, not hers. That was fine. He didn't care what she had to say about him. He was just happy not to have to deal with her anymore.

As for the media, who knew what would come next? That was probably in Nikki's hands. But she'd spent a lot of time on the story she'd spun today. Hopefully, she'd just stay quiet for a while and let everything die down. That would be the best thing, although he suspected he was being overly optimistic.

Sitting up, he grabbed his phone and punched in Keira's number. She probably didn't want to hear from him, but he needed to speak to her.

"Hello?" she said, a wary note in her voice.

"It's Dante."

"I know. Why are you calling?"

"Two reasons. I broke up with Nikki."

A longer silence than he would have expected followed his words. "Okay," she said finally. "Why?"

"A lot of reasons. She's leaving Whisper Lake tonight. I wanted you to know in case any of the media hang around town to ask you about her or us."

"Is her story about us all being friends going to hold?"

"I don't know. I'm sorry she ambushed you the way she did."

"I was surprised, but I wanted to help. I felt a little guilty that things weren't completely innocent between us."

"You have nothing to feel guilty about. And I didn't break up with her because of you. That's the truth, Keira."

Silence met his words. Then she said, "You mentioned you were calling for two reasons. What's the other reason?"

"When I left the rehab center today, I witnessed an argument between Mark Langley and a middle-aged, red-haired woman. She told him he was going to be sorry. He said he was already sorry. He told her it was over, and she said he was wrong. Then he jumped into his car and left. A moment later, she did the same."

"Really? Did he say her name?"

"No. He didn't say her name, and I don't know who she was."

"Maybe it's that woman, Mandy, the one who called him a few days ago when I was in his office. He said basically the same thing on the phone."

"I know you think this Mandy is the sister of the woman who died. Have you seen her photo online? Does she have red hair?"

"I never looked Mandy/Amanda up. I stopped digging. I thought I was being paranoid."

"Maybe you weren't."

"Maybe I wasn't. Thanks for telling me."

"Of course. Keira…" He wanted to say something, but he wasn't sure where to begin.

"Just say goodnight, Dante."

"I'll say goodnight, but I don't want to say goodbye."

"You will eventually."

"But that's not today. So, I'll see you around." He disconnected the call before she could say the word he didn't want to hear.

CHAPTER THIRTEEN

"I don't want to hurt you," Hannah said as she came into Keira's boutique late Friday afternoon.

Looking into her friend's troubled gaze, Keira steeled herself for what was coming. "Let's go in the back." She motioned for Connie to take care of their sole customer and then headed into the sewing room. "I know you're worried about your dress, Hannah," she said, as they moved into the next room. "The wedding is a week from tomorrow, and I haven't finished it yet. But I can promise you that it will be done." As Hannah opened her mouth, she rushed forward. "If for some reason, you don't want to wait, maybe you've found another dress you like better, it's fine. You can tell me. I'm very aware that my inability to finish the gown is stressing you out. I won't be hurt."

"It's stressing you out more than me," Hannah said, walking over to the gown that was hanging in plastic on a rack by the wall. "I told you it was beautiful weeks ago. But you keep insisting there's something more you want to do."

"There is. I want it to be perfect for you, Hannah."

Hannah turned to face her, giving her a bewildered smile. "Keira, I'm not perfect. I never have been. I have red hair and freckles and skin that hates the sun."

"You're beautiful, Hannah."

"I'm just me. And this dress is me. It doesn't need more."

"Just give me the weekend. If I can't do better, I'll call it a day."

"I just hate that you're killing yourself over something that I love."

"I'm not killing myself, but I have a vision, and I want to make it happen. You're just being nice, saying the dress is okay."

Hannah sighed and gave her a pointed look. "Seriously? Since when am I just nice, Keira?"

"Well…"

Hannah laughed. "That's right. We've known each other for a long time. I can be snarky and impatient and hold a grudge way too long. Like I said, I'm not perfect. Neither are you. And you need to deal with whatever is driving you toward this quest for perfection."

"Honestly, I don't know what it is. I'm just feeling stuck. It didn't happen with Chelsea's gowns, or her wedding dress, or her awards dress. The bridesmaids' dresses have gone well, but now I feel blocked."

"Because you're exhausted. You can't do everything, Keira. Last I looked, you weren't wearing a cape."

She sat down at her sewing table. "I could use a cape right about now."

Hannah took the seat adjacent to her. "I hate to add to your burden, but since you're too busy to check social media, I feel compelled to share some information you might need, unless you already know?"

"Know what?" she asked warily.

"The photos from your threesome date at the Lakeshore Bistro are online."

"It wasn't a threesome."

Hannah grinned. "Well, whatever you want to call it, the three of you looked very good together. Although, I could see by your expression that you did not want to be there."

"I didn't. I had no idea that Nikki had alerted the press. She just asked me to have a drink with her. I thought we'd chat. I'd explain that there was nothing going on with me and Dante. But she ambushed me, and she set Dante up as well."

"But you all went along with her?"

"There didn't seem to be another option, not with all those cameras focused on us." She paused, seeing something else in Hannah's gaze. "What aren't you telling me?"

"The photos were fine, but this afternoon Nikki went on social media to announce she'd broken up with Dante. She said that while she'd thought you were a friend, she'd learned that you were trying to steal Dante from her. She had a little tear dripping down her beautiful face."

"What?" she asked in shock. "None of that is true. Dante said he broke up with her right after I left, but it had nothing to do with me. They've been on the rocks for a while. They hadn't even seen each other in six weeks."

"I believe you, but Dante hasn't said anything publicly to refute Nikki's statements."

"I'm sure he doesn't want to feed the fire."

"He might need to respond, because you're the one getting consumed by that fire. He should defend you, Keira. She's dragging your name through the mud."

"I don't care what Nikki says."

"You should. You have a reputation, too."

"People in Whisper Lake know me. What the rest of the world thinks doesn't matter."

"What about your design business? That could be global. You have to protect yourself."

Hannah had a point, but she still didn't see any option but silence. "There's nothing I can say. I don't have a platform like Nikki does."

"Dante has a platform. You should talk to him about it."

"I'm trying not to talk to him at all," she muttered.

"Why?"

"Because talking to him is what got me into this mess."

Hannah gave her a sharp, searching look. "What happens now that he's not attached?"

"Nothing happens. He's still just passing through town. If we run into each other, we'll be friendly and polite, but that's it."

"Oh, come on. You kissed him. He kissed you. You passed *just friends* days ago."

"There's not going to be any more kissing."

"Well, that sucks. Your reputation is being shredded online, and you're not even getting the perks of this situation. If you're going to get reamed for allegedly stealing Dante from Nikki, why don't you just have some fun?"

"I can't."

"Why not? You're so serious all the time."

"It's not that I don't want to have fun." She paused and let out a sigh. "I like him too much already. I don't want to say goodbye to him now. Sleeping with him will only make it harder."

Hannah gave her a sympathetic smile. "That's true. You do tend to get emotionally involved. What can I do?"

"Go back in time and tell me I don't need a date for your wedding, so I won't go online and try to find one and then mistake Dante for my real but boring date."

"That part was not on me."

"It all started with you. And by the way, I am not bringing a plus one to your wedding, so you'll just have to deal with the awkward seating assignments. In fact, I'm happy to sit at the bar."

"Don't worry about that. It was never about the seating. I just didn't want you to feel like the odd man out."

"Because I'm the last single girl standing."

"Hey, Chloe is single now."

"It's not the same. She was married. She has a kid. But you don't have to worry about me. I am not in a hurry to couple up and walk down the aisle. I have a lot going on in my life. I don't need a man."

"Of course you don't *need* a man, but you still might want one. Anyway…" Hannah got to her feet. "I have to run. My brother is arriving tonight, and it's family dinner time."

"How is the family doing?"

"Everyone is good. My mom is sober and involved with a man

who seems to treat her well. My sister, Kelly, is turning out to be a very good mom. And Tyler is coming home, so I can't complain."

Hannah's family had been through a lot, so she was more than happy to know how great everything was now. "Was it difficult seeing your mom date again?"

"Yes. I didn't like it, especially because he seemed like a partier to me at first, and when my mom is involved with a man, she tends to lose track of her own sobriety. But that hasn't happened. He's cut back on his personal drinking and he seems to make her happy." She paused. "Is your mom still seeing her old friend?"

"Unfortunately, yes," she said, getting to her feet.

"Do you still have doubts about him?"

"I do," she admitted. She had even more after Dante's call the night before, but she hadn't had time to look into Mandy yet.

"Well, it's good to be careful."

"Unfortunately, it's my mother who's in the relationship, and the last thing she wants to be right now is careful." She walked Hannah back into the shop. "I'll have your dress to you by Monday."

"All right." Hannah gave her an impulsive hug. "It's all going to work out, Keira."

"I hope so. I just don't know how."

Dante's phone was blowing up when he left the rehab center Friday afternoon. There were texts from his brother, Micah, from his agent, Phil Aguardo, and his publicist, Elaine Robbins. From what he could see on his phone screen, Nikki's name was coming up a lot. *What the hell had she done now?*

He got into his car and called his agent first. He'd been with Phil since he was twenty years old. Over the past twelve years, they'd grown up together. Now, Phil managed a dozen professional athletes across a range of sports.

Phil picked up almost immediately. "Dante, have you seen what's going on?"

"No, I've been in the rehab center all day. But I have a lot of texts referring to Nikki. What did she do?"

"She made several social media posts claiming that you cheated on her with her former friend, the one in the photos from last night, and that you both lied to her. She feels like a fool for having believed your story. It goes on like that."

He blew out a frustrated breath. "It's all bullshit. I broke up with Nikki after she manipulated those ridiculously fake photos. And she and Keira met for ten minutes years ago. They're not friends."

"I figured. The media loves a good scandal, and you and Nikki have been a hot item for the last several months. What do you want to do?"

"Ignore it."

"That would be my usual advice," Phil said slowly.

"Not now?" he asked in surprise.

"It may go on longer if you don't respond. They're going to keep hounding you, and I don't want this to jeopardize your recovery."

"I won't let that happen. I can't believe she did this."

"I can," Phil said. "Nikki only dates high-profile men who raise her profile and give her more followers and more clicks."

"Why didn't you say that before? I thought you liked her."

"What's not to like? She's hot. And you were having fun. Not my business. Why don't you talk to Elaine and see if you can craft some kind of statement?"

"I told Nikki I'd let her play the breakup however she wanted. I just didn't realize she was going to smear Keira." Keira could be hurt, he realized, and his silence wouldn't help. "I'll think about what I want to do."

"Okay. Let's talk about your progress. I'm getting a lot of queries from team management."

"Tell them I'm working the rehab. Dr. Cole is coming up next week to check my progress. After that, I should know more."

"I will pass that on, but now I'm just asking for myself."

"It's up and down. The range of motion is getting better, but not as fast as I would like. I feel strong. I feel like there's improvement, but I don't want to over-analyze it. I want to just stay focused on getting better."

"I'm glad to hear you're feeling optimistic."

"I'm not sure I'd go that far," he said dryly.

"Give me a call after you talk to your doctor next week."

"Will do."

"If you need me to speak to Nikki's agent, I can also do that."

"No one controls Nikki. She'll do whatever she wants to do if it works for her benefit. But I appreciate the offer. I'll be in touch."

As he set down his phone on the console, he blew out a breath of frustration. *Why the hell had Nikki gone off on Keira?* He didn't care what she said about him, but to bring Keira into it when Nikki knew there was nothing going on between them…

Clearly, Nikki hadn't completely believed that, or even if she had, she'd just thought the story would be better if she played the betrayed woman. She wasn't completely wrong, either. He did have feelings for Keira. But their lives were not in the same place. It had been difficult enough to work things out with Nikki, who traveled as much as he did. But Major League Baseball didn't make its way through Whisper Lake.

He'd never be able to finish anything he started with Keira, so he couldn't start it, even though he really wanted to, even though his dreams were filled with her image, even though he could hear the sound of her laugh in his head.

He should talk to her about the lies Nikki was telling. But she wanted him to keep his distance. He had to make an exception for this. *Didn't he?*

As he drove out of the parking garage, a van immediately followed him. The man behind the wheel was the same man who'd gotten the first shot of him. He pressed his foot down harder on the gas. He wasn't going to talk to the press until he spoke to Keira.

He grabbed his phone and punched in her number, but she didn't answer. He tossed the phone onto the console and then decided to lose his tail before he tried to find her. The last thing he wanted to do was bring more trouble to her, although he had the feeling that trouble was going to find her whether he brought it to her or not.

CHAPTER FOURTEEN

As KEIRA LEFT the boutique through the back door just after four, she was shocked to find two photographers staked out in the parking lot: one middle-aged guy and a young twenty-something male. They'd been at the Lakeshore Bistro for Nikki's setup, but she'd thought they left town. They started shooting photos immediately, calling out question after question.

"Are you having an affair with Dante DeAngelis?"

"Are the two of you a couple?"

"Why did you betray Nikki?"

"Is Dante going to be able to play baseball again this season?"

She hesitated, wondering if she should try to answer any of their questions when the younger man asked, *"When did you and Dante start having sex?"*

No way was she talking to them! "No comment," she said, as she hurried toward her car. She quickly opened the door and got inside.

More shots were snapped as she drove out of the lot, her heart racing and her palms sweating. *Wasn't Nikki a better subject than she was? Or Dante, for that matter? Why the hell weren't they at the rehab center, chasing him down?*

Probably because they knew Dante wouldn't tell them anything. They might have thought she was an easier target.

Thank God she hadn't actually said anything. She'd been tempted, but that would have been a mistake. They would have spun her words around and made something else up.

As she drove away, she made a quick turn, then another. She knew this town like the back of her hand, and within minutes, she was able to get away. She was shocked that anyone would want to follow her. It seemed crazy, but Dante had tried to warn her that the tabloid press could be relentless. She might be a nobody, but she'd gotten caught in the middle of Dante and Nikki, and they were both celebrities. Hopefully, the press had gotten enough shots to be satisfied for now. She couldn't imagine that this story was really that interesting. There had to be celebrity breakups and plenty of legitimate threesomes to write about.

Putting the press out of her head, she headed toward the east shore, to the cabin where she'd met up with Dante several days earlier. A new stove was being delivered between five and seven, and she needed to sign for it and oversee the installation. This was another job she probably should have turned down, but her friend had trusted her to take care of everything and had insisted on adding an extra percentage point to a future sale to make sure she was compensated for her time.

She was actually happy to have something to do, and she wanted to be by herself for a while. She needed to figure out how to handle this new situation.

When she arrived at the cabin, she pulled her car into the attached garage and then entered the house. Everything was exactly as she'd left it several nights earlier. Since she had some time to wait, she pulled out her computer and sat down at the kitchen table. But as she opened the search engine, she was almost afraid to go online. She didn't want to see her name or image pop up. But it was probably fine as long as she stayed away from gossip sites and social media platforms.

Instead, she'd do a little more digging into Mark's life and see if she could find an image of Mandy. She was about to type in the name when her mom called.

"Hello? Is everything okay?" she asked immediately.

"It's fine. You always think something is wrong when I call," her mother replied. "I'm just waiting for Mark to arrive. Are you at the cabin?"

"Yes, I just got here. I'm not sure when the stove will arrive, probably close to seven, and who knows how long it will take to install. So, don't worry if I'm out late."

"That's fine." Her mother paused. "Dante just stopped by the house."

Her pulse jumped. "He did? Why?"

"He was looking for you. He told me that you've gotten caught up in some rumors about him. He's worried about you, and he wants to talk to you. He seemed very upset and sincere, so I told him where you were. He said he'd called you a few times, but you hadn't answered. Did I do the wrong thing?"

She wanted to say yes, because she did not want to talk to Dante. That's why she hadn't answered her phone. She didn't know what to say to him. Now that he'd broken up with Nikki, he'd removed at least one big barrier between them. But it wasn't enough, and she needed to think about how she wanted to deal with him.

"Keira?" her mother pressed, a worried note in her voice.

"It's okay, Mom."

"Are you sure?"

"Yes. I was going to call him. I just haven't had a chance."

"Oh, good. He said he broke up with his girlfriend."

"He's still leaving in a few weeks, Mom."

"Well, a lot can happen in a few weeks."

She walked into the living room as she heard a car out front. It was Dante. "He's here, Mom. I better go."

"All right."

As Dante got out of his car, she checked the vicinity for trailing photographers, but there were no other vehicles around. When he hit the porch, she slipped her phone into her pocket and opened the door. She motioned for him to enter, closing it quickly behind him.

"Did anyone follow you?" she asked.

"There was a guy behind me when I left the clinic, but I got rid of him. Are you all right?"

"Honestly, I'm not sure."

The air between them sizzled with tension as they stared at each other. *Why did he have to be so damn attractive?* Her body was tingling just from looking into his blue eyes, and she was incredibly distracted by his full mouth and the sexy stubble on his face. She drew in a shaky breath as his lips tightened.

"Keira…"

She waited for him to continue, but he seemed to have trouble finding the words. His hands curled into fists at his side.

"Are you angry?" she asked.

"Yes, I'm pissed. And I'm sorry. This whole situation is my fault."

"I can't argue with that."

"I never wanted Nikki to hurt you. I can't believe she went after you the way she did."

"I'm shocked, too."

"I had no idea she was going to do this. I hope you believe me."

"I believe you."

Relief flooded his gaze. Then he stepped forward and put his arms around her.

She shouldn't have gone into his embrace, but she did. She slipped her arms around his back, feeling powerful muscles under his thin T-shirt. She wanted to explore those muscles, and that was just the starting point of what she wanted. She told herself to get a grip. But her body was fighting her brain.

He tilted her face to his. She leaned into the kiss, closing her eyes, savoring the deliciously hot taste of his mouth. She told herself it was just for a second—one kiss. *If she was going to get torched online for breaking him and his girlfriend up, didn't she deserve this moment of madness?* That's all it would be. All it could be.

But he kissed so damn good. His mouth, her mouth—she didn't know where she ended and he began. She didn't know how long she could go without breathing, but she needed him more than she needed air.

And then her phone began to buzz and vibrate in her pocket. She broke away with a little gasp as reality brought her back down to earth.

She pulled out her phone and found enough breath to say, "Hello?"

"This is Arlington Appliance," a man said. "We'll be there in ten minutes."

"Okay. I'm here." She looked up from the phone and into Dante's beautiful blue eyes that were still sparking with desire.

"What's going on?" he asked.

"A stove is going to be delivered here in ten minutes."

"Right." He ran a hand through his hair. "Your mom said something about a delivery."

"Probably a timely interruption."

"I was thinking it was very *untimely.*"

Her body was screaming yes in agreement, but her brain was finally taking over. "Maybe not. This has gotten really complicated."

"It was very simple a minute ago."

"That was a minute ago."

"And the minute is over," he said dryly.

"Yes." She tucked her hair behind her ears and tried not to think about kissing him again. She needed to focus on all the problems that came with him, not all the heat. "There were photographers waiting in the parking lot when I left the store today."

He frowned. "What happened?"

"They were taking photos and shooting questions at me so fast I didn't have time to answer, not that I wanted to."

"What did they ask you?"

"If I broke you and Nikki up. When we first had sex. Whether you were going to play again. How I felt about betraying my friend."

"I'm sorry you had to deal with that."

"I've never faced that kind of intense scrutiny before. I haven't read what Nikki posted, but Hannah told me about it, and it sounds like she blamed everything about your breakup on me."

"I haven't read the posts either, but that's the report I got from my agent, my brother, and my publicist."

"Maybe I should have said something to those reporters."

"No. They would have spun your words." He gave her a grim look. "I shouldn't have broken up with Nikki until I left here. I just didn't want her hanging around, and she wasn't going to go if I wasn't brutally blunt. I tried to tell her before that we needed to take a break, but she wouldn't hear me."

"Because she was more into it than you were."

"I don't know if that's true."

"Come on, Dante, you can't keep playing it down. You've said all along that she's not your girlfriend, that it's not serious, but she's acting like she was your girlfriend, and you were serious. You're either not being honest with me or you're not being honest with yourself."

"You're wrong, Keira. I am being honest. It's Nikki who is making our relationship into something it wasn't. We met in February. A month later, I was off to spring training and then the season. We saw each other sporadically. She came to Denver right before I got the surgery, but she couldn't stand being in the hospital. She didn't even wait until the surgery was over to leave. I didn't see her for six weeks, until she showed up here."

She had to admit it didn't sound like that serious of a relationship. "I can't believe she left before your surgery was over. That was cold. Were you completely alone?"

"No. Danny and Micah came. They stayed a couple of days until I was able to take care of myself."

She was relieved to hear that. "I'm glad they were there for you. Why did you go to Denver for the surgery? Why didn't you have it in Miami?"

"Because Grayson's success rate with injuries like mine is phenomenally good. I wanted the best, and he's the best, so I went to Denver." He paused. "I actually didn't care that Nikki left. She's not good with medical issues, and I didn't have the energy to prop her up."

"You shouldn't have had to do that."

"I should have called it quits with her a while ago, but I've been so completely focused on my recovery that I just didn't want to get into it with her. She wasn't around. I didn't have a pressing need to have the talk."

"But last night you felt that need?"

"After the way she set us both up, yes. I'd had enough. She said she was going to tell people she broke up with me, but I didn't know she'd go after you. I should have figured she would. She's all about controlling the narrative, as you saw yesterday."

"She is very determined to do that. So, what now? Do we say something? Do we stay quiet? What's the play?"

"I'm not sure. I can talk to Nikki, but I don't know that I'll persuade her to come clean, not after she's made this so public. And speaking to her might make it worse."

He had a point. "If we don't say anything, will the press just eventually leave? How long will that take?"

"There's a chance they won't leave until I do. It's not just about you and me, although that's the spicier headline. It's also about my future in baseball. A lot of people want to know how my rehab is going, if I'm coming back." He paused. "I could leave, finish my rehab back in Denver or maybe even Miami. That would take the heat off you."

She immediately shook her head. "No. Your health is the most important thing, not this story. You should not leave rehab because of me."

"I don't want to complicate your life."

"Too late for that."

"I want to do something to make things easier for you."

"I don't think there's anything you can do." She squared her shoulders and lifted her chin. She wasn't going to be a victim or let this story run her life. "It will be fine. I can dodge the press. And even if they take photos of me, what are they going to see? I don't have time to waste on this situation. I have more pressing problems."

"Like Mark Langley?"

"He's one of those problems. He's having dinner right now with my mother. Hannah's wedding dress is the other issue. My design is not going well. I'm stuck and I don't know how to get myself unstuck."

"Well, I can't help you with the dress, but maybe I can help you with Langley."

"I was about to look for Mandy online."

"Why don't I help you?"

She hesitated. "I should say no. It feels like we're playing with fire."

A smile spread across his face. "It will only get as hot as you want it to get."

His flirty words sent another tingle down her spine. "That's the problem. I'm not making good decisions where you're concerned."

"We still have our clothes on, so the decisions haven't gotten that crazy."

"Maybe only because my phone rang." She wished she could retract her words as a sexy gleam entered his eyes.

"Interesting," he said.

"No, it's not." She paused as her phone buzzed once more. It was the same number as before. "Hello?"

"This is Arlington Appliance again. We, unfortunately, got a flat tire, and we need to wait for a repair. It will be about forty-five minutes before we get there."

His words brought both relief and worry, because the imminent arrival of the stove had been a good reason not to get into bed with Dante. But there was nothing she could do. "Okay," she said. "Let me know if that changes."

"Will do."

"What happened?" Dante asked as she hung up.

"The delivery is delayed. They got a flat tire."

"Interesting," he said again.

"No, it's not," she repeated.

"We have time to kill."

"To research Mandy," she said pointedly. "That's what I'm going to do. You can help or not."

"Oh, I'm helping. But I'm also hungry. Should I run out and get us some food? You haven't eaten, have you?"

"No. We could just order a pizza. I was actually going to do that."

"I'm in."

"What do you like?"

"Everything."

"That's easy."

"While you order the pizza, I'll start digging into Langley," he said, taking out his phone.

"Why don't we go into the kitchen? I've got my computer set up on the table."

As they walked down the hall, she called Dillard's and ordered a large pizza with everything except onions, and she was not going to analyze that decision. Because that might mean she had a plan, and she did not have a plan. She was just going to wait for a stove, share a pizza with Dante, and maybe find some dirt on Langley. That was it.

There was going to be no kissing, no naked fun…at least, she didn't think so.

CHAPTER FIFTEEN

As he and Keira settled in at the kitchen table, Dante couldn't help thinking about the last time they'd been there, sharing a meal, getting to know each other. It was weird, but this house was almost starting to feel like home, and it didn't belong to either of them. Maybe that was why it felt safe. It wasn't her life, and it wasn't his; it was a place to meet in the middle.

"Damn," Keira muttered, as she stared at her computer.

"Did you find something on Mandy?"

"No, I was actually checking my emails." She looked at him with disappointment in her gaze. "I think the fallout from Nikki's posts is just beginning."

"What happened?" He braced himself for another bad surprise.

"After Chelsea's red-carpet walk, I got some emails from stylists wanting me to design for their clients. They're all in the early stages of contact, but I just got a reply from one stating that her client won't be interested in pursuing a relationship with me now, because she's friends with Nikki."

His stomach twisted as he saw the distress in her eyes. "I'm sorry, Keira."

"Me, too."

He needed to fix this. "Look, Nikki isn't the only one with

connections. I can pull some strings, too. I can connect you to stylists. I've got an agent, a publicist, and friends in the media."

She immediately shook her head. "No, I don't want your help."

"Why not? I'm the reason you're getting screwed."

"It's just one stylist. Hopefully, the others won't bail."

"They might. I didn't realize until just this second that you and Nikki intersect in the world of fashion."

"I wouldn't say we intersect. I'm a small-town designer, who has made a few dresses. She's an international supermodel. I'm not in her sphere."

"You could be, one day. I can spread the word about how good you are."

"I don't think you should be talking about me at all. It will just add fuel to the fire."

"I have to do something. I got you into this."

She surprised him with a faint smile. "I actually got myself into this. I'm the one who sat down at your table and thought you were Danny."

"But I bought you fish tacos and got you out of that restaurant and into a photo with me."

"That's true, but I don't blame you for this, Dante. I blame myself, and I blame Nikki for being a cold-hearted bitch. I hope that's not too harsh."

He grinned. "You're not offending me. I just wish I'd seen that side of her a lot earlier."

"I'm sure you were distracted by her perfect body and her incredibly captivating face."

"She is pretty. But she's a shell. There's not much substance to her."

"She probably never needed to develop substance, looking the way she looks. Her whole career is based on her looking good in a picture."

"That's true. When we were together, everything was a photo op. And there was an endless number of parties." He thought about that crazy time for a moment. "It's very possible that dating Nikki played a factor in my injury."

She quirked a brow at his comment. "How so?"

"I was slacking off. Instead of working out on my off days, I was drinking a lot. I was hanging out on boats and taking photos when I should have been in the gym. I let my focus slip, and this is where I ended up."

"Maybe it was just overuse of your arm. You must have put tremendous pressure on your shoulder over the years. What did the doctor say?"

"That it could have been that or an odd tweak of a motion I'd done a hundred thousand times, or it could have been lack of training. Anyway, it is what it is. I can only move on from here. As for Nikki's attack on your business, I hope you'll consider my offer to help."

"I'll consider it, but frankly, Dante, I don't even have time for more business right now, especially design work. I'm struggling so much with Hannah's wedding dress, I'm losing confidence in myself. I always felt good when I designed, like I was doing exactly what I knew how to do. I thought of myself as creative, inventive, imaginative, but for some reason, I've gotten completely blocked. The wedding is a week from Saturday. I'm running out of time."

"What does Hannah think? Is she getting nervous?"

"No, because she thinks the dress is fine the way it is, but I know it's not. And she should have the perfect dress. She's my best friend. If I can't make a gown that is spectacular for her, then maybe I'm not that good."

He thought about her disparaging words. He was a little surprised by her pessimistic statement. She'd seemed very optimistic until now.

"What's really going on?" he asked.

"What do you mean?"

"Maybe the dress isn't what's bothering you. Perhaps you need to dig deeper."

"I don't know what you're getting at."

He thought about how best to express what he was thinking. "I was drafted out of community college. I'd been there two years, setting all kind of records, and I thought I was a superstar."

"It sounds like you were."

"Well, when I got to my first team in LA, they took one look at me and sent me down to the minors almost immediately. They said they wanted me to get experience. It was the right decision, but it wasn't what I wanted. I thought I was ready to be on the main stage, not playing games in a one-stoplight town in the middle of nowhere."

"So, what happened?"

"It turned out to be good for me. I got to pitch a lot and face different kinds of hitters, but it still felt like punishment. After a year, there was talk of bringing me up. I was very excited. But the more talk there was, the worse I started to pitch. It was like the closer I got to my dream, the more problems I encountered. My cockiness vanished. I was overthinking every move I made. I thought I had a hitch in my fastball. The sinker wasn't hitting its mark. I was annoyed with the mound, the dirt, my catcher, my infielders, even the weather. Oh, and the damn birds that would fly over during the late afternoon games, they really pissed me off."

She smiled. "How did you get out of it?"

"I got help from an unexpected person. The scorekeeper for our home games came up to me in the parking lot one night. He must have been close to eighty, but he'd been a player in his day, a pitcher, in fact. He told me to stop thinking about the next pitch, the next game, the next stage in my career. Just to focus on the ball and the batter in front of me. One hitter at a time. Put everything else out of my head. Don't look at the crowd. Don't look at the coach. Don't think about who's watching. I thought it was stupid advice. I barely let him finish before I took off. But the next game, I realized my mind kept sliding into the future. I was thinking about the next batter, the number four hitter, worrying about how I was going to get him out before he was even up. I was also scanning the crowd. I was watching for the scouts. I was measuring my success by the wrong things."

He took a breath, then continued. "When I finally just looked at the ball and the batter and pushed everything else out of my mind, the plate came into perfect focus. I pitched the ball, and the batter swung and missed. From that first strike, it just kept getting better. Concentration had always been the key to my success, but I'd gotten too far ahead of myself. I was so afraid of losing out on what I didn't have that I almost missed being able to get it—if that makes sense."

"It makes a lot of sense."

"Even though I didn't think I was afraid, I was."

"And you think I'm afraid."

He met her gaze. "It doesn't matter what I believe, only what you do."

She thought about his words. "I think I'm good, but I don't know how good. Am I talented enough to make it all the way? Or am I being overconfident? Living here in Whisper Lake, the world is very small. When I was in New York, I saw how cutthroat fashion was, how much power certain magazines or fashion houses or celebrities could wield over the industry. I think I'm talented enough to compete. But I don't know if I can make it. It's a big risk."

"How will you know unless you go for it?"

"I probably won't know. But going for it involves giving up other things that have been sustaining my mom and me, like the real-estate business and the boutique."

"Can you delegate?"

"Yes, but will things work as well as they do now if I'm not overseeing them? And then there's my mom. She's getting better. But is she truly capable of living independently? It's been a long time since she didn't have me looking out for her. Plus, I have immediate commitments, like Hannah's dress. I can't think about the future right now. I don't think I'm getting ahead of myself. I'm too wrapped up in the mess of the moment."

"I disagree. I think we just got to the heart of your problem."

"We did?"

"Yes." He rested his arms on the table as he gazed at her. "When you finish Hannah's dress, you will have to think about the future. But that's the problem—by not wanting to think about the future, you're actually thinking about it."

Her brows drew together as she considered his words. "That's convoluted but makes some sense."

"Maybe you can't finish the dress, because it's the last barrier before having to deal with your future plans."

Her eyes widened. "Wow. You might have just saved me a lot of money in therapy."

"Just throwing out an idea."

"I wish I could say you were wrong, but maybe you're not."

"Since I'm on a roll…"

"What?" she asked warily.

"Maybe your obsession with Mark Langley is because you subconsciously don't want your mom to be independent. If she's dating, if she has a man in her life who can also take care of her, you've just lost another one of your reasons for staying exactly where you are."

He thought he'd nailed it, but he also thought he'd probably pushed it a little too far. There was a gleam of anger in her eyes now.

"That would be a terrible thing for me to—break up my mom and Mark, because I need a reason to stay here."

"I said subconsciously, not deliberately."

She frowned as she let out a long breath. "I know what you said, and to be honest, I have questioned my motives. I do have some self-awareness. That's why I stopped digging. But since you're the one who saw Mark fighting with some woman, I feel compelled to do a little more research."

"You're right. I got carried away with my brainstorm. I'm really not qualified to analyze anyone."

"You made some good points," she conceded. "I liked your baseball story, hearing how you got past your fear. Maybe I can do something with that. I guess it's always easier to see through someone else's problems."

"Definitely easier," he admitted, pausing as the doorbell rang. "That must be the pizza." He pulled out his wallet. "I'll get it."

"No. I don't want anyone to see you here. I'll get it, and I already paid online."

"At least, let me do the tip," he said, handing her a ten.

"That's too much."

He shrugged. "We'll make someone's night."

As she left, he blew out a breath, knowing he'd gotten too far into her personal business, but he hadn't been able to stop himself, which was so unusual. But then everything about Keira made him want to be more and do more than he usually did. He'd also needed conversation to distract himself from wanting to kiss her again. Unfortunately, every time they stopped talking, the urge came right back. He probably should leave right after they ate, but he really didn't want to. And he rarely did things he didn't want to do.

Keira checked the peephole before answering the door, relieved to see it was Deke, a nineteen-year-old kid, who had delivered more pizzas to her than she cared to count. Deke was the son of the owner, Marian Dillard, and was currently going to school in Denver.

"Hey, Deke, are you back for the summer?" she asked. "I heard you're loving Denver."

"It has more action than here. What are you doing at this house? Having a party?"

"Waiting for a delivery. It's going to go on the market soon."

"Looks cool. Hey, I saw your picture online. Are you seeing Dante DeAngelis?"

"He's in town rehabbing his shoulder." She gave a more round-about answer than she wanted to, but it was hard to lie when Dante was sitting in the kitchen.

"I heard. His girlfriend says you broke 'em up."

"You can't believe everything you read online."

"But you know Dante, right? Is he going to be back this season? He's a fantastic pitcher."

"I'm not sure. Sorry." She took the pizza out of his hands and handed him the ten.

"Thanks," he said, his eyes widening when he saw the tip. "Glad I decided to bring this order out. The tourists have been stingy this week. If you see Dante, tell him I'm one of his biggest fans. I can't wait for him to be back on the mound."

"I will."

She took the pizza into the kitchen. Dante looked up from his phone. "That smells good."

"I hope you like it. By the way, our delivery boy said to tell you that he's your biggest fan, and he hopes you'll be back on the mound soon."

"He knew I was here?"

"No, but he saw our photos online, so he thought I might see you." She paused. "Maybe you should move your rental car into the garage. I'm sure the paparazzi know what it looks like, even if the pizza guy didn't."

"Good call."

"I'll open the garage door."

As Dante left the house, she walked into the garage and raised the door. While she was waiting for him, her mind went back to the conversation they'd had before the pizza arrived. She had to admit that Dante's analysis of her problems had struck a nerve. Maybe Hannah's wedding dress wasn't the real issue. Maybe it was about far more than that.

But since she couldn't do anything about the dress at this moment, she'd let that idea sit for a bit. Right now, she just wanted to eat and forget about the rest of the world and the future, even if that future was only an hour from now.

Keira couldn't believe how many times she smiled or laughed as she shared pizza with Dante. He seemed more relaxed than he had on any other occasion, and he was a really good storyteller. She liked that he told stories that didn't always show him doing something amazing.

There was no doubt he had a cocky confidence when it came to baseball, but he also had a self-deprecating charm that was pretty irresistible. In fact, she found her thoughts wandering throughout their meal, thinking about the curve of his mouth, the fullness of his lips, the light in his eyes when he smiled, the tenor of his voice when he talked about the things and the people that mattered to him.

She was a fool to think she could say goodbye to this guy and not hurt at least a little. But she was trying to stay in the present and not think about the future.

"Okay, that's enough stories from me," Dante said.

"You've had so many interesting experiences."

"It's been a ride."

"The ride is not over."

For the first time, a shadow moved through his gaze. "I hope not."

"I'm sorry. We weren't going to talk about tomorrow."

"It's never far from my mind, but we'll leave those thoughts for another day. Tell me what it was like to grow up here."

"It was wonderful. It was a carefree life. The town was a lot smaller. We rode our bikes everywhere. I had good friends. I knew everyone. Of course, when I was a teenager, I thought the town was way too small. I wanted more adventure and excitement. I wanted to see what was on the other side of the mountains."

"You must have found all that in New York."

"I did. It was amazing to go to school there and get my first job. It was a completely different world. I was going to plays, comedy clubs, and bars. It was a lot of fun. But sometimes I missed the lake and the mountains, having people know me when I walked into a store. New York was like being in a race all the time. Everything was fast. It was invigorating, but it was also tiring. I was working long hours for very little money, living with roommates in a tiny one-bedroom apartment."

"You must have stories from those days."

"Some of the designers and models I worked with were truly crazy. And I can't tell you how many times I had to run around town trying to track down someone's favorite food so they could make it through a photo shoot without being unhappy. There were a lot of divas."

"We have divas in baseball, too. Not me, of course."

"Of course not," she said with a laugh. "You've never made some poor intern try to find you a steak sandwich at six in the morning?"

"I am not an early riser. Did you really have to do that?"

"Yes, and this designer had to have the steak from a particular restaurant. I had to wake up the chef to get him to make it."

"Why would the chef agree?"

"The designer had a lot of parties in his restaurant."

"So, the designer got what they wanted, and the chef got something in return. What did you get?"

"A stress headache."

He smiled. "But you were willing to do whatever it took to get to where you wanted to go."

"I was. The longer I was there, the more opportunities I had. I was seeing a brighter light at the end of the tunnel. Then my mom got in the accident, and I dropped everything and came home. In the beginning, I thought it would just be for a few weeks or months, but it became clear very quickly that it would be a year or more. So, I quit my job and sold what I'd left behind. I never went back."

"Do you want to go back?"

"I don't know. That's a question for another day, too."

As they exchanged a long look, both very aware of the precariousness of their futures, the doorbell rang once more. "That must be the stove."

"I'll get out of the way."

"You can go back to the inn if you want," she said, as she got to her feet.

"No way. We still have to research Mandy and Langley. I'll go to the living room. I can get started while you deal with the stove."

"Okay." She grabbed her computer off the counter and handed it to him. "You can use this if you want. I bookmarked the article about the fire, too, if you're interested." She related her password as they headed toward the front door. She was happy Dante was staying. It didn't even matter if they found out anything; she just didn't want to say goodbye to him yet.

CHAPTER SIXTEEN

WHILE KEIRA WATCHED over the installation of the stove in the kitchen, Dante went on her computer and read the news article she'd saved. Then he moved on to Amanda Yates, or Mandy Yates, as she might be known. Her face popped up on a social media profile, and his heart skipped a beat. It was her—the woman with the dark-red hair who he'd seen in the parking garage with Langley. Keira had been right. Mandy was Amanda, Gretchen's sister.

He spent several minutes reading through Amanda's profiles on several sites. She had apparently been a teacher in Los Angeles at some point. But that ended several years ago. Her status was single, but there was mention of a divorce in some of her posts. He didn't see any children. Her birthdate wasn't public, but from the very few photos she had posted, she appeared to be in her late forties, early fifties.

She wasn't a particularly active poster. Months passed in between her posts, but as he read through the feed, it felt like she had an incredibly morbid fascination with her dead sister. There were mentions of Gretchen on her birthday, the anniversary of her death, in relation to a dog they'd once had. Mandy also posted photos of herself and her sister, saying that a piece of her heart had died with her. She said she'd gotten a divorce because her husband just couldn't stand how sad she was. There were hints of darkness in additional cryptic quotes about justice and revenge. She wrote in one post how unfair life was, how guilty people went free, while innocent people died.

Was she referring to Langley? Was it possible that Mark had something to do with that fire?

Frowning, he turned away from Mandy to search for additional information on the fire. Finally, he found one article that had slightly different information than the one that Keira had discovered. It said that the origin of the fire was believed to be a cigarette that had fallen between the cushions of the sofa. The only person who had been in the house at that time was the nanny, Gretchen Yates, who had perished. The assumption was that she'd been smoking and had dropped the cigarette. The Langley family had been vacationing in Malibu that weekend and were devastated by the news. There was a statement from Mark Langley: "We are beyond sad at the loss of Gretchen Yates, a trusted and loved member of the family."

If the fire was an accident, and Gretchen was to blame, where was Mandy's rage and desire for justice and revenge coming from?

He focused on Valerie Langley next, wondering about Mark's wife. But there was absolutely nothing on her. He couldn't find her on social media or in an online search. She had absolutely no online presence. Her son, Richard, didn't, either.

He looked up from the computer as Keira walked the installers to the door. Once they were gone, she came into the living room. "Sorry that took so long."

He realized it was dark outside now. "I didn't even realize. I was caught up in research."

She sat down next to him on the couch. "Did you find anything?"

"Yes. Mandy is Amanda, Gretchen's sister, and she's also the woman I saw in the parking garage."

Keira sucked in a breath. "That's interesting."

"Mandy is also obsessed with her sister's death." He flipped back through the pages online, bringing up Mandy's social media feed. "You can read through it, but she talks about someone needing to pay for her sister losing her life."

"Do you think she's talking about Mark?"

"She never mentions his name."

"I never found out how the fire started."

"I did. It was believed that the nanny was smoking before she went to bed, and that the lit cigarette slipped into the couch cushions and that's where the fire started. Mark and his family were away on vacation that weekend."

"That sounds like an accident."

"Maybe Mandy can't accept that."

"Maybe." She gave him a troubled look. "What do you think, Dante? You've been looking through all this for an hour. What does your gut say? Am I being paranoid? Is there something about Mark, Mandy, the fire, that I should be concerned about?"

He thought about the question. "If I hadn't witnessed the argument between them, I probably wouldn't be concerned, but there was real anger there. Now that we know the woman in the garage is Mandy, then I think this fire and Mark's relationship with Mandy is something your mother needs to know about."

"I just wish we had more to go on. My mom is crazy about him. She has dismissed my concerns as being ridiculous."

"Well, you can wait and see how their relationship goes, whether it gets serious or not. Are they having sex?"

She groaned with dismay at his question. "I don't know. I don't want to think about my mom having sex with anyone, much less this guy."

He smiled. "I get that. I try to avoid that subject with my father as well."

"You haven't told me much about your dad. Does he date? Is he involved with anyone? Do you have a stepmother?"

"I had one once, but their marriage only lasted five years. He seems to be very popular at the Italian Social Club. He's always going to parties there. But I don't see him that much, and I don't ask personal questions about his dating life, so who knows? In some ways, the man is a stranger to me."

"But you still know who he is. Sometimes, I wish I knew what my father was like, but my mother hates to talk about him. You'd think over time, she'd have a fond memory here and there, but if she does, she doesn't share them. Maybe they weren't that happy in their marriage." She took a breath. "I don't know why I keep sharing such personal information about my life. I never talk about my dad."

"I never talk about mine, either, but when I'm with you…"

Their gazes clung together for a long moment, the air going from comfortable to tense, but it was a good kind of tension, the kind of sizzle that usually led to more. But Keira was fighting their attraction, and he understood why. He should fight it, too. He didn't need more complications in his life, but he'd never been one to walk away from something or someone he wanted.

"It's easy," she said. "Talking to you."

"Right back at you. I have to say something, Keira, something I should have said before."

"What's that?"

"I know I upset you when I said you were using your mom as an excuse, and I don't want you to get the wrong idea. I know you've been through a lot with her, and I admire your sacrifice. You are an amazing daughter. And you want to protect her, and I can respect that."

She blinked some new moisture out of her eyes. "That's nice of you to say but taking care of someone you love isn't a sacrifice." She sniffed. "I'm so tired, my eyes are watering."

"That's a good excuse."

"I'm really not a crier."

"Me, either, except when I strike out. Then I can be a big baby," he joked.

"Does it even matter if you hit? I thought pitchers were only responsible for throwing strikes."

"Even though it's not what they pay me for, I think I'm a good hitter, and I don't like it when I don't do well."

"So, you cry?"

"Well, not anymore," he said dryly. "But when I was a little kid, after strikeouts, I had a lot of allergy attacks to explain my watery eyes."

"I can't see you crying."

"I worked really hard to be good. I hated when I wasn't living up to my expectations. No one could make me feel worse than myself."

"We have that in common. That's why that damn wedding dress is driving me crazy. But I'm going to look at it tomorrow with a fresh eye, and I might even think about what you said earlier, that maybe it's not just about the dress. But that's tomorrow."

"Still hours away," he murmured. "What do you want to do with the rest of the night?"

She swallowed hard, her eyes glittering with desire. "That's a loaded question."

"I know."

"We're supposed to just be friends, Dante. I don't want to make Nikki's story true."

"Her story doesn't matter. We know what's true."

"Do we?" she challenged. "Aren't we lying just a little when we don't acknowledge that we kissed before you broke up with her?"

"You're right. We did kiss. Maybe that was cheating."

"It was cheating, even if we want to pretend that it was just a moment of temporary insanity."

"The thing is, Keira, that moment didn't feel insane. It's the rest of my life that seems crazy. Kissing you felt right. I know I'm leaving, but that's not happening tonight or tomorrow, or even next week."

Indecision played through her eyes. "I can't deny I'm attracted to you. But you're not thinking about the future; you're thinking about right now."

"It's all that matters. Neither of us knows what's going to happen, but we can enjoy where we are." He paused. "Or not. I don't want to push you toward something you don't want. It's all good. We can be friends. I can go back to the inn. We don't have to take this any further. I don't want to hurt you, so whatever—"

"Stop talking," she interrupted, putting a finger across his lips.

His body tensed as he waited for her to continue.

She took her finger off his lips and framed his face with her hands. "I don't want to be just friends. I don't want to think about tomorrow. And I don't want to keep talking about kissing you. I just want to do it."

"Then do it."

Keira kissed Dante with a hunger that seemed almost insatiable. She'd been fighting her attraction for the last several days, but she wasn't fighting anymore. She wanted to explore his mouth, his body. She wanted to lose her mind over him, and she didn't think that would be difficult at all. Her pulse was pounding, her head was spinning, and there was a delicious heat running through her body.

As she broke away to take a much-needed breath, he threaded his fingers through her hair and brought her back to him. She liked the power in his kiss, the warmth of his lips, the sexy slide of his tongue against hers. It felt like they'd been doing this forever. No awkward moves. No feeling like it wasn't quite right. Because it was perfect.

Dante lifted his head, his eyes burning with desire. "Damn, Keira."

"I know," she whispered. "We're on fire."

"What do you want?"

"Well, I don't want to stop."

A happy light flashed through his deep-blue eyes. "Me, either."

As he lowered his head once more, she stopped him, realizing she wasn't exactly prepared for what she wanted to have happen. "Uh…"

He gave her a wary look. "Second thoughts already?"

"Not exactly. I don't have anything. You know, protection."

"I do."

"Really?"

"Don't question it," he said with a smile.

"Okay, I won't," she said, as he pulled her into another kiss.

"Is there a bedroom somewhere?" he asked.

She took his hand and jumped to her feet, leading him down the short hallway to the master bedroom. She felt nervous and excited as Dante stripped off his shirt, revealing a broad, tanned, muscular chest with just the perfect smattering of dark hair. Every muscle was defined and sculpted. Her mouth went dry.

"You really have been working out," she murmured.

"It's part of the job and the rehab."

Her gaze went to his shoulder. "I don't want to hurt you."

"As long as you don't make me throw you onto the bed, I think we're good."

"Hmm, we'll have to save that for another time."

He laughed. "I like the way you think. But I don't like how many clothes you have on."

"I'm a little intimidated by your perfect body."

"No, you're not," he said with a laugh.

She smiled back at him. "Okay, I'm not intimidated, I'm just getting really hot."

"Then let's take this off." He stepped forward and grabbed the hem of her shirt, helping her off with it, his gaze immediately dropping to her breasts. She'd worn a skimpy pink bra under her top, which Dante seemed to appreciate. He pulled her into his arms once more, and they kissed for several long minutes. She ran her hands up and down his back, loving the heat of his skin and the power of his muscles.

Dante did his own exploration, his fingers sliding down her spine, his hands settling on her waist. Her nerves tingled with anticipation of what was to come. She felt suddenly impatient to see more of him, to touch every inch of him.

His hands moved to the back of her bra, flicking open the snap with a deft hand. She broke away from his mouth to let the bra slip off her shoulders. And then she reached for the button on his jeans. They stripped off the rest of their clothes in mutual desperation, then kissed their way down to the mattress.

Dante gave every inch of her body the attention she so desperately craved. The chemistry between them was explosive. The fire got hotter with every touch. She wanted to slow things down, savor every feeling, but there was an urgency building that neither could ignore. Dante slipped on the condom and urged her on top of him, and she happily complied.

Their bodies moved together in hot, sweet, sexy madness, the climax as amazing as everything else.

As she slowly returned to reality, she gazed down at Dante, enjoying the sated look in his eyes. He took her face in his hands and pulled her down for a long kiss. Then she moved off him, rolling on to her side. She curled up next to him, resting her head on the pillow instead of his chest. "Are you all right? I didn't hurt your shoulder, did I?"

"No, you didn't hurt anything," he said with a happy grin. "You were amazing."

"So were you."

She ran her fingers down the side of his face, loving the shadow of beard that she'd felt all over her body just minutes earlier. He was such a handsome man. She leaned forward and kissed him, just because she needed that contact again.

He brought her in closer, deepening the kiss she'd started.

"You taste so good," he murmured.

"And you kiss really well."

"I wish I had more than one condom."

"Me, too, but I'm glad you had that one." She blew out a breath as they lay together in perfect comfort. A few minutes later, she said reluctantly, "I guess we should think about leaving."

"Not yet. It's so quiet here in the woods. I can't remember when I've been somewhere so still. The inn isn't loud, but there are noises: footsteps upstairs, voices in the hall. Out here, it feels like it's just you and me. No one else."

"Where do you live?" She smiled at her question. "Seems like probably something I should know."

"I have an apartment in Miami where I live during the season, and I have a condo in San Francisco for the off-season."

"Two different coasts."

"Two completely different vibes."

"Which do you like best?"

"San Francisco, but that's probably because it feels like home."

"I went to San Francisco once. We rode a cable car to the wharf. I loved the steep hills."

He smiled. "You and your love for steep hills…"

"The cable cars did go a little slow for my taste," she said with a laugh. "But the view of the bay was spectacular. We ate at an Italian restaurant in North Beach that was really good. I think the name was Rigoletto."

"I've eaten there many times."

"How funny. I wonder if we were there at the same time."

"When was this?"

"I was sixteen."

"I'm a year older than you, so I would have been living in the city then."

"Maybe we met a long time ago and never knew it."

He slid his fingers down her side, drawing a lovely trail of heat. "I would have remembered you."

"Were you always a charmer?"

His laugh was deliciously husky. "God, no. I fumbled my way through a lot of dates."

"I can't see that. You're way too good-looking. You had to be a confident teenager."

"I grew up with brothers. I didn't know how to talk to girls for a long time."

She wasn't buying his story. "I have a feeling talking wasn't really a requirement. You were a hot baseball player. Enough said."

"You know you're denigrating teenage girls as being shallow and superficial," he teased.

"Since I was a teenage girl, I'm allowed."

"What about you? Did you date in high school?"

"My first real boyfriend was Anthony Anderson. We were both

sixteen. He was a guitar player. He had long hair and a soulful voice, and I let myself believe he was singing every love song to me. He was a cool guy."

"How long did it last?"

"Not quite a year. He left Whisper Lake that summer to go to LA and play in some summer music program, and he never came back."

"Do you know what happened to him?"

"He got into a band. They toured in the US and Europe, but they never made it big. Last I heard, he was running a music store in LA and teaching music."

"Have you ever tried to contact him?"

"No. It was a teenage thing. I look back at most of the guys I liked when I was younger, and I wonder what the hell I was thinking. Anthony was a great musician, but he was also wild, and I was not. I could have never kept up with him, nor would I have wanted to. I was never a party girl. Even when I got to New York, I was the most boring girl in our apartment."

"You were working, pursuing your dream. I was boring, too, when it came to partying. I didn't want to jeopardize my fitness with too much alcohol. Nikki was an aberration."

"So, we're just two boring people."

"Hey, we were not boring tonight."

She smiled, loving how easy it was to talk to him. "That's true. So, tell me something about yourself that no one else knows, not your fans, or your agent or publicist, something personal, and if it's embarrassing, you get an extra point."

"A point, huh? Okay. I love to compete."

She could see the new energy in his eyes. "What have you got?"

He thought for a moment. "There's actually a lot that people don't know about me."

"I'm intrigued."

He laughed. "Don't be. It's hard to be super exciting when you have a singular purpose in life."

"No point for that."

"That wasn't my answer. You want embarrassing?"

"Yeah, something like sitting down at the wrong guy's table and assuming he's your date."

"That was not embarrassing. That was lucky."

"It was both for me," she admitted.

"All right. Here's one. I was twenty-five. One of my friends was getting married, and I was in charge of the bachelor party, which involved hiring a stripper. I was texting with the stripper one night, and at the same time, I was getting texts from a woman I had just started seeing."

"Uh-oh, I think I know where this is going."

"I got the text threads mixed up, and I asked the woman I wanted to date how far she would strip down and did she do lap dances?"

She laughed. "That's a good one. What did she say?"

"She said I was creepy and to never text her again. I tried to explain, but she blocked my number."

"That's worth a point."

"Well, I'm not playing this game alone. You tell me something embarrassing, something that precedes you assuming I was your date."

"Remember when I said I wasn't really a party girl? Well, that's partly because I had a very bad experience with vodka shots when I was working in New York. I got drunk at a Fashion Week party, and I was trying to find the bathroom, but there was a long line, so I headed to the patio, but I didn't make it. I threw up on the very expensive shoes of an incredibly talented Spanish designer named Manuel Valdez. He was not happy."

"I bet. What did he do?"

"He sent the bill for the shoes to my employer. Since I didn't have the money to pay, my boss said she'd pay it if I watched her monster kids for a three-day weekend. And when I say monster, I mean wild children. They threw toys at me. They painted on the walls, and they dumped spaghetti sauce into my purse."

"I'm surprised. I would have thought that kids would love you."

"They hated me, but they really hated their mom, who had

dumped their dad and was off with her new boyfriend. We managed to come to a peaceful agreement on the last day. But I learned my lesson. No more vodka shots."

"That's worth a point."

"Hey, it should be worth two."

"Now who's the competitive one?"

"Me. I am competitive. Maybe not like a pro athlete, but I like to win. It's much more fun than losing."

His smile broadened. "Definitely more fun."

She let out a sigh. "This is so nice. And I don't want to get out of this bed, but I think we should probably go home soon."

"We have a little more time, don't we?"

"More time…but no more condoms."

"We can do some other stuff," he said with a spark of mischief in his eyes.

"We already did other stuff."

"I was just getting started."

"You are very tempting."

"I want to show you the benefit of not being just friends."

"You've already done that."

He ran his fingers through her hair as he gazed into her eyes. "I like you, Keira."

A shiver ran down her spine. "I kind of figured, but it's nice to hear."

"I haven't been able to stop thinking about you since we first met."

"You've been on my mind, too, even when I didn't want you to be. And no matter what happens, I want you to know that I don't have any regrets."

"It's not morning yet."

"The sun won't change my mind," she said, hoping that was true. "I wanted to be with you tonight. Whatever comes next, even if it's nothing, is fine."

A frown played across his lips. "This is starting to sound like goodbye."

"No, it's not goodbye. I'm not ready for that yet."

"Good. Can I see you tomorrow?"

"Well, if you come by McLaren Park around noon, my friend Gianna's stepdaughter will be playing softball, and I'll be cheering her on. It's Hailey's ninth birthday, so I'm going out to support her and the team."

Indecision played through his eyes. "Softball, huh? I don't know. I've been avoiding anything related to baseball."

"It's just going to be little girls who can barely hit. I want you to meet Gianna and her husband, Zach. Chloe will probably be there, too. Jake is the coach, so Hannah will also show up."

"Maybe I can meet you after."

She didn't love his answer. It made her feel like everything was on his terms. And it was, wasn't it? She wasn't having regrets, but she did feel like she'd just gotten a wake-up call. He was so consumed by his injury, his feelings about baseball, that he couldn't even watch a little kid's game, even if it meant spending time with her and her friends. "Sure, all right," she said shortly, sliding away from him. "I should get home."

He sat up, his brows drawing together as he frowned. "You're mad."

"I'm not."

"Yes, you are. The one thing I've liked about you the most is that you're really honest."

He had a point. "Fine. Your decision about tomorrow just makes me realize how much baseball controls your life. I don't want to forget that."

"It's not controlling me." He licked his lips, his gaze darkening. "I need to explain."

"No, you don't."

"Yes, I do. I'm not that great at expressing my feelings, but here goes."

She waited as he searched for words, fascinated by the play of emotions going through his eyes.

"Watching a baseball game feels like putting salt in an open wound," he said. "It reminds me of where I started, a little kid playing a game that became my whole life. Baseball kept me going after my mom died. Baseball gave me purpose. And being good at it gave me something to feel happy about." He paused. "Pitching is the one thing I'm really good at, Keira. I don't know who I am if I'm not a pitcher. I don't know what I'll do next, and facing that uncertainty is terrifying. Maybe that sounds selfish. No. It doesn't sound selfish; it *is* selfish," he added. "You want me to meet your friends, and I'm making a little kid's game about me and my problems."

His brutally honest and self-revealing words made her feel bad. "I'm sorry, Dante. I didn't realize what I was asking."

"How could you?"

"I was thoughtless."

"No, you weren't. You asked me a normal question, and I made it weird."

"Well, you did do that."

A slow smile spread across his mouth. "I haven't been this honest with anyone ever, Keira. In my family, if I had a problem with someone or they had a problem with me, we usually just resolved it by hitting each other in the face. Same thing with my teammates."

She grinned back at him. "You spend a lot of time with guys."

"Too much testosterone," he agreed. "But talking to you…I don't know. I can't seem to stop telling you how I feel. It's like I've turned into someone else."

"Don't you dare say a woman," she warned.

He laughed. "I wasn't going to say that. Because I've been with a lot of women who cannot get honest, either."

"A lot, huh?" she muttered.

"Maybe not a lot, but some."

"We were just talking about being honest," she reminded him.

"Right."

"So how do you feel now that you've shared your worries with me?"

"Strange and a little unsettled."

"You can trust me, Dante. Whatever you say to me will never go any further."

"I believe that." He met her gaze. "And I have to admit, I haven't always been able to trust that someone will keep my secrets."

"You don't have to worry about that with me. As much as I don't want to see you leave any time soon, I really, really want you to get better and get back to the mound. I want you to be happy."

"Thanks. I'll come to the game tomorrow."

"No. You don't have to do that. It's not a big deal. We're actually going out on Adam's boat tomorrow after the game. Adam is Lizzie's brother."

"The cop, right?"

"Yes. Why don't you join us for that? If you want to. No pressure. It's nice to see the lake from the water."

"It sounds great. And for the record, I want you to be happy, too."

"I'm extremely happy right now," she said, lightening the mood. "And just so you know, pitching is definitely not the only thing you're really good at."

"I'm glad you think so, because I am not ready to let you out of this bed, not without showing you what else I can do."

"You really are an overachiever, aren't you?"

He laughed. "This will be worth more than one point."

"I'll be the judge of that."

He gave her a gentle push, rolling her onto her back, and lowered his lips to her stomach, sliding his tongue around her belly button, sending all kinds of delicious chills through her body. She closed her eyes and let him have his way with her. Then it would be her turn.

CHAPTER SEVENTEEN

SATURDAY MORNING, Dante didn't wake up until his alarm went off at eight. He felt tired but really happy. After leaving the cabin around two o'clock in the morning, he hadn't gotten more than four hours of sleep. He wished they'd been able to spend the whole night together, which was odd, since he rarely wished for that. But Keira was different in so many ways.

He'd followed her home from the cabin, making sure she was in her house before heading back to the inn. It was late enough that everything was quiet. He hoped the tabloid reporters had left the area, but that was probably being too optimistic. He just wished they'd concentrate only on him and leave Keira alone, but that was also a foolish thought.

He hated that Keira was having to deal with the press and also with Nikki's lies. She didn't deserve to have her reputation shredded online, but he was glad she hadn't shut him out because of it. He'd had more fun with her than he could remember having with a woman, and that wasn't just because of the great sex they'd shared. It was everything else, too.

He'd liked being with her. And he'd enjoyed talking to her. He'd told her things he hadn't told anyone, and he felt a little lighter today, maybe because he'd let some of the fear and worry out.

After a quick shower, he dressed and headed down the stairs, eager to grab breakfast before he headed to rehab. Today's session would only be two hours, but he wanted to have the energy to do it well. He walked into the dining room, filled his plate with fruit and eggs, grabbed a cup of coffee, and then looked for an empty table. There were several open. It was early, and most of the guests were probably taking a slower start to the day. But Mark Langley was up and sitting at a table by himself, sipping coffee as he gazed at his phone. He wasn't wearing a suit today, but he wore a short-sleeve button-down blue shirt with tan chinos, looking casual but also put together.

He hadn't planned on sitting with anyone at breakfast, but it seemed like too good of an opportunity to pass up. He moved over to Langley's table and said, "Mind if I join you?"

"Of course not." Mark tipped his head toward the open chair as he set down his phone. "How are you today?"

"Good. I'm heading to the rehab center in a few. Wanted to get some food first."

"How's your rehab going?"

"Very well. The center and the therapists are impressive."

A gleam of pride entered Mark's eyes. "I'm happy to hear that. We're still rolling out some of our services, but I believe the rehabilitation center will eventually be one of the finest in the country."

"I believe you're right. How did you end up here in Whisper Lake? Were you working at another center before this?"

"Yes. I was at a clinic in Las Vegas, but I needed a change, and the mountains seemed perfect. Plus, I wanted the opportunity to manage such a new and cutting-edge facility."

"I can understand that."

"You've become good friends with Keira, haven't you?"

"I have."

"She probably told you that her mother and I grew up together."

"She mentioned that you dated in high school."

"We did, and it's been great getting to know Ruth again. We

hadn't seen each other in years, but it feels like we picked up right where we left off."

"She doesn't seem different to you? Keira said her mother had an accident and a serious brain injury."

"She doesn't remember some things that I do, but she seems like she's doing very well," Mark replied. "I'm sorry she had to go through all that. But she's a fighter. She always has been. She raised Keira pretty much on her own."

"That's what I heard. Did you know Keira's father?"

"No. I never met him, but what I heard about him, I didn't like much. He always sounded selfish and narcissistic. But Ruth was in love with him. She says now she was too young when they married. She didn't realize what he was like. When you're young, you don't look too closely at things. You skip over red flags and ignore alarm bells, because attraction is a powerful thing."

"Are you speaking about Ruth or yourself?" he asked curiously, as Mark seemed to have gone off into the past.

Mark started, as if surprised and displeased he'd said so much. "Both, I suppose. I was married for thirteen years, but it was only good for the first three." Mark shrugged. "It was a mistake, but I got my son out of it, so I'll never regret the choices I made."

"Where is your son now?"

"He lives in Los Angeles."

"Do you see him often?"

"Unfortunately, no. My son blamed me for the divorce. There were so many things he didn't understand."

"Maybe one day he will. Does your ex-wife live in Los Angeles?"

"She passed away a few years ago."

That was new information. "I'm sorry to hear that."

"It was sad. But we hadn't been together in a long time, so I didn't really know her anymore."

"Now you've reconnected with an old flame. I always think it's interesting when people who dated in high school find each other again decades later. It seems like it might be meant to be."

"We'll see. It is nice to talk to someone who shares some of the same memories." Mark lifted his coffee mug to his lips and took a sip. Then he said, "I'm not sure Keira thinks too highly of me. She seems suspicious of my motives."

"Keira seems to be a very fair-minded person," he said. "Maybe you should talk to her. Tell her more about yourself. She just wants to protect her mom. If you're up front with her, and you get to know each other, I'm sure she'll give you a chance."

"I hope so. Ruth is very important to me. I'd like to get to know Keira better. I definitely want Ruth's daughter on my side."

Mark said all the right things, but there was still something about him, something in his conversation that felt a little too smooth. He needed to shake him up a little, see if he could surprise him into saying something. "It's none of my business, but I was in the parking garage the other day and caught the end of a somewhat intense argument between yourself and a woman with dark-red hair. I hope everything is all right."

Mark stiffened. "I didn't see you."

"I hope she wasn't a dissatisfied patient."

"No. She has nothing to do with the clinic. I apologize if that was awkward."

"More concerning than anything else. She seemed very angry."

"She's just going through some personal issues. I've been trying to help her out."

"She's a friend then."

"Not really a friend." Mark checked his watch. "I should leave. Ruth and I are going to the farmers' market to pick up some fresh vegetables and fruit." Langley pushed back his chair and stood up. "I'm sure we'll talk again soon."

"I'm sure we will. We're on the same floor."

"Yes." Mark paused. "The woman I was arguing with, she's someone from my past. Did you mention her to Keira?"

"I did," he admitted.

"I should probably talk to Keira then."

"You should. From what I know, Keira and her mother are very tight. If you want something with Ruth, you're going to need her daughter to get on board."

"You're right. I'm going to make that a top priority. Have a good day."

"You, too." As Mark left, he wondered if he'd made a mistake in admitting that he'd told Keira about Mandy. On one hand, it gave Mark time to come up with a story to explain the argument with Mandy. But on the other hand, Mark had also been put on notice that his relationship with Mandy was more public than he'd realized. Mark could either share the nature of that relationship with Keira and her mother, or he could go for a cover-up. Whichever choice he made would be revealing. Hopefully Keira would see it that way.

He finished his coffee and then headed out the door. He needed to get to rehab, and then he was going to have to face his past at a child's softball game. Even though Keira had told him to skip it, to meet them at the harbor at two, he was going to make the game. He'd never let fear control him; he wasn't going to start now. And besides that, he really wanted to see Keira again.

Keira arrived at the park at the beginning of the second inning. Chloe and Hannah were standing off to the side of the first-base dugout, watching Chloe's almost three-year-old son, Leo, dig in the dirt along the fence.

"Hi there," she said. "Looks like someone is getting dirty."

Chloe smiled. "He found a stick, and that's all it took."

"How's the game going? Has Hailey batted yet?"

"No, her team is in the field," Hannah interjected. "She's at second base."

"I see her." She gave Hailey a wave as the little girl looked in their direction.

Hailey smiled and gave a small wave back before turning her attention to the girl in the batter's box.

Jake, who was standing in the dugout nearby, shot them all a look. "Don't distract my players," he said.

Hannah rolled her eyes. "Jake is taking his coaching role way too seriously."

"It's nice of him to do it," Chloe said.

"He was just going to sponsor the team until the coach had to have his appendix out. Zach couldn't do it, because he has his hands full designing Justin's new office complex. It's going to be something else, from what I hear."

"I'll bet. More business coming to Whisper Lake," she said. "And more jobs."

"The town is growing fast," Chloe agreed. "I might have to hire more help. We're busy seven days a week now. It's all good, but I'm used to having more downtime."

"I know what you mean. The shop is busy, too." She paused as Gianna came over to join them.

"Keira, thanks for coming," Gianna said.

"No problem. I'm hoping our girl gets a hit for her birthday."

"That would be lovely, but she's been struggling a little, so who knows?" Gianna paused, giving her a thoughtful look. "I'd love to know how you're doing, Keira, with everything that's going on, beyond the two-word text you sent saying: I'm fine."

"I'm fine," she reiterated.

Hannah gave a scoffing laugh. "No way you're fine."

"Is there anything we can do to fight the lies that woman is telling about you?" Chloe asked. "I'm not usually on social media, but I could get on there and post something."

"We all could," Gianna said.

"No. I don't want any of you to do anything. It will blow over eventually, and the people I care about know the lies aren't true. I didn't break up Nikki and Dante, and I only met Nikki once a long time ago. I didn't betray my girlfriend."

"Of course you didn't. You would never do that," Gianna declared. "The three of us know that better than anyone."

She looked around her circle of friends and smiled, thinking of how many years they'd known each other, loved each other, supported each other. These women would always have her back, and she would have theirs. "Thanks," she said. "To be totally honest, though, there is something between Dante and me. There's an attraction, a chemistry."

"Really?" Gianna asked, a new light in her eyes.

"But," she added hastily, "it's not going anywhere. Dante is only in town for another two weeks. We're just going to be…friends."

"Kissing friends?" Hannah asked.

"Maybe," she conceded. "Let's not make a big thing about it. We're just going to have fun and that's it. And now that you know that, I hope you will not act weird around him when he comes on the boat with us later. I invited him. I hope that's okay."

"It's more than okay," Gianna said. "And we'll be good."

"I know you and Chloe will be good…" She gave Hannah a pointed look.

"I'll be good, too," Hannah said dryly.

"And I'm afraid I won't be there, so I'm going to expect a full report at some point," Chloe said. "I also want to say, Keira, that you should have some fun. Even when you think a relationship might last forever, it doesn't always make it." She cleared her throat. "Sorry, I took that a little too dark."

"I vote for fun, too," Gianna said. "I spent way too much time trying to figure out Mr. Right, even accepting a few engagement rings along the way because I kept thinking I just wanted to get married. But all those guys were wrong. When I saw Zach again, I knew that I'd been trying to force something that wasn't there."

"I have no words of wisdom," Hannah put in. "I just think Dante is hot and you're hot and you could be really hot together."

She grinned. "I can always trust you to keep it simple."

"Maybe he could be your plus one for the wedding," Hannah added, a sparkle in her eyes.

"Stop obsessing over my plus one," she ordered. "But I'll think about it. I don't know where things are going to go with us."

"I know," Hannah said.

She made a face at Hannah. "You don't know everything."

"I know this. Dante is walking toward us."

She whirled around in surprise, seeing Dante make his way

down the right-field line. After what he'd told her the night before, she hadn't expected to see him before the boat trip. But here he was, looking incredibly sexy in faded jeans and a dark-orange T-shirt, his thick brown hair blowing in the warm breeze. Her heart flip-flopped in her chest, her mind flashing back to the beautiful memories they'd made the night before.

She moved away from her friends to greet him. "I can't believe you're here," she said. "I thought you were going to meet us at the boat."

He smiled as he gazed into her eyes. "I didn't want to waste time that I could spend with you."

Her heart sped up at his husky words. "What about the baseball?"

"I think I can handle it. As long as you're here."

"I'm here," she said.

"I want to kiss you. But…"

She sucked in a quick breath. "But?" she echoed.

"There are a lot of people looking at us."

She glanced over her shoulders, seeing her friends gazing at them with unapologetic curiosity. "We could give them something to see."

He grinned. "I thought you'd want to keep our relationship private."

"Our relationship has never been private." She put her hands on his shoulders as she stole a much-needed kiss. "There. It's done."

"For now," he promised.

"For now," she agreed.

They stared at each other for a long minute, with the air sizzling between them, but a sudden cheer broke the trance they seemed to be in.

She turned toward the field as a fly ball headed straight for Hailey. She caught it and another cheer broke out. "That's Hailey," she said. As Hailey ran toward the dugout, she shouted, "Good catch, Hailey."

Hailey looked over at her with a big smile on her face as her team got ready to hit.

When she turned back to Dante, she saw a smile play around the corners of his mouth. "What?"

"Making the last out of the inning when you're on defense is always the best feeling."

"I bet. So, this isn't bringing only bad memories?"

"Surprisingly not. Her face was so full of joy. I remember that feeling."

"I'm sure you felt it a lot, considering how good you are at the game."

"Baseball is still a game of percentages. The best hitters in the league get out seventy percent of the time, and I try to raise that to a hundred percent of the time if I can."

"Hmm, I never thought of it that way. There's more failure than success."

"That's why the success is so sweet. It's a difficult game. But when you win, it feels amazing."

"I'd love to see you play."

His smile dimmed. "Maybe you will. Who knows?"

"I know," she said confidently. "I have faith in you."

"If I could will my arm to work, I would, but it's not that simple. It's not about desire."

"I understand, Dante. You have a real injury to deal with. But you're working hard, and you have a great rehab facility and an excellent doctor. I think you'll make it back."

"Hopefully. But I didn't come here to talk about my game. Why don't you introduce me to your friends? I know Hannah, but not the other two."

"Okay." They walked down the sideline, joining up with Hannah, Chloe, Gianna, and also Zach, who had just arrived. She introduced him to everyone, but there wasn't time for prying questions as Hailey came up to bat.

They cheered her on, but after two swings and two misses, Hailey hit a weak ball to the pitcher and was thrown out at first. Her smile turned into a dejected frown as she walked back to the dugout, and no amount of cheering and support seemed to change that.

"She's so hard on herself," Gianna murmured.

"I keep telling her it's just a game. She's here to have fun," Zach put in. "But that almost makes her angrier."

"I agree," Gianna said. "Last game, I said nice try, and she almost bit my head off."

"I hated when anyone said that to me," Dante said, drawing all eyes to him.

"Really?" Gianna asked curiously. "Why?"

"Because I was disappointed in myself. I couldn't hear what anyone else had to say. I just knew that I'd failed, and it pissed me off." He cleared his throat. "But your little girl is not me, so…"

"No, that makes sense," Zach said with a nod. "I never felt that way when I was playing sports. I just figured I'd do better the next time, even if that wasn't true. I guess I wasn't hard on myself at all." He gave Dante a thoughtful look. "How did your parents handle you?"

"Oh, don't go by my parents," Dante replied. "My mom would just serve me up a big bowl of pasta after a game. That was her go-to solution for everything bad that happened. My dad never showed up to see me play, so he had no idea what was going on, nor did he care. But you should keep on supporting Hailey. She'll appreciate it even if she can't show it."

"Leo, stop eating the dirt," Chloe said suddenly, interrupting their conversation to grab her son off the ground. He had dirt smeared across his mouth. "Anyone have a fix for this problem?"

"Not me," Dante said with a laugh. "I never ate dirt."

"I think we're going to head home," Chloe said. "I have a gift for Hailey in my car."

"I'll come with you to get it," Gianna said.

As they left, Zach moved closer to Dante and started talking about baseball and kids.

Hannah slid next to her and gave her a little smile. "Nice kiss, but a little G-rated."

"We're in public."

"True. But I can still see that you are so into him."

"I am," she admitted. "For however long it lasts."

"Live in the moment."

"That's what I'm going to do."

As the inning ended, Jake came over to the fence, motioning for Zach and Dante to come over. A moment later, to her amazement, Dante gave her a wry smile and a shrug as he headed toward the dugout. "I'm going to coach first base," he said.

"Have fun."

As Dante moved to the field, Zach rejoined them. "Dante said he could give Hailey some tips later on her swing."

She was surprised again. "That's great."

"He seems like a nice guy."

"Keira definitely thinks so," Hannah said with a laugh.

She made a face at her friend. "You be quiet."

"When am I ever quiet?"

She didn't bother to answer, her attention moving to Dante. As each girl hit and reached first base, he had a little chat with them. She had no idea what he was saying, but the girls seemed to be completely captivated. *How could she blame them?* She was completely captivated, too.

CHAPTER EIGHTEEN

DANTE COULDN'T BELIEVE he'd gotten talked into coaching, but it was actually fun. The kids were eager to learn. They listened to whatever he said, and they laughed and smiled so easily. Even Hailey, who definitely had an intensity that reminded him of himself, relaxed when he talked to her. And after the game, with an empty field, he found himself helping Hailey and her friend Megan with some hitting.

With Jake pitching and Zach shagging balls, he coached each girl on her stance and talked about watching the ball and not getting too tense. Within fifteen minutes, their success at connecting with the ball went up about ninety percent. Most of the families had left by the time they finished, but Gianna and Keira were still sitting in the stands. He walked over to join them as Jake and Zach got the equipment together.

"Nice job, Coach," Keira teased.

"Thanks for doing that," Gianna added, as she got off the bench. "I've never seen Hailey hit so well."

"Hopefully it sticks," he said.

"I'm going to help Hailey get her things together. You're coming out on the boat with us, right?" Gianna asked. "I'd love to get to know you better."

"Yes. I'm looking forward to it."

"Good," Gianna said with a smile.

As Gianna left, he looked at Keira, and even though he'd just told Gianna he was looking forward to the boat party, he was really more interested in getting Keira alone. "How long is this boat trip?"

"Several hours. There will be plenty of food and drinks." Her smile grew more tentative. "Are you having second thoughts?"

"No, just wishing we could be alone."

Her dark-brown eyes sparkled at that comment. "Maybe we can be alone later."

"I hope so."

"I'd bail on the boat, but it's Hailey's birthday."

"I get it. And it sounds like fun."

"It will be fun, I promise. How was your rehab today?"

"It went well, a shorter session this morning, but I felt good about it." He paused as another team began to arrive at the field. "I guess we should go. Do you have your car? I walked here."

"You did? That's a good walk from the inn."

"It's a beautiful day."

"And no one accosted you?"

"Nope. No one waiting outside rehab or the inn. Maybe the press is over us. It's a little surprising, but I'll take it." As they walked toward the parking lot, he added, "By the way, I had break-fast with Mark Langley this morning."

She stopped abruptly. "What did he say?"

"Not a lot, but I did tell him I'd witnessed an argument between him and a woman. He did not tell me her name. He made some vague reference to her being an old friend going through some issues in her life."

"Anything else?"

"He wanted to know if I'd mentioned her to you. I said I had. I hope that wasn't the wrong answer, but I'm curious to see if it will compel him to speak to your mother or you about Mandy."

"Maybe it will."

"He knows you're suspicious of him, Keira. He said he'd like to get to know you better because he's very interested in continuing his friendship with your mom. I suggested he talk to you."

"Okay. But I'm a little worried that now he has time to make something up."

"It's a possibility, but he also knows that he has to say something. Maybe that will give you another clue to pursue or will ease your mind. He also mentioned that his wife passed away a few years ago."

"That's interesting. I couldn't find anything on her, although I have to admit I didn't look that hard. I was focusing on him and Mandy. Did he say anything else about her?"

"Only that his son blamed him for the divorce and that he and his son are not close."

"I wonder why Richard blamed him for the divorce."

"He didn't say."

"Did you mention the fire?"

"I didn't want to go that far. Did you talk to your mom about Mandy?"

"I didn't get a chance. She had an early breakfast with a good friend of hers, and then Mark took her to the farmers' market. They're going to spend the day together. But the three of us are supposed to have dinner together tomorrow night, so I need to find time for a discussion very soon."

As they reached the parking lot, he was distracted by the squeal of tires and a van pulling into the lot.

"Dammit," he said, as two male photographers jumped out of a car. They raced forward, snapping photos with each step.

"Should we run?" Keira asked.

"No," he said, as he looked into her eyes. "Let's not run."

She gave him a searching look. "Okay. Whatever you think."

He hoped her trust in him wasn't misplaced.

Questions were shouted out at them as a dozen more photos were snapped.

"Here's the deal," Dante said, ending the barrage of questions. "My breakup with Nikki Voltari had nothing to do with Keira. Nikki and I simply want different things from life. Keira did not steal me away from Nikki. She was never friends with Nikki, and she has done nothing wrong. She's a really good person who simply got caught up in the drama that Nikki created to increase her followers." He raised a hand as more questions were shot at them. "I just have one more thing to say. I'm here in Whisper Lake to rehab my shoulder. The center here is one of the best in the country. I plan to be back in Miami when my rehab is over, and I can get back to my team. My goal is to be as fit as I ever was, but that will depend on the work I do here, work that I can't do with you all chasing me around. That's it. That's the whole story. You can take a million more pictures, but there's nothing else to say."

As he urged Keira toward her car, one of the photogs said, "We hope you get back on the mound, Dante."

"I hope so, too."

He jumped into the passenger seat while Keira got behind the wheel. She started the car and drove out of the lot. They both watched the mirrors as they left, but no one was following.

Keira turned to look at him as she came to a stoplight. "Thanks for saying that about me."

"I told the truth. I'm not sure they believed it."

"I don't care. You said it. That's what matters to me."

He wanted to tell her that she was what mattered to him, but the light turned green, and she turned her gaze back to the road. There would be time to tell her. However, as they drove toward the harbor, he knew that time was not his friend. And there would be other things he had to tell her—like goodbye. But he wasn't going to think about that.

———

The afternoon flew by as they cruised around the lake, stopping to swim and innertube, as well as explore some of the hidden coves with the water a beautiful turquoise blue. Adam and Brodie took turns driving the boat with Chelsea, Hannah, and Jake hanging out up front. Keira was at the back of the boat with Dante, Gianna, and Zach as well as Hailey and her friend, Megan. At the moment,

Dante and Zach were getting the girls onto the innertube for another ride. She smiled as she watched Dante help Hailey adjust her life jacket. He was good with kids. In fact, he was good with everyone. It felt like he'd been part of her group of friends for years instead of a little over a week, and that put an ache in her heart. Because he would be gone soon, and moments like this would just be a memory.

She pushed that painful thought out of her head. She would be sad later. Today, she would just enjoy being with him.

"I like him," Gianna said, breaking into her reverie as she sat down on the bench next to her. "Dante fits right in."

"I was thinking the same thing," she admitted.

"Hailey talked about him in the car. She's a big fan, by the way. She said he told her that when people say *nice try*, they're just showing their support. Hopefully, she'll remember that the next time I forget and tell her that I'm proud of her for trying her best. Dante seemed to really understand Hailey's mindset."

"He did," she muttered, distracted as Dante stripped off his shirt, his muscled chest glistening in the sunlight.

"Oh, my," Gianna said with a laugh as she waved a hand in front of her face. "It's getting hotter by the minute."

"It sure is," she said with a grin.

"Do you want a drink to cool off? I made some strawberry lemonade. It won't be as good as a cold shower, but you can always jump in the lake."

"Sure. And I'm fine."

"Tell that to the flush on your face."

"That's from the sun."

Gianna laughed, then got up to get the lemonade.

As she glanced back at Dante, she had to silently admit that he was bringing the heat to her face, too. Her body tingled with memories from the night before, the taste of his mouth, the feel and weight of his body on hers, the rough edges of his impatient fingers, the way they'd come together with wild impatience and almost desperate hunger. She couldn't remember ever feeling like that. Maybe she was making it better than it was. Maybe she'd need to be with him again to find out for sure.

"Here you go," Gianna said a moment later, handing her a cold glass of lemonade.

She took a grateful drink, dragging her gaze away from Dante as Chelsea sat down with her and Gianna.

"I haven't had a chance to talk to you since the awards show," Chelsea said. "I told everyone you made my dress. I hope you're getting calls."

"I've had several stylists reach out."

"That's great."

"We'll see. One person already changed her mind after Nikki posted her lies about me online."

"Are you serious?" Gianna said. "That's terrible. Can't you sue her or something?"

"That's the last thing I want to do. I just want her to stop talking and move on with her life."

"Can Dante get her to stop talking?" Chelsea asked.

"He broke up with her. It wasn't the other way around. Nikki is pissed. She's going to do what she thinks is best for her brand. It's fine."

"It's not fine," Chelsea said. "Maybe I can do something."

"What can you do?" Gianna asked with interest.

"I have contacts in the fashion world. If she wants to make it difficult for you, maybe I should make it difficult for her," Chelsea replied, a fierce look in her eyes.

"Oh, I don't want you to do anything like that," she said quickly. "I appreciate the defense, but it's not necessary. It was one stylist. Hopefully, the others won't bail. Nikki can't know everyone, right?"

"She's pretty popular," Gianna muttered. "Maybe you should consider Chelsea's offer."

"I don't even have to take Nikki down," Chelsea added. "I can just talk you up."

"You already did that by wearing my dress. And to be honest,

Dante volunteered to do the same thing. But I don't want people to reach out to me because they're doing someone a favor. Besides, I'm really busy right now with the wedding dresses, and the shop, and the realty business. I don't need any more design work right now."

"I just hate that she's getting away with this," Chelsea said.

"I hate it, too," Gianna said.

"What does everyone hate?" Adam Cole asked as he joined the group. Adam had on a T-shirt and board shorts, looking more relaxed than she'd seen him in a long time.

"More like *who* do we hate," Chelsea told her brother. "And it's Nikki Voltari, the supermodel spreading rumors about Keira."

"Oh, yeah, I heard about that," Adam said. "Sorry, Keira."

"Thanks. It will all die down, I'm sure. Let's not talk about it anymore. I just want to enjoy the day."

"Then I better speed this boat up," he said with a grin. "I know how much you like to go fast."

"I do, but this is Hailey's party."

"And the girls are done tubing, so we can take off on a faster ride," he said.

"If we're going faster, I'm moving up front," Gianna said.

"Me, too," Chelsea agreed.

Dante came over to her as her friends moved away. "Your nose is starting to burn," he said.

"I just put on more sunscreen," she said. "You're very tan."

"I live in Miami."

"You must go on boats a lot."

"A fair amount, but this is one of the best parties I've been to in a while."

"I find that difficult to believe since you're at a kid's birthday party."

"With you," he said with a smile, leaning in to give her a quick kiss. "Hmm. You taste like strawberries."

She held up the glass in her hand. "Strawberry lemonade. Want a sip?"

"I'd rather taste your lips."

She cleared her throat, seeing Hailey and Megan moving in their direction. "Let's keep this G-rated."

"Until later?"

She saw the promise in his eyes. "Yes."

"Then you better give me a drink."

She handed him the glass. "You can finish it."

"Thanks." He swigged it down in two long gulps. Then he grabbed her hand as the boat suddenly took off. "Whoa."

"Adam said he was going to give us a faster ride," she told him. "He knows I like to go fast."

He smiled. "I think you like to go slow, too."

"G-rated," she reminded him.

He laughed. "Got it."

The rest of the afternoon passed in a blur of laughter, stories, drinks, food, and finally birthday cake. It was after seven when they finally docked at the harbor and got off the boat. She felt relaxed and happy but also eager to spend some time alone with Dante. She drove him back to the inn and pulled into the parking lot.

Dante looked over at her. "You're coming in, right?"

"I don't think you can stop me," she said with a laugh.

He leaned over, cupped the back of her neck, and pulled her in for a kiss. She didn't know if he meant it to be brief, but once her mouth was under his, she wanted more. They kissed for long minutes until they were steaming up the car.

"Let's go inside," he said breathlessly. "Race you."

"I don't think I can beat you in a foot race," she said, as she jumped out of the car. But she jogged alongside him as they ran up the steps to the porch.

He got to the door first. "I won. That means you have to pay up."

"We didn't make a bet."

"I made one in my head. It involves you getting naked."

"Sh-sh," she said, socking him in the arm.

"No one is around. So, are you going to pay up?"

"I just might."

Dante opened the door, and they hurried inside. She hoped Lizzie wouldn't be at the front desk, because that would only slow them down. Unfortunately, Lizzie was there, and she wasn't alone. There was a tall, handsome man standing in front of the check-in counter, wearing worn jeans, ripped at the knee, and a navy-blue T-shirt with a beer logo. His light-brown hair was on the long side, and his blue eyes seemed very familiar.

CHAPTER NINETEEN

"Micah? What the hell are you doing here?" Dante asked.

Micah? Dante's brother?

"Nice to see you, too," Micah said with a laugh. "Who's your friend? Or do I even need to ask?" Micah stepped forward, a curious gleam in his eyes. "You must be Keira."

"I am. How did you know?"

"Your face is all over the internet."

"Right. I almost forgot," she mumbled.

"What are you doing here, Micah?" Dante asked again.

"I wanted to see how you were doing. So, here I am. I've gotten myself a room, thanks to Lizzie."

"He was in luck," Lizzie said. "I had a cancellation."

"How long are you staying? I have rehab Monday through Saturday. I'm really busy," Dante said.

"Don't worry. I have to leave Monday morning, but I thought I'd check in on you and see what Whisper Lake is all about."

At his words, Keira realized that any thought of getting naked with Dante had just been blocked by his brother's arrival. She felt an absurd sense of disappointment. But she wasn't going to stand in the way of their brotherly reunion. "You guys should catch up," she said. "Lizzie, do you have time to have a drink with me?"

"I do," Lizzie replied. "I'm actually glad you stopped in. I want to hear about the birthday party."

"Hey, you don't have to go, Keira," Micah said. "If I'm interrupting something, I can go find some food on my own."

"No, don't be silly. You and Dante should go out. It's a Saturday night. The town is hopping. If you want to see Whisper Lake, this is a great time." She turned to Dante. "We'll talk another time."

"We will," he promised. Turning back to his brother, he added, "Do you want to drop your bag off?"

"Sounds good. I'll be back in a few minutes."

As Micah went upstairs, Lizzie cleared her throat. "I'll pour us some wine. Want to meet me on the patio, Keira?"

"Sure. I'll be right there."

Left alone, Dante gave her a rueful smile. "Sorry about this."

"Don't apologize."

"I had no idea Micah was going to show up here."

"He's worried about you. It's nice that he came."

"Yeah, but I had a lot of plans for tonight, and none of them included him. As soon as he's gone…"

"Give me a call," she finished.

He sighed. "Sometimes I want to kill my brother."

She smiled. "Just enjoy it. Have fun with Micah. We can get together next week. We have time."

He frowned at her words. "Not as much as I'd like."

"We agreed not to think about the future too much, or we'll miss what we have right now."

"What I have right now is an annoying little brother in town."

Despite his statement, she could hear the love in his voice. Dante needed his family. It was nice that one of his brothers had showed up to support him. As Micah came downstairs, she gave him a quick kiss and then headed out to the patio.

Lizzie was waiting with a bottle of wine and a cheese tray.

She shook her head in amazement. "Did you just whip that up?"

Lizzie laughed. "No, I put it out for happy hour earlier, but hardly anyone was around today, so I had a lot left over. How was the boat party?"

"Very, very fun. We missed you and Justin."

"I was sad not to make it, but Shay was off today, and Justin had to fly back to San Francisco for a few days." Lizzie paused. "Did you take Dante on the boat?"

"I did. He got along really well with everyone."

"Why wouldn't he? He's a nice guy."

"He *is* a good guy," she agreed.

"And you two are…"

"Having fun and not over-analyzing."

"Sounds good. Too bad his brother showed up, huh? The look on your faces… I know that's not what you planned for the evening."

She flushed at the knowing gleam in Lizzie's eyes. "It definitely was not, but I'm glad his brother came to see him. He could probably use some family support."

"How's everything else going with you? Is your mom still seeing Mr. Langley?"

"Yes," she said with a sigh. "They were planning to spend the day together and God knows what they're doing now."

Lizzie laughed. "I can't imagine my parents dating anyone."

"You're lucky that they're still happily married to each other."

"Thirty-eight years and going strong."

"That's amazing."

"It is. I hope Justin and I go the distance. Of course, we have to get married first."

"Have you set a date yet—one that will stick? First, it was going to be this summer, then you were talking about fall…"

"Now, maybe spring," Lizzie said with a helpless shrug. "We want to do it when Justin has time to relax, and I can be away from the inn. We want to take a long honeymoon. Anyway, we'll see what happens. We're not in a hurry. But I will let you know as soon as I know. I'll want you to make my dress."

"You might want to wait and see how happy Hannah is before you decide that."

"Why? What are you talking about? I already saw Hannah's dress, and it's beautiful."

"It's not quite right, and I'm running out of time to fix it. I should probably be doing that now."

"It's Saturday night. You can take a break and tackle it in the morning."

"I know."

"By the way, getting back to Mr. Langley," Lizzie began. "He had a visitor today. She got really agitated when I said he wasn't here."

She sat up straighter. "Did she have red hair?"

Lizzie looked at her in surprise. "She did. Why? Do you know her?"

"No, but Dante told me that Mark had an argument with a red-haired woman a few days ago. He was curious about it, and so am I. Did she give you her name?"

"No. She asked for his room number. I didn't give it to her. I said I'd leave him a message, and she thought about that. Then she said she'd like to write him a note, so I gave her paper and a pen, and she went into the living room and took about fifteen minutes to write her message."

"Do you know what it said?"

"No. I wouldn't read his private message. I put it in an envelope and slid it under his door." Lizzie paused. "But the woman did say something odd to me."

"What was that?"

"She said Mark seems like a nice guy, but people should be careful around him."

"That doesn't sound good."

Lizzie shrugged. "Maybe she's a jilted lover."

"Maybe." She didn't like that this woman was hanging around and trying to talk to Mark. She didn't like the warning she'd left, either. She needed to speak to her mother, but she had to do it when her mom wasn't with Mark. Hopefully, she'd be able to get her alone later tonight or tomorrow morning.

"I thought you werc loncly, bored, and depressed," Micah said as he sipped his beer. "I was wrong. Let's talk about Keira."

Dante set his beer down, thinking it was ironic that they were talking about Keira at Micky's Bar and Grill, where it all started. "Keira is…amazing."

Micah raised a brow. "Amazing, huh? That's an impressive adjective for you."

"She's an impressive woman."

"Is it true then? She broke up you and Nikki?"

"No. Nikki and I were done a long time ago. I just didn't have the energy to break up with her until she showed up here in town and manipulated the press and reminded me exactly who she was."

"She was hot."

"She was a lot of other things, too. Actually, that's not true. She was basically one-dimensional. It was all about being a celebrity, an influencer. Everything was a photo opportunity. She was never really with me, even when she was with me. She just wanted me in her pictures."

"I'm sure it was more than that."

"It wasn't. What I can't stand is how she spun our breakup into some kind of crazy betrayal. She even pretended that Keira was her friend. They met once for ten minutes like eight years ago. Nikki didn't even remember her until Keira mentioned it."

"But you do like Keira. Nikki must have picked up on that."

"Maybe she did. I don't know. I just want her to move on and for the tabloids to leave me alone."

"You generate a lot of clicks, Dante. I wouldn't expect this to end anytime soon."

He shrugged. "I talked to the reporters today. We'll see if they are happy enough with what I said to leave us alone."

"What did you say?"

"I defended Keira. I told them I was here to rehab, and my plan was to be back to my team when I was done. Whether they believe it or not, I don't know, but I had to say it."

"Is that the plan? Is your shoulder going to be ready for the pressure you want to put on it?"

"I sure as hell hope so. I don't know who I am without the game. It's been a part of me since I was six years old."

"Well, to me, you'll still be a pain in the ass."

"Nice," he said dryly.

Micah leaned forward, his gaze turning more serious. "You know what I've always admired about you, Dante?"

"What?"

"You never quit, even when the odds are long. You push on. This is just another challenge for you. You'll figure your way through it. You always do."

He appreciated his brother's words. "I won't give up, but ultimately my body has to be as strong as my desire."

"What does the doctor say?"

"That he'll be able to tell me more when he sees me next week. Until then, I just have to do the work to get better. Now, tell me what's going on with you and the food truck."

Micah sighed. "That's a conversation for another time. Did you know that Dad is hooking up with Valentina?"

"Valentina from next door?" he asked in shock. Valentina had been friends with his mother.

"Yes. I saw her leaving his condo early one morning. He said she was there to drop something off, but I don't think that was the truth. She was all flushed and there was a guilty look in her eyes."

"Damn. Why did you have to put that picture in my head? I don't want to think of Valentina being flushed and guilty."

"Because I wanted to get it out of my head," Micah returned. "It's better that he's dating her than some girl who's our age, right?"

"I'd prefer if he wasn't dating anyone." He realized as he finished the statement that he was sounding a lot like Keira. "Although, Dad has a right to be happy."

"Sure," Micah agreed. "But I like Valentina. She made us so many cookies after Mom died. In the long run, I don't think Dad will make her happy. He just doesn't seem to have the ability to see beyond himself."

"No, he doesn't. Valentina should know that about him. Or maybe he's different with her."

"Possibly. I just have to say that I'm glad I had you, Danny, and Paul around. Because growing up with him alone would have been horrible."

"We were lucky to have each other."

"You know you still have us, right? Because you've been pushing us away since you got hurt."

"I know," he admitted. "I just haven't felt like I could talk about anything."

"You don't have to talk. Just let us be there for you."

"I'm doing better now. Not just the arm, but mentally. I even watched a kid's softball game today."

Micah raised a brow. "Seriously? You went to a ballgame?"

"Yes. I thought the memories would make me feel worse. They'd remind me of what I might be losing, but they didn't. They just reminded me of good times." He paused. "I can't really explain it."

"The game was always your escape. Now your escape might be cut off. It's not surprising that would bother you, but it sounds like you've got a handle on it." Micah gave him a speculative look. "Does your new outlook have anything to do with Keira?"

"Possibly. But enough about me. Are you seeing anyone? What about that girl—Carly? Is she still around?"

Micah let out another sigh. "That relationship died about the same time as the food truck."

"Then we better get another round of beers," he said, motioning for the waitress.

CHAPTER TWENTY

KEIRA GOT UP EARLY on Sunday, dropped her mother at church, and then headed to her boutique. Her mother's friend, Lois, would bring her home after their Sunday brunch, so she had a few hours on her own. After that, she hoped to speak to her mother before Mark came over to cook them all dinner. She needed them to have a heart-to-heart conversation that was long overdue.

She had thought about bringing it all up before church, but they'd been running late, and she hadn't wanted to start a conversation they couldn't finish. But today was the day. No more stalling. Today was actually the day for a lot of things. She was going to tackle Hannah's wedding dress and make some final decisions.

After parking in the lot behind her store, which was closed on Sundays, she walked through the back door and into her sewing and design room. She set down her bag and headed straight to the rack where Hannah's dress was hanging.

Her conversation with Dante on Friday night had given her a lot to think about.

She took the dress out of the plastic and put it on a dress form. She walked around it slowly, noting every lace detail, every line, and every seam. The hem was perfect. The bodice had a beautiful sweetheart neckline with a sexy cut, but it wasn't too much. *So, where was the problem?*

Hannah had told her from the very beginning that she wanted to look sexy and be comfortable at the same time. She didn't want anything too laced up, or that made it look like she was trying too hard to be something she wasn't. She wanted the gown to feel like her.

As she stared at the lace and beads she had recently added to the three-quarter-length sleeve, she realized her enhancements didn't work. They were too fussy. It wasn't Hannah who was trying too hard; it was her.

Why?

The question ran around in her head. She knew the answer now, and it was exactly what Dante had suggested. It wasn't about the dress. It was about the future. Once she finished the gown, she would have to decide what to do next. She would have to decide who she was—a part-time Realtor, part-time shop owner, or a part-time designer. She was beginning to realize that she couldn't do them all well. She had to pick a lane. She had to stop pretending she could do everything, because the truth was, her *everything* was turning into half-hearted mediocrity.

She took the dress off the form and laid it on the table, immediately stripping off the sleeve work. Within minutes, she lost herself in the gown. It suddenly became very clear where she had gone wrong, where she had tried to fix something that had nothing to do with the dress.

She didn't know how much time had passed until her phone started buzzing. She looked up from her work and grabbed her phone out of her bag. Her mother's name flashed across the screen.

"Hi, Mom." She glanced at the clock on the wall, realizing it was almost two. She'd been working on the dress since nine.

"How's it going?" her mother asked.

"Good. I figured out my problem with Hannah's dress."

"I'm so glad. I know it was bothering you."

"What are you doing? Are you back home?"

"Yes. Lois and I are playing cards with Susan and Donna. I just took a break to unpack the groceries Mark had delivered for the meal he's cooking us tonight. There's so much food I was thinking that Dante should join us."

"Dante's brother came into town last night. He's only staying until tomorrow, so they'll probably spend the day together."

"Oh, well, you could invite them both."

"Uh, I don't know. I think it's best if we leave them out of dinner."

"Why don't you just ask Dante? I'd really like to get to know him better. And wouldn't you be interested in learning more about him from his brother? It seems like a good opportunity."

Clearly, her mother was matchmaking. "It's probably better if I don't learn more."

"Because you like him too much already?"

"Maybe."

"Just ask Dante. If he says no, fine, but if he doesn't, then that's great."

"I'll think about it." She paused as another call came in. "Actually, he's calling me now."

"Let me know," her mom said.

As her mother hung up, she took Dante's call. "Hi."

"Hey," he said, his husky voice sending a thrill through her.

She really was in trouble if just the sound of his voice got her hot. She cleared her throat. "What are you up to?"

"My brother and I just completed a very long bike ride around the lake."

"That sounds fun and exhausting."

"It was great. It felt good to work out in the sun. What have you been doing?"

"Working on Hannah's dress. I figured out where I went wrong. I have to admit you made me look at it with a new perspective."

"I'm glad I could help. By the way, Micah told me that there are new photos of us online. I didn't look at them, but he said the stories were fairly positive and focusing more on my rehabilitation than on you."

"Really? I'm not still a boyfriend stealer?"

"Apparently, you're the mystery woman who is nursing me back to health."

"I guess that's better."

"You can look them up if you want."

"No, thanks. I'm just hoping the reporters won't be back."

"There's not much of a story left to tell here in Whisper Lake. Apparently, Nikki has also been photographed with a new man, so she has changed up her narrative. I think we may be okay."

"That's good."

"It is, but I'm *not* good. I miss you, Keira. What are you doing later? Want to hang out with my brother and me?"

"I'm having dinner with my mother and Mark. She would love for you and your brother to join us, but I told her I didn't think you'd want to."

"I want to," he said immediately.

"Really? I think your brother would probably prefer to hang out with you alone at some nice restaurant in town."

"Hey, he showed up without notice. He can go wherever I want to go."

She smiled at his dismissive tone. "Maybe you should ask him."

"We'll be there. What time?"

"Five thirty."

"Perfect. Have you spoken to your mom about Mark yet?"

"No. She's with her friends today. They're playing cards. Hopefully, I can speak to her before dinner, which could make this meal very awkward. Are you sure you want to put Micah through that?"

"He'll be fine. I'll get him up to speed and suggest my brother ask Mark pointed and personal questions. He's very good at that."

She heard the dry note in his voice. "I guess you've been getting a lot of those questions."

"Yes, and I'm ready to expand our group to include you, your mother, and Mark."

"If you're sure."

"I am. I want to see you tonight, even if we will have way too many chaperones."

She smiled to herself. "I want to see you, too." She ended the call and then punched in her mom's number to let her know that Dante and his brother would be joining them.

Keira arrived home a little after four, having finally finished Hannah's dress. She couldn't wait to show it to her. But it would be good to have a night to sleep on it and take one more look before she delivered it to Hannah tomorrow. When she walked into the kitchen, she tossed her keys and bag on the counter, noting an array of grocery items on the counter. It looked like Mark was planning to cook a feast.

The kitchen door swung open, and her mother came in with a vase of flowers in her hands and a very happy smile on her face. "Look what just arrived."

"They're beautiful. I assume they're from Mark."

Her mother nodded as she set the vase on the counter. She pulled out the card and read it silently, her smile broadening.

"Well, what does he say?" Keira asked. "Or is it private?"

"Beautiful flowers for my beautiful girl." Her mother lifted her gaze to Keira's. "He used to call me that in high school. When we went to the prom, he had the corsage sent to me earlier in the day, and he wrote the same thing: beautiful flowers for a beautiful girl. Not that I'm a girl anymore, nor am I beautiful."

"Wrong on both counts," she said, feeling it was now going to be even more difficult to douse her mother's joy with some cold, hard truth, but she couldn't keep putting it off. "Can we talk before the guys get here?"

"Of course."

"Let's sit down."

Her mother's gaze turned wary. "That sounds ominous."

She took a seat at the table and waited for her mother to join her.

"I know you have concerns about how much time we're spending together, but I know what I'm doing," her mom said, as she sat down. "I know Mark; you don't. You have to trust my opinion."

"Did you know that there was a fire at his house when he lived in LA? It happened right before he divorced his wife. His nanny died in the fire."

Her mother stared back at her, surprise in her gaze. "What are you talking about?"

"Do you want me to repeat it?"

"Mark never mentioned a fire in his house, but it sounds like it was a long time ago. How did it start? How did the woman die?"

"It apparently started with a lit cigarette in the sofa."

"And Mark was there?"

"No. Mark, his wife, and his son were away that weekend."

"Oh. Well, where did you hear this?"

"It doesn't matter. It's concerning to me that he never told you about it."

"Well, he hasn't told me everything about his past, so it's not that concerning to me. I mean, it's very sad that a woman died, but I don't understand why you and I are talking about it. There are things that have happened to me that I haven't told Mark about." She paused. "You've been digging into his life, haven't you?"

"Yes. He showed up out of nowhere and he's been very aggressive in getting reacquainted with you."

"We're catching up, Keira. We mostly talk about high school and friends we remember from the past. Or we talk about our kids or what we've been doing the last ten years. But our former spouses have not been a real topic of conversation. Is that it? Is that all you have?"

"No, it's not all. The nanny's sister, Mandy, has posted a lot of things about the fire and the loss of her sister online. She talks about someone needing to pay. And I believe she's referring to Mark."

"Why would Mark have to pay for a fire that started when he wasn't home?"

"I don't know, but Mandy is here in town. Dante saw her arguing with Mark in the parking garage at the rehab center, and

Lizzie told me that a red-haired woman stopped by the inn yesterday and made some cryptic accusations about needing to be careful around Mark, because he's unpredictable. If you put all the pieces together, Mark could be in some sort of trouble, and I don't want you caught in the middle of it."

"A red-haired woman," her mother mused. "I saw a woman with red hair sitting in her car outside the house today when Lois and I came back from church. She had the windows down and she gave us a funny look, but after we got out of the car and went into the house, she drove off."

She didn't like the idea that Mandy had been here at the house. "You need to talk to Mark about this woman."

"I don't want to pry into Mark's life. It's not my business. He's entitled to his privacy."

"What if he's involved with this woman? What if he's not as single as he claims to be? And the fact that this woman came here to your house makes me uncomfortable."

"She wasn't doing anything. She was just in her car, and you don't know if it was the same woman."

"I can show you a picture."

Her mother held up her hand. "Keira, I appreciate that you want to protect me. But I trust Mark, and if there's something for me to know, he'll tell me."

She blew out a breath of frustration. "Mom, you need to trust me more than Mark."

"Well, of course I trust you, Keira. But you've been suspicious of Mark from the start. I think you've gotten so used to taking care of me that you don't realize I'm better now. I can make decisions for myself. My mind is clear."

"I'm glad, Mom. But you can be blinded by love even when your brain is clear."

"I know I've made mistakes about men and romantic relationships, but I'm a different woman now. Mark is someone I knew and loved a long time ago. It's not like I picked him off the street. Can't you just give him a chance?"

"I'd be more willing to do that if this angry woman wasn't hanging around."

"All right. I'll talk to Mark about her. But I don't want you to bring her up tonight. Mark wants to get to know you, and that won't happen if we start off with accusations. Can we have a nice dinner and then I'll talk to him tomorrow?"

"All right," she reluctantly agreed. "I won't bring her up tonight."

"Thank you. Now, I'm going to take a shower and change. You should do the same. Put on something pretty for Dante," her mom added with a smile.

She rolled her eyes, but she did follow her mother upstairs to change into a short floral dress.

CHAPTER TWENTY-ONE

DANTE FELT INEXPLICABLY nervous as he rang Keira's doorbell. It wasn't about meeting her mom or talking to Mark. It also wasn't about bringing his brother along to a dinner that could very likely get uncomfortable. It was all about her.

He couldn't get Keira off his mind. It had been a long time since anyone or anything besides baseball had taken up so much space in his head. He told himself it was because he wasn't playing right now, but that wasn't the only reason he couldn't stop thinking about her. She'd gotten under his skin, and that made him feel both happy and unsettled, because he liked to be in control of his emotions. It was how he had gotten to the top of his game. He didn't feel in control now, but he was going to have to live in that space, because the front door had opened and the subject of his thoughts was standing right in front of him, looking even more beautiful than he remembered.

Keira wore a coral-red sundress with tiny white flowers that clung to her curves and showed off her tanned legs. Her brown hair fell in soft waves over her bare shoulders, her eyes sparkling, her smile bright. He didn't know how long he looked at her, but it must have been too long, because Micah cleared his throat.

"Hello," Micah said.

"Hi," Keira said belatedly.

"We brought wine," Micah added. He held up two bottles. "Red and white. We weren't sure what you were serving."

"I'm not completely sure, either. Our chef is apparently delayed, but hopefully he'll be here soon. Come in." She stepped back and waved them inside.

Keira's home was beautifully decorated and felt both comfortable and cool, with dark hardwood floors, exposed beams, and large windows that brought in the light.

"Nice house," Micah commented.

"Thanks. It was originally my grandmother's, but after she passed, my mom did a complete remodel. She picked out all the art." Keira lowered her voice. "Just so you know, she's very proud of it and loves compliments."

He gave her a smile. "Noted. Did you get your artistic talent from your mom?"

"Maybe. We both love art, but she can't sew a hem, much less draw a dress. If I got my sewing skills from anyone, it was from my grandmother." As she spoke, she led them down the hall and into the kitchen. She pulled out wine glasses. "Shall we start with the white? It looks cold, and it's such a warm day."

"Sounds good to me," he said.

"I'm in," Micah added.

She opened the wine and filled three glasses and then suggested they go out to the patio. Her mother was changing and would be with them shortly.

The pool area was just as inviting as the rest of the house, with two seating areas at either end of the pool. Keira directed them to the one closest to the kitchen, where two large umbrellas offered shade for both a dining table and a couch and two chairs. An impressive built-in brick outdoor kitchen filled out the space.

"Is that a pizza oven next to the barbecue?" Micah asked.

"Yes. We put it in about ten years ago," she said, as she sat down on the couch. "It's great and very fun for parties. We love to entertain out here."

He could see why she would. He took the seat next to her while Micah grabbed the chair across from them.

"Who's in charge of parties—you or your mom?" Micah enquired.

"That has always been me," she said with a laugh. "I love a good pool party. I usually host one on the Fourth of July, but this year was just too busy." She paused. "Dante told me you're a chef, Micah. I think he said you have a food truck."

"I *had* a food truck, but it's having a lot of mechanical issues, so I'm debating my next move."

Micah's words were light and casual, but Dante sensed an undertone that he didn't understand. He'd tried to broach the subject earlier in the day, but Micah had shut him down. Since he hadn't wanted to talk about baseball and his future, he'd had to leave Micah and his career plans alone. Maybe Keira would get more information out of him.

"Can you get it fixed?" Keira asked.

"I could, but I'm not sure it's the direction I want to continue going in. I'll see." Micah paused as Ruth stepped onto the patio. "This must be your mother."

Both he and Micah got to their feet. Ruth looked bright and pretty tonight, wearing a short-sleeve light-blue dress.

"Hello, Dante. It's nice to see you again," Ruth said.

"You, too," he replied. "This is my brother, Micah—Ruth Blake."

"Nice to meet you," Micah said. "Your house is great."

"Thank you. Keira takes good care of our home and of me."

"Is Mark on his way?" Keira asked her mother.

"No. He just called." Her lips tightened. "I'm afraid I have some bad news. Mark won't be able to make dinner. An emergency came up at work, something only he can handle, apparently. He's very sorry."

Dante wondered what kind of emergency would take Mark to the rehab center on a Sunday evening. It wasn't like he was a doctor. He could see the same question in Keira's gaze, but she didn't speak it aloud.

"I know he wanted to do this," Ruth added. "And I wanted the two of you to get to know each other, Keira." Disappointment filled her gaze.

"We'll do it another time," Keira said. "We can still have dinner. Mark sent over a lot of groceries. What was he going to make?"

"I have no idea. I think there was lamb and a lot of vegetables. I don't really know. Maybe we should just order a pizza."

"Oh, no," Micah said. "If there's lamb in the kitchen, I am definitely making it. I'm a chef, so I can probably come up with something tasty."

"We can't put you to work," Keira protested.

"I'd be happy to do it. I'd love to cook you a meal."

"Are you sure?" Ruth asked.

"Absolutely. Do you mind if I just forage in the refrigerator and come up with a meal?"

"I'd be very happy for you to do that," Ruth said. "I'll show you where we put things."

As Micah and Ruth moved into the house, Dante sat back down next to Keira, immediately pulling her into his arms and taking the kiss that had been on his mind since the last time his mouth had touched hers. She tasted even sweeter than the wine on her lips, and he felt like an addict who'd finally gotten the hit he desperately needed.

She kissed him back with the same hungry desperation, making him feel that he wasn't alone in this crazy attraction that they had for each other. He wished Micah and her mother were far, far away, but he was very aware that one or both could come back at any minute. He reluctantly lifted his mouth from hers. "We had a moment. I had to take it."

"I'm glad you did." She licked her lips, making his groin tighten once more. "When is your brother leaving?"

"Tomorrow morning. We could get together later tonight at the inn."

"No. You should spend your time with Micah."

"We've been together all day. We'll have had enough of each other. And believe me, he would understand."

"Still. It would be better to wait until he's gone."

"All right," he said, seeing the firm look in her eyes. "Let's change the subject. What do you make of Mark not showing up?"

"It's very strange. This whole dinner was his idea. By the way, I talked to my mom about Mandy, the argument in the parking garage, the fact that Mandy was looking for Mark at the inn—"

"Wait," he interrupted. "When was she at the inn?"

"Oh, that's right, you don't know. When I was talking to Lizzie after you and Micah went to dinner last night, she said that a red-haired woman came looking for Mark and was agitated that he wasn't there. She took a long time to write him a message, which Lizzie did not read, but did deliver to Mark's room. Lizzie also said that Mandy made some cryptic remark about no one should trust Mark. She didn't know what that meant."

"So, Mandy is still in town."

"Yes. When I told my mom about her, she said she saw a red-haired woman sitting in a car in front of this house when she came back from church with her friend. The woman drove off after they went into the house. I don't like that Mandy was here. She must have thought that Mark and my mom were together."

"Maybe it's good that they weren't."

"Exactly." A troubled glint entered her gaze. "But if this woman is even a little off, I don't want her around my mom."

"What did your mother say?"

"She dismissed the whole thing. It's Mark's private business, and he doesn't have to tell her everything. She hasn't told him everything. She said she knows him, and she trusts him. She did agree to talk to him, but she didn't want to do it tonight. Now, she won't have that opportunity, anyway. I wonder if he cancelled because he needed to see Mandy."

"Who knows?" He didn't like the idea of Mandy being in front of the house, either. If she was stalking Mark, then Ruth could be an obstacle in her path. "If your mother won't confront Mark, maybe you need to do it, Keira. Or I'll do it. He has the room next to mine. I can knock on his door and tell him what we know."

"I appreciate that, but I think I'd rather do it myself, if my mother won't." She blew out a breath. "Anyway, that's all going to have to wait. I can't say I'm totally unhappy about him not showing up. I worked a lot today, and now we can just have a nice dinner. I'm sorry your brother has to cook. It was very generous of him to offer."

"He loves to cook. It will be a good meal."

"But he's supposed to be having a fun weekend."

"Cooking is fun for him. Or at least it used to be. I'm not sure what's going on with him now. He's very mysterious about his food truck." He paused as Ruth rejoined them, a glass of wine in her hand. "Does Micah have everything under control?"

"He seems to," Ruth replied. "He insisted I come out here and have a drink. But I think you should go and help him, Keira. I'll entertain Dante."

He could see the determined glint in Ruth's eyes. So could Keira.

"All right," Keira said, as she got up. "But don't ask Dante twenty questions." She gave her mom a pointed, warning look and then headed into the kitchen.

As Keira left, he smiled at Ruth. "You can ask me as many questions as you want."

"Actually, I thought you might have some questions for me."

"About?"

"My lovely daughter. Would you like to know more about her?"

"I would," he admitted. "What was Keira like when she was a little girl?"

"Stubborn, independent, and creative. She was also very active. She always had a ton of energy. In the winter, she would spend hours skiing or snowboarding. She was a bit of a daredevil. Gave me a few gray hairs, I'll tell you. In the summers, she'd paddle-board or swim or spend time with her friends. Actually, whatever she did, she rarely did it alone. She had a great group of girlfriends. Most of whom still live here."

"I've met some of them. They are great."

"I don't know if Keira told you, but we've always been close. It was just the two of us for a long time. I was really sad when she went to college in New York, but I was also excited for her. I wanted to see where she would take her artistic talent. Unfortunately, I had my accident, and she gave up everything to come back and take care of me. My daughter is one of the most loyal, generous, loving people you'll ever meet."

"It's great how close you are."

"We get along really well. Sometimes we butt heads, but what mother and daughter don't? Are you close to your family?"

"With my brothers, yes. My mom died when I was young, and my father retreated from the family after that. My brothers and I raised ourselves with a little help from my grandmother."

"I'm sorry about your mother."

"Thanks. I wish now I'd known her better. But when I was a kid, I just thought of her as Mom. I never asked her about her life before I was born. I heard bits and pieces, but I feel like I didn't really know the woman she was."

"I'm sure your father or grandmother could help."

"My grandmother passed away several years ago, and my father hates to talk about my mother. He basically leaves the room if her name comes up."

"It must be painful for him."

"I suppose."

"What do you remember about your mom?"

"She liked to cook. I didn't, so I didn't hang out with her in the kitchen. But Micah did. I think cooking keeps him close to her memory. I wish I had that." He thought for a moment. "She also liked to dance. There was always music on in the house, and she was dancing to it, even if she was folding laundry. Sometimes when my father would come home, she'd grab his hand and make him spin her around." He stopped abruptly, surprised by the image in his head. "I can't believe I just remembered that."

"Memories are precious. Mine were gone for a while. They've mostly come back, and I'm grateful for each and every one of them now. Mark has helped me remember a lot of my youth. It's so lovely to revisit that time. Keira isn't a fan of Mark's, but she doesn't know him the way I do. I don't think Keira realizes that I had a life before she was born, either, and Mark was part of that."

"That makes sense," he said slowly. "But from what I know of Keira, she's a fair person. If she has doubts about someone, maybe it's smart to listen to those doubts, or talk them out with her."

"We did that a little today. I heard what she said, but I do know that Keira has gotten overprotective since my accident, so I have to weigh emotion with facts. But I will speak to Mark." She cleared her throat. "What about you and Keira? Are you falling for my daughter? Am I being too nosy?"

"Yes and yes," he said with a smile.

"I think she likes you, too. But it's complicated, isn't it?"

"Very much so."

"The best things usually are. I just hope that I'm not one of the complications that keeps the two of you apart. Keira has given up so much for me. I want her to have her life."

"I think she'd say she's doing exactly that."

"Oh, I know she'd say that. But it wouldn't be true. She's always been more of a giver than a taker."

He thought about her words. "I think I've been the opposite."

"Tell me about yourself, Dante."

"What do you want to know?"

A smile played across her lips. "Whatever you want to tell me."

"What was it like growing up with Dante?" Keira asked Micah as she sat at the kitchen counter, sipping her wine and watching him cook. She'd offered to help chop something, but Micah had waved her off and was moving around the kitchen at the speed of light.

"Frustrating," Micah said with a laugh. "Hard to follow in the footsteps of a kid who does everything really, really well."

"You mean sports?"

"And school. He wasn't just great at baseball, he got straight As."

"Seriously? When did he have time to study?"

"Late at night. He was a night owl."

"I always got a lot done late at night, too. It's so quiet; it's easier to focus. What about you, Micah?"

"I like nights. Working in restaurants, I'd always volunteer to close, so I could play around in the kitchen, make my own creations, and think about one day having my own restaurant."

"Is that still the goal?"

"I don't know. I'm not sure where I'm headed next, but I'll figure it out. I can always go to work for someone. I'd just like to have more autonomy, which is not easy to find." Micah paused as he put the lamb in the oven. Then he said, "Dante tells me you'd like to be a full-time designer one day, but you have a lot of other responsibilities right now."

"Yes. I have lots of autonomy, but that also means I have an enormous amount of work. I design on the side right now, but I am interested in making that a priority. I just have things to figure out." She sniffed. "It already smells good in here."

"I'm just getting started."

"I'm sorry we're making you work for your dinner."

"This isn't work, and I'm happy to do it. Plus, I get a chance to talk to you. And I'm curious to get to know the woman my brother is so taken with."

She flushed at his words. "I don't know about that."

"Trust me, I know my brother. The way he talks about you— it's not like anything I've heard before."

"Really?"

"Really," he echoed. "Baseball has always been his passion. There have been plenty of women who have tried to divert some of that passion to themselves, but they didn't even make a dent."

"Maybe this is just a weird time for Dante. He doesn't have to choose between baseball and seeing me, because there is no ball-game for him."

"That's true," Micah said, a somber note in his voice. "I'm hoping he hears what he wants to hear tomorrow."

"Tomorrow?"

"He's meeting with his orthopedic surgeon."

"He said Grayson was coming to check on him, but I didn't realize it was tomorrow. He must be stressing about that."

"He's trying not to think about it. Dante has a way of locking away things that bother him and not taking them out until he has to. I guess it's how he keeps his focus. He doesn't let distractions take over."

"How do you think he would react if he couldn't pitch the way he used to?"

"I hate to even think about it. Baseball has been his entire life. It was the way he connected to our dad. It was his escape when our mom died. The ballpark was his happy place. It's where he found himself, found a purpose to keep going. I don't know what he would do if he lost it all."

She could feel the pain of Micah's words. "I hope he won't have to face that. I want him to keep doing what he loves."

"So do I." He paused, giving her a smile. "You've been good for him. He was in a dark place after the surgery. He's like a different person now."

"His arm is getting better, so he's feeling better."

"And you've gotten him talking. He said he's told you more stuff than he's ever told anyone. How did you make that happen?"

"I have no idea," she said with a laugh. "When we first met, I felt like I was the one rambling on about everything. I'm very different from Dante. I don't lock anything away. When I'm feeling something, I tend to talk about it."

"Maybe you inspired him to talk, too."

"If I helped, I'm glad." She sipped her wine. "Tell me some Dante stories, and the more embarrassing the better."

He laughed. "Let me see…"

It was almost seven when the four of them sat down together to eat. Keira felt like she'd gotten some insight into Dante: the kid, the man, the ballplayer, and the annoying older brother. She had a feeling that Dante had probably gotten similar inside information from her mom.

"This is the best lamb I've ever had," her mother said, as she tasted a bite of the well-seasoned meat.

"Thanks," Micah said. "Your kitchen was well-stocked."

"But Micah knew exactly what to do with all the herbs," she interjected. "I never really know how to use spices appropriately."

"It's trial and error," Micah said.

"I would have to agree," Dante put in. "And I've tasted a lot of Micah's errors over the years."

"Very funny," Micah drawled.

She smiled at the fond, teasing look that passed between the brothers. "Micah said he started cooking for everyone after your mom died."

"He did," Dante agreed. "We were his guinea pigs. Those early years were rough, but by the time we got to high school, he was very good."

"The DeAngelis brothers never quit, do they?" she asked.

"Never," Dante and Micah echoed together, then laughed.

"Well, I think it was smart of you to take up cooking," her mother told Micah. "Cooking is the way to a woman's heart."

"I thought it was the way to a man's heart," she countered.

Her mother shook her head. "No. Women often do all the cooking. When the man cooks, he's more likely to win her over."

She smiled at Dante. "Did you hear that?"

"I wouldn't hold your breath," he returned with a dry smile. "Any other tips, Ruth? If a man can't cook?"

"Humor. If you can laugh with someone, there's a good chance you can stay together." A smile parted her lips. "Mark and I laugh a lot. He's quite funny. He has a very sarcastic, dry sense of humor. He's very quick. I enjoy how fast he can find a joke. I really wish he'd been able to come tonight. But even if he's not here, we can enjoy the food that he dropped off and that Micah cooked so excellently."

"I'll drink to that." Keira lifted her wine glass. She really didn't want to hear any more about the amazing Mark at this moment. She clinked glasses around the table and then went back to her meal.

When Micah brought out the dessert, a tart with fresh strawberries and cream, she was even more impressed. "You really need to be in a restaurant," she told Micah. "Or get that food truck fixed. You're too good just to cook for friends and family."

"Thanks," Micah said. "Tonight gave me a chance to remember how fun it is just to make something out of a bunch of ingredients I hadn't picked out. I've gotten so bogged down with the business angle, I almost forgot how much I love to experiment with my cooking. I had a chance to slow down, look at my priorities." His gaze moved to Dante. "And what's really important to me."

Something passed between the two brothers. She couldn't read the message, but she suspected Micah was making a point about Dante and his priorities. But Dante's arm was going to make his choice, not his brain.

"Maybe it's the mountains, the beautiful lake, this nice town," Micah continued. "It has a good vibe. It opens your eyes."

"I love Whisper Lake," her mom said. "But sometimes I think the mountains act as barriers, instead of motivators. We have everything we think we need right here, but maybe we don't."

She met her mother's gaze. "I know you're talking about me."

"Not completely," her mom denied. "I was just thinking that Micah found clarity when he left his home and came here. Maybe it's leaving your comfort zone that really makes the difference, not the location. Not that I want you to leave, Keira. I just don't want to be the reason you stay."

"Mom, you don't have to worry about that." She didn't want to have this conversation with her mother now, not with Dante and Micah listening in.

"But I do worry about you, Keira," her mom continued. "I was the reason you came back. It wasn't your choice. You've taken such good care of me. However, I worry that you're missing out on the life you were meant to have."

"I make my own choices. And I don't think being happy is about geography; it's about who you are with and what you do with your life." She cleared her throat, realizing she was getting too close to her issues with Dante. "Let's talk about something else. What were you and Dante laughing about when I called you in for dinner? I have a feeling you were talking about me."

"I'm afraid I can't reveal that," Dante said, a smile playing around the corners of his mouth.

"That answer will drive her crazy," her mother said. "Keira hates when people have a secret."

"I do hate that." She gave Dante a pointed look. "So, spill."

"Your mom told me about the time you tried to dye your hair blonde and ended up a greenish-yellow color," he said.

She groaned. "You told him that story, Mom?"

"He mentioned how we both have the same beautiful brown hair, and I told him that in middle school you really wanted to be blonde like Chloe and Gianna, so you tried to dye your hair, but it turned green and yellow, and you couldn't go to school for a week until we got your hair fixed."

"Why did you want to be blonde?" Dante asked.

"I'm pretty sure there was a boy involved. I was thirteen and stupid. I'm sure you did dumb things at that age."

"Did he ever," Micah said.

"Hold on," Dante interrupted, putting up a hand. "I think we've all shared enough family stories for one night."

"That's true," she agreed. "I'm going to clear the plates."

"I'll help." Dante got to his feet.

"And I'll keep your mom company," Micah said.

They cleared the plates from the table, making several trips in and out of the kitchen before she started to rinse and load the dishwasher. "I can take care of this," she told Dante, "if you want to hang with my mom and your brother."

"No. I want to hang with you." He slid his arms around her

waist, nuzzling her neck until she turned her face to catch a hot kiss. "Nice," he murmured.

"It is nice, but I need to finish the dishes."

"Am I distracting you?"

"You know you are."

"Maybe I should do the dishes for you. Win you over. Your mom seems to think that men doing household tasks is just the ticket for that."

"I wouldn't take advice from my mother. She's been single most of my life, and her choices in men have never been the best. I don't think Mark will be an exception."

"She really is taken with him."

"He's definitely her favorite topic of conversation." She paused. "When I was talking to Micah, he mentioned that you're seeing Grayson tomorrow. I didn't realize it was that soon."

"It was supposed to be Thursday, but he had to change it, because he has to be back in Denver that day."

"Are you worried about it?"

"There's nothing I can do, so whatever it is, it is."

"That's very Zen-like."

He made a face at her. "I'm not feeling Zen, but I can't predict what the diagnosis will be, so I just have to wait."

"I'm sorry. I shouldn't have brought it up."

"It's not a problem. I'm hoping for the best, but we'll see. I've only been in rehab for a week, so it may be too early for a definitive answer. If there has been good progress, that will be something I can work from."

"Does it feel like you've made progress?"

"It does, but whether or not I can throw a ninety-mile-an-hour fastball is another story."

"I hope you get good news."

"Thanks. So, I'll see you tomorrow night?"

She grimaced. "I forgot I'm having Hannah and all the brides-maids to the shop after closing tomorrow. I'm doing final fittings and then we're going to get dinner. I could possibly meet you later. Unless you want to wait and see what Grayson says…"

"No. Whatever he says about my shoulder has nothing to do with us. You can come by as late as you want. I'll be at the inn. And I'll be very prepared this time, so if you can spend the night…"

"I can do that." She smiled and leaned into another long, sexy kiss that made her wish it was already tomorrow.

CHAPTER TWENTY-TWO

DANTE HAD an MRI in the morning, followed by his normal rehab session, with a quick break for lunch and then an afternoon work-out. It was close to four when he went to meet with his surgeon, Dr. Grayson Cole. Grayson was tall, with dark hair and blue eyes. He wore a white physician's coat over tan slacks and a light-blue shirt. They shook hands, and then Grayson asked him to sit on the exam table.

"How's it going?" Grayson asked.

"That's what I'm here to find out. I assume you spoke to the therapists." He had no time or energy for small talk. He was feeling too tense for that.

"I have spoken to your therapists. I also have the results of your MRI, but before we get into all that, I want to do an examination, so I can make my own assessments."

"I'm ready." He didn't like the fact that Grayson didn't want to give him the results of the MRI. He tried not to make anything of it. Worrying wouldn't change anything.

For the next twenty minutes, Grayson put him through a series of strength, flexibility, and range of motion moves, rotating his shoulder and arm in various directions. It took all of his inner strength not to ask questions during the assessment.

Finally, after Grayson finished making some notes in the chart, he looked back at him. "You're doing well."

"I hope you're going to elaborate."

"The results of your MRI are very good."

"What does that mean? Am I going to be able to pitch again?" It was really the only question he needed answered.

"There's a little more rehab work to be done, but you're on your way to a complete recovery."

"Seriously?" He couldn't believe what he was hearing. "No limitations?"

"No. But I'd like you to finish the week of rehab here. After that, you can go back to Miami and work with your team's PT for several more weeks before you get back into the rotation. I'd aim for an early August return. I know that's still a month away, but I want you to go slow, so there aren't any setbacks. Can you do that?"

"Absolutely. This is great news."

"You've put in the work, Dante."

"Only after you put in the work. Thanks, Doc. You're giving me back my life."

"I'm glad I could help."

"You did more than that." He was still trying to wrap his head around the fact that he could leave Whisper Lake by the weekend. His excitement ebbed as he realized how much sooner he would have to say goodbye to Keira. His departure date had always loomed over them, but now it was even closer.

"How have you been enjoying Whisper Lake? Is Lizzie treating you right?" Grayson asked.

"This town is amazing, and your sister treats me better than my family."

"She always wanted to run an inn where she could be the hostess all the time."

"She's very good at it. How long are you staying?"

"Just until tomorrow morning. As you know, I had to reschedule a surgery for Thursday, so I can't spend the holiday here as I planned."

"Thanks for coming to check my progress."

"I had some other business as well, and it's always nice to see my siblings. I'm going to have dinner with them tonight." Grayson paused. "I would caution you to continue to be careful with any heavy lifting or extreme sports for another few weeks."

"No worries there."

"All right then. That's it."

"I can't quite believe it."

Grayson smiled. "You'll get there. Take care of yourself. Let me know if you need anything."

"I will. Thanks again." As he left the exam room, he pulled out his phone. He had so many people he wanted to call to share the good news. Keira was at the top of the list. But he hesitated. He didn't want to call or text her to tell her he would be leaving town a week early. They were getting together later tonight. He would tell her then.

However, he could tell Micah. He sent his brother a text as he headed toward the parking garage. When he stepped off the elevator, he was surprised to see Mark and a security guard standing by Mark's car.

As he got closer, he realized that there were long scratch marks on the side of the vehicle as well as the hood.

"What happened?" he asked.

Mark stiffened when he saw him. "Vandalism," he replied.

"Looks like someone keyed your car. Was your vehicle the only one hit?"

"It looks that way."

He glanced around the garage, noting the security camera not too far away. "Did the camera catch who did it?"

"Unfortunately not. But we're in the process of getting a better security gate, so this won't be a problem in the future. I'm sure it was just kids."

And he was equally sure it wasn't a kid at all. It was Mandy. He wanted to challenge Mark, but he and the security guard were already walking toward the entrance to the garage. That question would have to wait.

He got into his rental car, his mood no longer quite as exuberant as it had been. Before he went back to Miami, he needed to help Keira figure out what was going on with Mark.

If Mandy had keyed his car, then who knew what she would do next?

———

As Keira closed the shop on Monday afternoon, she checked her phone, wondering why she hadn't heard from Dante about his meeting with his doctor. She worried that he'd gotten bad news. Or maybe it was just the opposite: he'd gotten good news, and he didn't want to tell her he was leaving soon. Her gut twisted at that thought. She didn't want him to leave, but she did want him to be healed. Unfortunately, she couldn't have both.

Her phone buzzed, and she jumped to answer it, relieved to see Dante's name flash across her screen.

"Hi," she said. "I've been wondering what's going on. How did it go with Grayson?"

"It was good."

"That's great. I'm so happy for you. Are you happy? I can't tell."

"I'm thrilled. I'm just still trying to believe it's true."

"You can go back to pitching?"

"Not right away, but soon. Grayson thinks I'll make a full recovery. I'll give you the details tonight. We're still meeting up later, right?"

For a split second, she thought maybe she should say no, because every second they spent together was going to leave one more painful memory to deal with. But she couldn't say no, because she needed to see him. "Yes," she said. "It will probably be close to ten."

"I'll be waiting. Have fun with your friends."

"I will. Bye." She let out a breath as she set down her phone. She told herself to be happy for him, but all she could feel was selfish unhappiness that he was leaving, probably sooner than she'd thought. She needed to get over that feeling before she met up with him.

The door to her shop opened, and she immediately put a smile on her face as Hannah, Gianna, and Chloe came through the door.

"I brought wine." Gianna held up a bottle. "Do we need glasses?"

"I have some plastic wine glasses in the back," she replied. The door opened again, and Chelsea and Lizzie walked in. "Looks like we're all here," she said, as she came around the counter and locked the door behind them. Then they headed into the back room.

Hannah filled wine glasses as Keira started with the bridesmaids. She'd tucked Hannah's dress away. She didn't want her to see it until she tried it on.

Happy chatter went on as each one of the women took their turn in front of the mirror. Lizzie's hem needed a minor tweak as she'd decided to wear a different pair of shoes. But Chloe and Gianna's gowns were perfect. Chelsea was the last to try her dress on, and it fit like a glove, although it seemed a bit tighter than she remembered.

Chelsea turned away from the mirror with an odd expression in her eyes.

"What's wrong?" she asked. "If it's too snug, I can let out a seam. I may have miscalculated."

"You didn't," Chelsea replied. "I wasn't going to say anything because I don't want to take the attention away from Hannah—"

"What are you talking about?" Hannah asked.

Chelsea glanced at Lizzie.

"Just do it," Lizzie urged.

"Oh, my God," Hannah interrupted. "Are you pregnant, Chelsea?"

"Yes!" Chelsea's dazzling smile was incredibly bright. "Almost eight weeks. I didn't think I'd show at all yet."

"That's amazing," Hannah said as she hugged Chelsea. The rest of the women followed, and she was the last.

"I'm so happy for you," she said. "This is great news."

"Brodie and I are thrilled. He's already buying baby stuff. I keep telling him we have plenty of time. We don't even know if it's a boy or a girl yet. And the doctor said I should wait three months to say anything, but I was starting to worry that the dress might not fit and I'd have to give you an excuse, like I ate too many donuts."

She smiled. "The dress looks lovely, but I can let it out if you want."

"I think I'm good. I only have a week to go."

"Well, let me make a small adjustment," she said, eyeing the dress once more. "I'll make the alterations in the morning, and you can try it on tomorrow afternoon."

"I hate to give you more work."

"For a baby, I would remake the entire dress," she said with a laugh, feeling very emotional. She looked over at Lizzie, who was dabbing at her eyes. "You're going to be an aunt."

"I know. I'm so glad Chelsea told you, because I was having trouble keeping it in."

"Is this why you keep changing your wedding plans?" she asked.

"Partly. I do want Chelsea to be in the wedding, so Justin and I are now thinking after she has the baby would be good."

"Whatever you want, Lizzie. I'll waddle down the aisle in a maternity dress for you," Chelsea proclaimed. "Hey, Keira, how are you at designing maternity clothes?"

"Honestly, I've never tried."

"It could be a new market for you," Chelsea said.

"Considering how many of my friends are coupling up, I think you're right." She felt a twinge of what could only be considered more selfish yearning that she hadn't found her love and wasn't anywhere close to a wedding or a baby. Although it was possible she had found her man, he just wasn't someone she could keep.

"Let's have a toast," Gianna said. She stopped abruptly. "Now, I know why you didn't want any wine earlier, Chelsea."

"Let's wait on the toast until we go to dinner," Chelsea said. "I can toast with sparkling water. But now I'm going to get out of this dress and then Hannah will try on hers. Because that's why we're here."

"Don't worry," Hannah said, giving Chelsea a pointed look. "You're not stealing my thunder."

"Well, still. Let me change."

As Chelsea got out of her gown, Keira helped Hannah on with her wedding dress and then led her to the pedestal in front of the big mirror. She hadn't changed a lot on the dress, but she had altered enough that it felt like a different gown than the one Hannah had seen before. She watched Hannah's expression in the mirror, feeling joy at the happy gleam that lit up her face.

"Wow, I look incredible," Hannah said.

Her bridesmaids agreed with a stunning array of adjectives: beautiful, gorgeous, and sexy.

Hannah turned around, meeting her gaze. "I thought it was pretty before, Keira—the first and second time I tried it on—but now it's perfect. What did you do?"

"I basically got rid of everything I did last time. And I accentuated your boobs," she added with a laugh.

"Thank God for that. Seriously, Keira. You outdid yourself, and I didn't even think that was possible. What was the breakthrough?"

"I was putting a lot of things on your dress that weren't about your dress at all."

"Well, that's cryptic." Hannah gave her a searching gaze.

"It's not important. All that matters is that you're happy and that you're going to be a beautiful bride."

"It's exactly what I wanted. I knew you were the right woman for this job."

"I'm glad you're happy. Jake's eyes are going to pop out when he sees you in that."

"Wait until you see the lingerie I bought for the honeymoon," Hannah said with a mischievous smile.

She grinned back at her. "Maybe it's good for Jake that you know CPR."

"Probably," she said with a laugh. "Now get me out of this. Let's go to dinner and drink wine and toast to Chelsea's baby."

"You got it."

They left her shop about twenty minutes later and headed down the street for dinner. For the next two hours, she gossiped with her friends, and it was just the distraction she needed. While the men in their lives came up, they also talked about their jobs, their families, what was happening in town and in the world, what books they were reading, and what TV shows they were binging. It was a great catch-up that had been too long in coming.

Their evening wound down around nine. As they paid the check and left the restaurant, her mind turned to Dante. She was eager to see him, impatient to hear more about what the doctor had said, even though she knew that his good news would be her bad news.

They walked back to her store and hugged their goodbyes. Then she got into her car and headed to the inn.

Lizzie was taking Chelsea home, so she didn't see her when she arrived. The reception area was empty, so she jogged up the stairs to Dante's room.

He answered her knock immediately, pulling her inside the room for a smoldering kiss before she could get one word out. There was so much to say, but he didn't seem interested in talking, and since she was afraid of having the conversation they needed to have, she was fine to leave any discussion for later.

She threw her arms around his neck and savored each kiss more than the last. She wanted to drink him in until she was drunk on the heady feelings bubbling up inside of her.

Dante walked her back against the wall, and she loved the feeling of being trapped between a deliciously hard man and a solid wall. As he lifted his mouth from hers, he gave her a look so filled with desire that her entire body tingled. She felt breathless and impatient and very, very needy.

This man—this gorgeous, rugged, athletically built man—was beyond her wildest imagination. She'd never felt this over-whelmed, not just by him, but by her emotions, her hunger. She wanted to strip off his clothes and trace every inch of him with her mouth. She wanted to touch him and taste him, and then pull his body into hers. She wanted to feel his power and strength.

"Damn," he whispered. "You are so beautiful, Keira." His blue eyes glittered with appreciation. "I want us to go slow, take our time."

"We have all night and you said you were really prepared, so… We can mix it up. Fast, then slow or slow, then fast."

"It's not going to be slow."

"Good. You know I like speed. The more reckless, the better." She tugged at the hem of his T-shirt. "Let's get these clothes off."

He stepped just far enough away to yank off his shirt and kick off his jeans. Then he grabbed her by both arms, turned her around, and pulled the zipper of her dress down to her waist. She stepped out of the dress as he unhooked the clasp on her bra and then his hands were on her panties, pushing them down her hips. She turned back around as the last two items of clothing dropped to the floor.

Dante claimed her mouth once more, sliding his lips down the side of her neck as his hands played with her breasts. Her nerves were on fire, burning with need and impatience. But Dante had apparently changed his mind about going fast, as he explored her body with his mouth and his hands, teasing every sensitive spot until her legs went weak.

He pulled her over to the bed and they fell onto the soft mattress together, getting tangled up in each other as the heat between them got hotter. She wanted to feel him everywhere. She wanted his body over hers, under hers, next to hers. A desperation to make this memory count took over. She needed him to know her, really know her. She wanted to imprint her touch on his body, on his mind, so he would never forget her. Because she knew she would never forget him.

Breathless, heart pounding, nerves tingling, they came together in a perfect collision of need, desire, and what felt a lot like love. She felt overwhelmed with emotion as she floated back down to earth. She could laugh. She could cry. She didn't know which way it would go, because there were too many feelings running through her, and following those feelings came the thoughts and the questions.

She closed her eyes, wanting to hold them back, wanting to just linger in this moment, to enjoy being with Dante. She concentrated on the weighty feel of his arm on her waist as he rolled up next to her, his lips nuzzling the corner of her ear, a spot she'd never thought was so sensitive until Dante had found it.

"Do you want to go to sleep?" he murmured.

She smiled at the husky note in his voice and slowly opened her eyes. "No. I was just trying to catch my breath."

"Breathing is highly overrated," he said with a satisfied smile. "Especially when your mouth is on mine. I can't seem to get enough."

"Maybe that's why I feel so light-headed."

"I feel it, too."

"Do you?" she couldn't help questioning. "Because I've never felt like this before. You're really good at all of this."

"We're good together, Keira. Sorry for grabbing you when you walked in the door. I just… I'd missed you all day."

"Don't apologize. I liked it—all of it."

"Me, too. How was your night tonight?"

"It was really good. Everyone has their dress and they're happy."

"Including Hannah?"

"Most of all. She tried on her gown, and she looked absolutely perfect. I thought she might cry. I thought I might cry. But somehow we managed to hold it together."

"It all worked out."

"It did. You were right, Dante. It wasn't about the dress. It was about me. I was letting the gown become the target of all my frustration and indecision about my career choices. Once I really looked at it and I pictured Hannah wearing it, I realized I'd been trying to fix something that wasn't even broken."

"You must be relieved."

"I am. The wedding is on Saturday, with the rehearsal dinner on Friday and the Fourth of July on Wednesday. I didn't want to be worrying about the dress up until the last minute."

"Now you can worry about other things," he teased.

She smiled. "I'm really not such a big worrier, but the past week has been stressful. Not just the wedding, but Mark and my mom, all my business stuff."

"Did your mom talk to Langley? Did she find out why he didn't come to dinner?"

"She said he apologized again, and that they were going to get together tomorrow evening for a long chat. She did not want to bring up the fire or Mandy on the phone, so that conversation will happen when they meet—maybe. I'm not sure she'll ever bring it up."

"She needs to."

Her gaze narrowed at the suddenly tense look on Dante's face. "Why? Did something happen?"

"Yes. When I left the rehab center today, Mark was with a security guard in the parking garage. Someone had scratched his car with a key or some other hard object."

"Are you serious? Was it Mandy?"

"Mark said he thought it was kids. He also told me that the security camera didn't cover his spot. I saw the camera, and he was lying about that. I believe he knows exactly who keyed his car. He said they're adding a new security gate to the garage entrance. But my gut tells me this wasn't a random act of vandalism."

"It had to be Mandy. Why won't he admit that? Why not go to the police if she's harassing him?"

"There has to be a significant reason."

"Like maybe Mark did something to cause that fire," she suggested. "Maybe he is in some way responsible for the death of the nanny."

"He was out of town."

"That's what the reports said. But Mandy is blaming him for the death of her sister. I have to question why. Is she crazy? Or did he have something to do with it?"

"Short of asking him flat out, I have no idea how we'll figure that out."

"Maybe that's what I'll do. I'll lay it all on the line. I'll tell him I'm worried that this woman has shown up at the inn and at my mom's house and if she did key his car, then she could be dangerous."

"Want company when you do that?"

"I wouldn't say no," she told him.

"Then we'll do it together. I think we make a good team."

She tensed at his words. "Speaking of teams, you still need to tell me about what Grayson said. If you want to."

"Of course I want to. As I mentioned on the phone, it went better than I expected. I'm actually ahead of schedule. Grayson wants me to finish out this week of therapy, but then I'm free to go back to Miami and work with the team PT for another few weeks as I make my way back into the pitching rotation."

"That's great, Dante. The best news. Why aren't you jumping up and down on the bed right now?"

"I'd rather jump with you. Next round," he said with a grin. "But seriously, I'm trying not to get too far ahead of myself. There's still work to do, and I have no idea how long it will take to find some of my pitches, but I can start looking for them in a few weeks."

"I'm so happy for you. This is what you wanted—a complete recovery."

"It is what I wanted, but I'm very aware that it cuts our time short, Keira." His voice took on a sober note. "That's why I'm not jumping up and down. It's a mix of good news and bad."

She nodded, trying not to show any of the disappointment she was feeling. "We both knew it was coming."

"Unfortunately, sooner than we thought, but we still have the rest of this week."

"When are you leaving?"

"Probably Saturday morning."

Her heart sank. "Wow. Saturday. That is fast."

"Until then, I want to spend every minute I have away from rehab with you."

She wanted to spend that time with him, too, but she had multiple jobs and a wedding coming up. There wouldn't be that many minutes to give to him. Maybe she should end things now. Because seeing him for five more days and living through an endless circle of heartbreaking emotion seemed like a very bad idea. She would be a wreck at the end of it.

Although, to be honest, she'd probably be a wreck, even if tonight was the last night. She'd made the mistake of getting emotionally involved with a man who was leaving.

"Keira," he said, his gaze darkening. "It's not going to be easy for me to say goodbye, either."

"But you have to. You have to go back to your life and live out your dream. Being a ballplayer is who you are."

He frowned a little at her words. "It is," he agreed.

There seemed to be a new ambivalence to his statement. Or maybe she was just imagining that.

"Did you tell your coach?" she asked.

"Yes, I let everyone know."

"They must be thrilled."

"They are. I just wish you could go with me."

"I don't think I'd do well in Miami. Too hot and humid. My hair would frizz right up," she said lightly. "And I have so much here: my mom, my businesses, and my friends."

"I understand. I wish they had a baseball team here."

She gave him a sad smile. "Me, too."

His fingers ran down her arm, drawing a little shiver that had nothing to do with the cold. "Can you stay the night?"

She hesitated for just a second, torn between wanting to stay with him and wanting to protect her heart. But it was too late for that. "I can stay, even though I shouldn't. This is going to be hard."

He cupped her face with his hand and gave her a long, tender kiss. "Let's be in the moment as long as we can."

She was going to try her best, but this time their kiss felt bittersweet.

CHAPTER TWENTY-THREE

DANTE WOKE up Tuesday morning to an unsettling quiet and a very cool other side of the bed. He abruptly sat up. There was no sign of Keira in the adjoining bathroom, and her clothes were gone. He fell back against the pillows with a frustrated groan. He knew he shouldn't have closed his eyes last night. He'd stayed up longer than Keira, but the long day had eventually caught up to him, and he'd drifted off, hoping that they could talk more in the morning, because the second time they'd made love had felt like goodbye, and that had bothered him more than he could put into words.

But there was no conversation to have now. Keira had left, and he didn't know when he would see her again. He hoped she hadn't decided to call it quits because he was leaving earlier than expected, because they still had five days to be together—to talk, to laugh, to have incredible, mind-blowing sex. *Who would want to give up five days of that kind of pleasure?*

He knew the answer. Keira probably thought it would be easier if it were just over now. He'd seen that thought float through her eyes last night, right after he'd told her his news. He'd managed to persuade her to stay, to keep enjoying the moment they were in, but he had a feeling that moment was over.

He blew out a breath as he stared up at the ceiling. It wasn't going to be easy to leave her. That was a new feeling for him. He'd never had a problem leaving a woman, a relationship, a city, his family... He'd always looked ahead instead of back. That probably wasn't a trait to brag about, but it was the truth. He'd always put his dream ahead of everything else, and it had paid off. Every move he'd made had been a good one, a step closer to ultimate success. But this time felt different.

The past two months had come with a lot of self-analysis and fear for the future. He'd had to face the possibility his career might be over, and even though the injury was now just going to be a blip on his record, a short time away from the big stage of his life, he had changed because of it.

He had been forced to think about a life without the game he loved, and it had been terrifying. He loved being a pitcher. He loved baseball. He loved the guys on his team and the fans who came out to cheer them on. He'd been forced to imagine a life where he didn't get to go out and pitch, where he didn't hear the roar of a crowd or feel the pressure of a game on the line, and his future had seemed bleak until he met Keira. She had wrapped him up in her smiles and her arms and her body. She'd brought him back to life, made him realize that what he did for a living wasn't all that he was.

He could talk to Keira in a way he'd never talked to anyone else. They'd gotten deep so fast and so easily. He knew her, and she knew him. It hadn't all been serious. They'd laughed a lot. In fact, being with Keira had brought simple joys back into his life. She'd opened up a new world to him, one where he was just one of a gang of fun, friendly people, who lived and loved without being on a stage, without running from the tabloids, without needing to be better all the time. It had been an incredible break.

But that's all it had been—a break. His life was in Miami, and Keira's life was here. They couldn't be together. Unless...

Could he find a way? But what way? Could they do long distance? Could he come back to Whisper Lake in the off-season? Would that be enough?

The baseball season was March to the end of October. That

didn't leave many months for any other kind of life. And he wasn't close to retirement, not if his arm was truly back to normal. He could play another six to eight years.

And what about Keira's dreams?

Even if she were willing to follow him to Miami, how could he let her do that? She needed to think about putting herself first. If she was going to move anywhere, she should go to New York. She was too good not to do what she was meant to do. But she put other people before herself.

They really were opposites. He'd always put himself first, and she never had. Maybe they needed to rub off on each other. He needed to think more about other people, and she needed to think less.

He sighed once more as his brain grappled with unsolvable problems. Finally, he got out of bed and hit the shower. He needed to get to rehab and keep working on his recovery. At least it looked like his arm could be fixed. He didn't know about anything else. But he did know that he wasn't ready to end it with Keira; he just needed to convince her that five more happy days were worth whatever else might be coming.

Keira started getting texts from Dante shortly after lunchtime, but she didn't reply. She didn't know what she wanted to say. He wanted to get together for dinner. He wanted to take her out. And yesterday she would have said yes in a heartbeat, but now…she was torn. She liked him way too much, and she sensed a world of hurt coming her way. *Why make everything worse by drawing out their goodbye?* And it would be worse, because every day she fell a little more in love with him.

It was crazy. They hadn't known each other very long, but she couldn't deny her feelings. She'd dated enough men in her life to know what she wanted, and Dante checked off a lot of boxes, except the big one. He didn't live in Whisper Lake. He didn't have a life in this town. He'd asked her before if that was a deal breaker.

She hadn't said it was, but maybe she hadn't been honest with herself.

She looked up as the door opened and two teenagers walked in. She gave them a smile as they asked where the sale rack was. She waved them toward the back corner of the store.

A woman came in next, wearing a very stylish dress with stiletto heels and dark sunglasses. The jewelry around her neck was stunning and eye-catching. She was definitely not a local.

She came up to the counter and removed her glasses. "Keira Blake?"

"Yes. Can I help you?"

"I'm Margot Devane. I've emailed you several times. My client, Jessica Stillman, is very interested in your work."

"Of course. I'm sorry. It's been a busy week. Ms. Stillman wants a dress for an awards show in October. Is that right?"

"She does. But now she's doing a movie festival in Rome in September where she'll have several events that need very special outfits. She'd like to discuss everything with you as soon as possible. She loved Chelsea Cole's dress. She feels that you're someone who will give her something original."

"I'm so happy to hear that."

"Good. Because this is an incredible opportunity. I'll be honest with you. I've tried to have her work with designers in LA where I'm located, and she has turned everyone down. She wants you, and she sent me here to tell you that she won't take no for an answer. She'd like you to come to LA as soon as possible for a meeting."

"Uh." She was a little overwhelmed by Margot's words. "I have a lot going on this week. I have a wedding on Saturday, and I have my businesses to run."

"Are you saying you don't want to meet her?"

She licked her lips. *What the hell was she thinking?* "No, I'm not saying that. I would love to meet her, but it would have to be next week at the earliest. If she wants to talk before then, we could do a video chat."

"No, she wants to get to know you in person. Why don't we try for next Monday?"

"Next Monday?" she echoed. "That might be a little soon."

"Working with Jessica will be incredibly lucrative for you. I really don't understand your hesitation. She's one of the hottest actresses in Hollywood right now."

"I know, and I am very honored—really. I just have some family issues."

"All right, but I'll need an answer by Friday." Margot handed her a card. "I look forward to setting up your trip. It's my job to get Jessica what she wants, and she wants you. Let's make this work for both of us."

She picked up the card. "I'll let you know by Friday. Thanks for the offer."

"You can thank me when you get to LA."

She let out a breath as Margot left and stared at the card in her hand. She felt like she'd just been handed a ticket to something amazing. The other people who had emailed her after the awards show had either not responded back to her email or had dropped out after all the bad press she'd received, but Jessica either hadn't seen that press or didn't care. Dressing her for several events could be huge. But this ticket to something amazing would require her to make some tough decisions about her future.

She'd been feeling overwhelmed for the past year. She couldn't add one more thing to her plate without getting rid of something. *But what?*

A wave of panic ran through her. Her gut was churning. It was just too much. She was already feeling emotional about losing Dante. Now, she had to make a life-changing decision about her career. She didn't want to do that. She wanted to dive into bed and pull the covers over her head.

There was also no guarantee Jessica would hire her even if she did fly to Los Angeles and talk to her. She could be put through a series of test designs and in the end, Jessica might decide not to use her and then all that time would be wasted. It was a risk. *But wasn't it just the risk she wanted?* This could be the beginning of her own design business, one that went beyond her friends.

As the teenage girls brought clothes up to the counter, she put down the card and focused on what she had to do right now. It was actually a relief. She knew how to sell clothes in her boutique and make customers happy. The rest she still had to figure out.

Dante was annoyed that Keira hadn't texted him back by the end of the day. She was clearly avoiding him, and he didn't know what to do about it. *Should he give her space? Or should he try to force her into talking to him?* If he gave her space, he might never see her again. On the other hand, if he pushed too hard, he might reach the same result. She might just tell him to his face that she was done.

He paced in front of the window as the clock struck five. He definitely needed to get out of his room at the inn, because the bed just reminded him of Keira and the night they'd spent together.

Restless, he decided to go downstairs and check out Lizzie's daily happy hour.

As he stepped into the hall, he saw someone coming out of Mark Langley's room. To his shock, it was the red-haired woman. She froze when she saw him, a guilty look flashing across her face.

"Hello," he said.

She gave him a nod and then hurried toward the stairs. He realized as she disappeared that she hadn't shut Mark's door. He moved down the hall and knocked on the door. With no answer, he pushed it open, about to say hello when he realized that Mark wasn't there, and the room looked like it had been ransacked.

There was writing on the wall—three words: YOU WILL PAY.

Damn! He backed out of the room, careful not to touch anything, and jogged down the stairs to the lobby. He saw Lizzie in the dining room, talking to one of the other guests. He walked in and hovered nearby until she gave him a questioning look.

"Sorry to interrupt," he said. "I need to speak to you right away."

"Okay. Is something wrong?"

"Yes." He motioned for her to follow him.

"I'll talk to you later, Susan," Lizzie said to the woman, then followed him back to the lobby. "What's going on, Dante?"

"You need to see this." He headed up the stairs with her right on his heels.

"Is there something wrong with your room?" she asked.

"Not my room. Mark Langley's room." When they got to the third floor, he led her to the open door. "I saw a woman come out of this room a few minutes ago. She left the door ajar. I was going to shut it or let Mark know it was open, and then I saw this."

Lizzie stepped into the room and gasped, her gaze darting from the upturned drawers to the ripped pillows on the bed, the slashed fabric on the recliner, and the threatening words on the wall. "Oh, my God," she murmured, putting a hand to her mouth in shock. "Who did this?"

"A woman with red hair. I saw her come out of the room. She gave me an odd look and then rushed down the stairs."

Lizzie met his gaze. "There was a woman matching that description who came by last week. She was looking for Mark. I told him she'd left him a message. I put it on his desk."

He walked over to the desk and saw a piece of paper with a few handwritten scrawled lines: *You should have protected my sister and not your wife. You're going to keep paying until I tell you it's time to stop.*

"Sounds like blackmail," he muttered.

Lizzie read the note over his shoulder. "It does sound like that."

"Mark must have decided to stop paying." His gaze swept the room. "She left him a bigger message."

"I have to call Adam." Lizzie pulled her phone out of her pocket. "Can you wait here while I do that? He might want to ask you what you saw."

"Of course."

She got in touch with Adam fairly quickly and after a brief conversation, she ended the call, saying, "He's five minutes away. He said not to touch anything." Lizzie looked around the scene with pain in her eyes. "She really destroyed this room. She must have taken a knife or scissors to that recliner. It was donated to me by my dad. My mom said he should give it up because he was spending too much time in it. So, he drove it up here, thinking one of my guests would like it. Everything in this room was chosen with love." She wiped her eyes. "It's silly to be so personally attached."

"It's not silly, and I'm sorry." For Lizzie, this wasn't just an inn. It was truly her home, a home that had just been ripped apart.

"I wonder how she got in. It's easy enough to get into the building but not the rooms. They're all coded to the keycard."

"Maybe you should call Mark Langley."

"Good idea." She looked through her phone, then punched in a number. "It's going to voicemail," she said a moment later. "Mr. Langley, this is Lizzie Cole. There's been an incident at the inn with your room. Please call me as soon as you can. It's urgent."

As she finished her message, he walked around, careful not to disturb anything. The woman hadn't just used a knife or scissors on the recliner; she'd cut up Mark's clothes and slashed the sheets and pillows. There was a personal vindictiveness to everything he saw, a burning hatred, and it was very unsettling.

"I should have stopped her," he muttered. "I didn't know what she'd done."

"How could you know? And why would you stop her? She could have just been visiting Mark."

"Mark's car was scratched yesterday. He said it was probably kids, but I think it was her. I know they had an argument several days ago."

"What about?"

"No idea."

"Keira has been suspicious about him from the beginning. I thought she was being overprotective of her mom. She's been taking care of her for so long, she worries about everything, but her instinct might have been right."

"I think it was." He needed to give Keira a heads-up about

what had happened here. But before he could pull out his phone, Adam arrived.

Since both he and Lizzie had seen the red-haired woman, they came up with a good description between them. When he was done answering Adam's questions, he headed downstairs, jumped into his car, and went looking for Keira. He wasn't going to leave yet another text message or voicemail. He was going to find her and talk to her.

Her car wasn't at her shop, and there were no lights on in the building, so he went to her house. Adam would probably be close behind him, just in case Langley was with Ruth Blake, but he didn't want to waste another minute before he filled Keira in. He couldn't help thinking that he now had a very good reason for getting in touch with her. Unfortunately, he was bringing nothing but more bad news.

CHAPTER TWENTY-FOUR

KEIRA SIGHED when she opened the door to find Dante on the porch. She'd just gotten home and had hoped not to have a conversation with him tonight. "I know I owe you a text. It's been really busy. I'm not ignoring you."

"Yes, you are," he said bluntly. "And you do owe me a text, but that's not why I'm here."

She looked at him in surprise. "Why are you here then?"

"Mark's room was vandalized at the inn. It was completely trashed, with threatening words written on the wall: *YOU WILL PAY*. Mark's clothes were shredded. It's bad, Keira."

Her eyes widened, her stomach churning at his words. "That's crazy. You think it was Mandy?"

"I know it was. I saw her leave his room. Where's your mom?"

"She's not here. She left me a text saying she and Mark went for a drive."

"You should call her, ask her to come home now, but don't tell her why."

She frowned and waved him into the house. Then she walked over to the table in the entry to get her phone. "I don't know that she'll come home if I don't say why."

"You can't tip her off."

"Why not?"

"Because we don't know what's happening, and if she's with Mark, it would just be better if he didn't know what was going on until the police are talking to him."

"The police are involved?"

"Yes. Lizzie called Adam. She also called Mark, but he didn't answer. I know Adam is going to look for Mark, but if your mother is with him, and you can get him to bring her home, then we can get her here before we get into anything else."

"You're scaring me a little."

"Sorry. I don't think your mom is in danger. The crazy woman is clearly after Mark."

"And we need to know why," she said with new determination in her voice. She called her mom. For a moment, she thought it was going to voicemail, but then her mom's voice came across the line.

"Hi, Keira. What's up?" her mom asked, a light note in her voice. Nothing sounded wrong. That was a good sign.

"I was wondering if you're almost home. I really need to talk to you."

"Is something wrong?"

"Not wrong, just concerning. I know you're out with Mark, but I have to speak to you. It's important."

"What's this about, honey?"

She searched wildly for a reason that might make sense. As her gaze lit on Dante's attractive face, she had her answer. "It's about Dante. He's leaving sooner than I thought, and I need your advice."

"Okay, well, we were heading back anyway. We picked up a pizza if you're hungry. Mark was hoping you might be around."

"Great. He's welcome to come in and stay for dinner. I just need a few minutes with you alone, if he doesn't mind."

"Of course not, and I'm glad that will work out. I've wanted us all to sit down together."

"See you soon." She looked at Dante. "Sorry I mentioned you. I needed an excuse."

"I figured."

"They're on their way back from picking up a pizza. They'll be here soon."

"Good. I'm going to stay."

She nodded. Their eyes met, their gazes clinging together, unspoken words and emotions flowing between them.

"Why were you avoiding me today?" he asked.

She sucked in a quick breath. She wanted to evade the question, but he wasn't going to let her get away with that, so she decided to be honest. "I think it might be better if we didn't see each other anymore."

"We had a good time last night. We have a good time every time we're together."

"But our time is ending, and frankly, I'm not handling it very well."

His gaze softened. "Keira, I know this is difficult."

"It is, but it shouldn't be. I went into this knowing it was a short-term thing, a summer fling—fun, easy, and forgettable."

"I never thought it was going to be forgettable."

"Well, it turns out it won't be, at least not for me. I got too emotionally involved, and I know myself, Dante. It's not going to get easier the more time we spend together. We should just smile and wish each other well."

A cloud of dark shadows filled his gaze. "I'm here until Saturday. Do you really want to waste the time we have left?"

"I do and I don't. I've been conflicted all day, which is why I didn't text you back. But now that you're standing in front of me, I know the answer."

He met her gaze and his lips tightened. "And the answer is we're done."

"Yes. I had a good time with you. The only regret I have is that we don't have more time. But I'm really glad I sat down at your table and thought you were my date."

"Me, too. I wish you'd change your mind."

"I know, but it wouldn't be the same. The end would just be looming over us."

She could see he wanted to argue. Dante was the kind of man

who got what he wanted. But a car pulled up out front. Her mother and Mark had arrived.

She opened the front door as they made their way into the house with two large pizza boxes and a bottle of wine. Her mother looked at Dante in surprise.

"I didn't know you were here, Dante."

"I just arrived," he said.

"I hope you'll stay for pizza," Mark said, as they all walked toward the kitchen. "We got plenty."

When they entered the kitchen, Mark set down the pizzas and offered to open the wine.

"That sounds good," her mother told Mark. "I know Keira needs to speak to me for a few minutes. You and Dante can entertain each other while we're gone."

"No need for that," she said. "We all need to talk."

Her mother gave her a confused look. "About what?"

"Let's sit down at the table." She pulled out a chair and sat down as the others did the same.

"This isn't about Dante, is it?" her mother asked.

"No, it's about Mark," she replied, her gaze moving from her mom to Mark.

He looked straight back at her. "All right," he said. "I'm happy to talk about whatever you want to discuss."

"Well, I'm not," her mom said with a look of annoyance on her face. "Keira. I told you I would talk to Mark on my own."

"Have you?" she challenged.

"Not yet, but I will."

"Well, time has run out. Dante, why don't you tell Mark what happened at the inn?"

"At the inn?" Mark echoed.

"Your room was vandalized tonight," Dante said. "Lizzie left you a message. The police also want to talk to you. Didn't you get those calls?"

"I saw a couple of voicemails, but I was driving. I didn't have time to listen to them. What happened to my room?"

"I ran into the woman you were arguing with a few days ago in the hallway outside your room. She gave me an odd look and then ran down the stairs. I noticed your door was still ajar, so I went over to let you know. When I opened the door, I realized the room had been trashed. There was a threatening message on the wall that said: *YOU WILL PAY.* I got Lizzie. She called her brother, who is a police detective, and I'm sure they're both trying to reach you."

Mark had paled during Dante's explanation. He pulled out his phone. "Yes, I have several voicemails. I should listen to them."

"Before you do that, you need to tell us who this woman is and why she's threatening you," Keira said.

"Keira," her mother interrupted. "This is Mark's business, not ours."

"This woman could be dangerous, Mom. You're spending time with Mark, and he's someone's target. I don't want you to get hurt. Mark needs to decide if he wants to see you and tell us the truth, or if he wants to leave and take care of his own business. But I'm not going to stand by and do nothing." She blew out a breath, knowing she'd probably overstepped, too, but she didn't care.

"Keira is right," Mark said, turning to her mother. "I believed I could handle the situation, Ruth, like I've done in the past, but Mandy is in a bad place. I thought she left town yesterday. She promised me she was leaving, but apparently that didn't happen."

"When did she promise?" Dante asked. "Was it after she scratched your car? We both know that's who did it."

"Yes, it was after that," Mark admitted. "I met with Mandy, and I told her that the police were getting involved, that she was captured on the security camera, and that I would only stop her from being charged if she left town. She said she would go."

"Who is this woman?" Keira asked. "What does she want you to pay for?"

"A long time ago, fifteen years now, there was a fire at my home. I was out of town with my wife and son. But our nanny, Gretchen, was in the house, and she died in the fire. She was Mandy's sister."

"Why does Mandy blame you for that if you weren't even there?" Dante asked.

"It's a long story."

"It's time to tell it," Keira said.

Mark's lips tightened, but then he gave a short nod. "All right. I will tell you the story. I didn't know until months after the fire that my wife had left our vacation rental and gone back to the house to talk to Gretchen. She did it in the middle of the night, and she was back before the police called early the next morning."

Her pulse leapt at his response. "Your wife set the fire?"

"I need to back up," Mark said. "You have to understand the context of what was going on."

"Take your time," her mother encouraged.

He gave her a grateful smile. "Thank you, Ruth. My wife, Valerie, had mental health issues, some of which she took medication for. But when she would go off the meds, she would become unbalanced, paranoid, and unpredictable. I knew things were getting rocky with her, which is why I suggested a weekend away at the beach. We went to Malibu. It was less than an hour away from our house, but she loved the water, and I thought it would calm her down. I wanted us to reconnect as a family. When she was off her meds, she barely paid attention to our son, Richard. I knew that he was feeling neglected."

Mark cleared his throat. "That night," he continued, "Valerie started a fight with me. She accused me of having an affair with Gretchen, which was not true. I was not involved with the nanny, and I told Valerie that several times. She said she was so angry she was going to sleep in the extra bedroom. I didn't question it. I was relieved to have a break. I didn't want to fight with her, and I especially didn't want to do it in front of Richard. But sometime that night, after I went to bed, she took the car and drove back to the house. She later told me that she woke Gretchen up and made her come downstairs. Gretchen also denied anything was going on, and she apparently went back up the stairs while Valerie decided to drink and smoke cigarettes in the living room. At some point, Valerie left the house, but she also left her cigarette in the couch and it started the fire. There was a bottle of alcohol on the cushions and that blew up the fire. The police thought that Gretchen had been drinking and smoking before she went upstairs and that she had no idea what happened. She died in her bed."

"That's awful," her mother said, putting a comforting hand on Mark's arm.

"You said you didn't find this out for months," Keira interrupted, not wanting her mother to get Mark off track. "How is that possible?"

"Valerie was asleep in the guest room when I got the call about the fire," he replied. "I woke her up. She was disoriented. I dropped her and Richard off with Valerie's sister when I went to the house and spoke to the police. Later that day, when I got back to my sister-in-law's house, she said that Valerie was having a breakdown. I got her to the hospital, where she was admitted. I think she had tremendous guilt, and it was eating her up inside, so she couldn't speak. She couldn't do anything. She was basically catatonic. She was in a psychiatric facility for eight months before she finally started to come back to life. And then she started telling me stories about the fire. I honestly didn't know if they were true or not. I just knew that I had to protect my son. I divorced Valerie, and I took Richard to San Francisco. To this day, he blames me for taking him away from his mother and also for abandoning her when she was sick. But I didn't do that. I paid for her to get help for ten years after that. I wanted her to get better, but I couldn't have her around Richard unless she was stable."

"That makes sense," her mom said. "You had to protect your child."

"Why didn't you go to the police?" she asked. "Why didn't you tell them what Valerie did?"

His eyes turned bleak. "It had been almost a year since it happened, and I didn't even know if Valerie was telling me the truth. Or if she'd made up another story in her head."

"There was no proof that she went to the house that night?" Dante asked.

"None. We didn't have a security camera. None of our neighbors did, either. It was the middle of the night. I read the police report. No one came forward saying they'd seen anything. There was also no camera at the house in Malibu where we were staying. I suppose there might have been some way the police could have checked traffic cameras to see if our car was caught on any, but I didn't want to put Valerie or my son through an investigation that wouldn't change anything. Maybe that was wrong. But I just wanted to take Richard away from it all."

"Let's get back to Mandy," Dante interjected. "When did she find out that your wife set the fire? And why didn't she go to the police?"

"Mandy found out six years ago. My wife was sick, dying from cancer. She decided it was time to pay for her sins, so she told Mandy. She wanted to cleanse her soul."

"And then Mandy started blackmailing you," Keira guessed.

"Yes," he said, meeting her gaze. "Mandy threatened to go to the police and also to tell my son that his mother was a murderer. Valerie was finally in a better space. Richard was a freshman in college. He was actually happy. The truth would have destroyed them both, so I paid. It eased my guilt, too, to be honest. But Mandy wanted more and more and more. Right before I moved here, I told Mandy I was done paying her. My son is twenty-four now. He's an adult. He has his own life, and if he finds out the truth now, hopefully, he can handle it." Mark turned to her mother. "I was going to tell you, Ruth. But every time we were together, it was so much fun; I didn't want it to end, and I thought it might if you knew I was dealing with a blackmailer."

"Mandy came to this house," Keira put in. "You didn't think she could be a problem for my mother?"

Surprise filled his eyes. "She came here? When?"

"Sunday," her mother answered. "I assume it was her. There was a red-haired woman sitting in a car outside of the house."

"She must have been following me around this week. I never saw her. I'm sorry, Ruth. I should have told you."

"I can understand why you didn't," her mother said.

Keira sucked in a sharp breath as her mother let Mark off the hook. "I can't," she said harshly.

"It was complicated," her mother said, giving her a pointed look, then gazing back at Mark. "And it was part of your past."

"But Mandy isn't in the past," she interjected, bringing their attention back to her. "She's causing trouble. And we don't know if she's done."

"Keira is right," Dante said. "Mandy cut up your clothes, Mark. There was a personal vindictiveness to her destruction. You need to tell the police everything you told us."

"I agree. I'll do that now." Mark got to his feet. "I'm going to step into the other room."

As Mark left, Keira looked at her mom. "Do you believe he told us the whole story?"

"Yes. I believed every word," her mother said, without a trace of doubt in her eyes. "Didn't you?"

"I don't know," she admitted.

"You do know. You heard what he had to say. You just don't want to let go of your suspicions because you don't want him to be with me," her mother said sharply.

Was her mother right? Was she holding onto her suspicions for that reason? "I do want you to be happy, Mom, but I still think you should be careful. We don't know if this is Mark's only secret."

"I believe it is." She stood up. "I'm going to check on Mark."

She looked at Dante as her mom headed down the hall. "What do you think? You're probably the most objective person in this situation."

Dante gave her a thoughtful look. "I'm inclined to believe him."

"So it's two against one."

"Is it?" he challenged.

She sighed. "Maybe not. It's a bizarre story, but it felt true. I wouldn't mind hearing Mandy's side. I hope Adam can catch her."

"She won't be able to move around so freely now that the police are looking for her. She knows I saw her come out of Mark's room, so her best bet would be to leave town and disappear."

"I would think so, too, but she seems determined to get him to pay. Maybe she thinks he will do so now that she's shown the lengths to which she's willing to go."

"In which case, she'll contact him, and I'm sure the police will use him to get to her."

"Good point." As the doorbell rang, she added, "That must be Adam. I want to hear what he has to say."

"So do I. Is it okay if I stay?"

"Sure," she said, as they stood up. "But when Mark leaves, you need to leave, too."

He met her gaze. "I know. I got the message. We're over."

She let out a sigh. "Unfortunately, yes. But we shouldn't think of it as a bad thing. It's only happening because your arm is better. I am happy for you, Dante. It might not look that way, but I want you to have your life back. I really do."

"Thanks. That means a lot."

"And we had fun, so…" She drew in a shaky breath. "That's what I'm going to remember."

Shadows filled his gaze. "I hope that's what you remember, because I never wanted to hurt you."

"You didn't," she said. And she meant it. Because he hadn't hurt her; she'd hurt herself by falling for a man who was always going to say goodbye.

CHAPTER TWENTY-FIVE

KEIRA LOOKED out her kitchen window on Wednesday morning. The Fourth of July promised to be a hot, sunny day that would end in spectacular fireworks, but she wasn't in the mood for any more explosive surprises. The night before had had too many. After Adam had a long discussion with Mark, where much of the same information he'd revealed to them had been shared once more, all three men had left. Mark and Dante had gone back to the inn while Adam was off to look for Mandy.

She and her mother had eaten some cold pizza in an uncomfortable silence before her mom declared she was exhausted and didn't want to talk about anything. She'd then gone up to her room and closed the door.

She'd decided to go to bed, too, but sleep hadn't come fast or easy. Her brain had jumped from one worry to the next. *Could she trust that Mark had told them the entire truth? Could her mother possibly get caught up in this feud between Mark and Mandy?*

When she forced her mind off that subject, she'd thought about her surprise visit from Margot, her request that she come to LA as soon as possible to meet with Jessica. Her dream job could be days away. *But how could she make that work with everything else going on?*

And then there was Dante. He wanted her to spend the week with him. He didn't want to waste the time they had left, but she was afraid of falling more in love with him. His departure was going to hurt. On the other hand, she was depriving herself of a lot more fun.

But it wasn't fun anymore. It was just over.

She turned away from the window and started the coffeemaker. Then she popped bread into the toaster and sliced up an avocado and a tomato. She munched on that as she waited for the pot to fill. When it was done, she filled a large mug with coffee and took a grateful sip.

Her mother walked into the kitchen. "Good morning," she said, a cool note in her voice.

"Morning. Coffee is ready. Can I get you something to eat?"

"I'll just take coffee. I'm not really hungry."

She filled a mug and took it over to the table, sitting down across from her mom. "Did you sleep?"

"A little. You?"

"Same. Have you heard from Mark?"

"Yes. I just spoke to him. When he got back to the inn last night, the room was really bad, so he checked out and went to the Sunset Lodge. This morning, he spoke again to Adam. They haven't picked up Mandy yet, but they did see her car on a traffic camera, on Highway 10, heading out of the mountains."

She was relieved to hear that. "So, she's gone."

"They think so. They're going to watch the Denver airport and also alert the police department in Los Angeles, where she lives."

"I wonder if she'll go home. She must know the police are looking for her."

"Mark says she has a brother who lives in Fresno, California. Maybe she'll go there. I'm sure they'll find her, and this should be the end of her blackmail."

"What do you think about everything now, Mom?"

"Mark was in a very difficult situation. I'm not saying I would have made the same choices, but I understand why he did what he did. It's not easy to be married to someone who is that unstable, and his child had to come first."

"I agree with that, but a woman died because of his wife, and she never had to answer for it."

"That's true. Mark said there was a part of him that always hoped she had just made it up in her head the way she'd made up so many other things. That because they fought over Gretchen and then Gretchen died, Valerie thought she was responsible but wasn't."

"That sounds like an excuse, a way for Mark to rationalize not going to the police."

"Possibly. You've been looking for a reason not to like him, and you certainly got one."

She frowned. "This isn't my fault, Mom. I didn't make this up. Mark did what he did. And I'm not even the one who brought it all out; that was Mandy."

"I know. I'm not blaming you. I'm just sorry you were right."

"I'm kind of sorry, too."

Her mother met her gaze. "Why?"

"Because you like him."

"I do like him. All the old feelings from when I was a teenager have come back. He makes me feel young again. I'm not injured or ailing when we're together; I'm just me. I don't want it to end."

"It doesn't bother you that he kept so much from you?"

"I think he would have told me eventually. He said that again this morning. He feels bad that Mandy showed up here at the house and he didn't know about it. He didn't think she was dangerous to anyone, but after seeing his room last night, he realized he hadn't seen how out of control she was. He said he felt bad for her when she first came to him. She'd just gone through a bitter divorce and she'd lost her last remaining parent. She has a brother, but everyone else is gone. And she needed money. She needed someone to take care of her."

"And he wanted to do that."

"Yes. It wasn't just blackmail; it was also guilt. He wasn't responsible for what happened, for that fire. He had no idea his wife had left the house. And he believes the fire was truly an accident. But he still felt like Gretchen's death was his fault. Maybe he should have forced Valerie to get medical help, but she was very resistant. She wouldn't take her meds. She wouldn't see a doctor. He felt helpless."

"I can see how he might feel that way."

"I'm glad you can see that, because life is complicated, Keira. Most people aren't all good or all bad; they're complex and they're flawed."

"I know." She let out a heavy breath. "Is Mark going to tell his son?"

"I urged him to do that. He needs to tell Richard everything before Mandy does. His son should hear the truth from him. He agreed."

"What about the two of you? Where do you go from here?"

"You won't like my answer."

She gave her a tired smile. "You want to keep seeing him."

"Yes. I'm sorry if that makes you unhappy, but I've been alone for a long time. I've found someone I enjoy spending time with, and he feels the same way. We're not going to get married or live together. We just want time to get to know each other again. Can you handle that?"

"I guess I'll have to. I'm going to need to know a lot more about him before he gets my unrestricted approval."

"That's fair enough. Now that I've shared my plans, what about you? What's happening with Dante?"

"His arm is better, and he got the okay from his doctor to go back to pitching. He's leaving town on Saturday."

"Oh, Keira." Her mother gave her a sympathetic look. "I'm sorry."

"I'll survive."

"I don't want you to just survive. I want you to live. I want you to have everything you've ever dreamed about. But, mostly, I don't want to be the reason you don't have the life you're meant to have. I'm good now, Keira. I can get by on my own or with a little help from my friends. You don't have to stay here with me. I am so grateful for everything you've done. But I love you more than life, which is why I want you to go and do whatever you want to do."

She blinked back a rush of emotion. "Are you trying to kick me out?"

"I'm giving you permission to leave, if you want to. You're so talented, Keira. If you want to go back to New York, you should. If you want to follow that handsome baseball player to Florida, you can. Brenda can manage the real-estate business. I'm sure you can find someone to take over the store. You just have to decide what you want, what you really want. And then don't think about anyone else. You've been generous for too long. It's time to be selfish."

"I love being with you, Mom. It's always been us. We're a team."

"A good team," her mother agreed. "We'll always be that to each other. But we both know you need to do something different. Whatever it is, I'll support you. And I want to be clear: this has nothing to do with Mark being in town. This is just about you and me."

"I got it. Thanks."

"Now give me a hug."

She got up and gave her mom a long hug, feeling like another turning point had arrived earlier than she'd thought.

"So, any idea what you are going to do?" her mom asked, as she took her coffee mug to the sink.

"Today or for the long-term?"

"Let's start with today. Are you going to the beach or out on a boat with your friends before the fireworks?"

"I'm not sure," she said vaguely. "I'm going to head down to the store and get caught up on some paperwork. After that, I'll see."

"It's a holiday; you can take a day off. Or are you trying to avoid Dante?"

"You think you know everything," she said with a dry smile.

"I do know you. He's not gone yet, Keira. Maybe you should take this time to find out how you really feel about him."

"Unfortunately, I already know."

Dante spent most of the day on a bike ride. He'd wanted to be outdoors, but he hadn't really wanted to be with anyone except Keira. He'd hoped she would call him, but she hadn't. By seven in the evening, he was tired of his own company. He headed down to the beach, where Lizzie was hosting a picnic dinner before the fireworks. He hoped Keira would be there, but even if she were, she'd probably try to avoid him.

When he arrived at the beach, he found Lizzie standing by a buffet table filled with food, while Zach and Jake tended to meat on a grill. Hannah and Adam were sitting at one of the tables, drinking beer and snacking on chips. He waved to Lizzie, then joined the group at the table.

"Hello, Dante," Hannah said with a smile. "Is Keira with you?"

"No," he said shortly, surprised that one of Keira's best friends didn't seem to know they weren't seeing each other anymore.

"I hope she's not still working. When is she coming?"

"I'm not sure."

Hannah gave him a sharp look. "Are you two having a thing?"

"No, we're having nothing."

"Oh. So, she's avoiding you, which is probably why she's not here."

"If that's the reason, I'll leave."

"Don't be silly." Hannah leaned over and grabbed a beer out of a cooler. "Have a drink. I'm going to give Keira a call."

As she got up, he opened the beer and took a swig.

"Looks like you needed that," Adam said dryly. "Women problems?"

"Seems like those two words usually go together."

"Can't argue with you."

"But I'm glad to get a chance to talk to you. Is there any news on Mandy?"

"We haven't been able to locate her yet. She last used her credit card at a gas station about thirty miles away yesterday evening around seven. Nothing since then, but we'll find her eventually."

"I'm sure it's not a crime that is at the top of the list."

"Are you kidding? She destroyed one of my sister's guest rooms. Trust me, it's very high on my list. I will make sure she pays for what she did."

"I'm glad to hear that. What do you think of Mark Langley?"

"He has been very forthcoming. I will, however, follow up with the LAPD later this week on that fire from fifteen years ago to make sure Langley's story lines up with what is in their reports. And I'll be interested in talking to Mandy when we find her, but from what I saw, I think she got desperate when he decided to stop paying for her silence. She wanted to do something to shake him up, make him pay again. But she went way too far, and now she's going to be the one to pay."

He nodded, seeing the determined glint in Adam's eyes. Adam would get to the bottom of the situation. He'd do it not only because it was his job, but also because his sister had suffered a loss. Adam seemed to be an overachiever like his siblings, so he had confidence that he'd get the answers they all wanted.

Their conversation was interrupted as everyone came over to the table, bringing plates of food, one of which was plopped down in front of him. He found himself squeezed into the middle of the group. Keira's friends were smart and funny, but he couldn't enjoy himself because Keira wasn't there. And he hated the idea that she was missing the party because of him.

When they'd finished eating, he excused himself on the pretense of getting another drink, but once he'd dumped his plate into the trash, he kept on walking. There was a good chance he wouldn't see this group again before he left, and he didn't want to get caught up in goodbyes.

The crowd at the beach had thickened as the time for fireworks drew near, and he was definitely going against the swarm of people moving toward the sand to get a good spot for the fireworks. Eventually he made his way out of the area and walked down the block to where he'd parked his car.

He was almost to his vehicle when he ran into Mark and Ruth. Mark had a blanket under one arm and a picnic basket in his hand.

Ruth gave him a surprised smile. "Dante. You're not leaving, are you?"

"Yes, I'm going back to the inn."

"The fireworks are starting soon. You don't want to miss them."

"I'm not big on fireworks." He should have left it at that, but for some reason, he couldn't. "Is Keira joining you?"

"No. She's not interested in the fireworks tonight, either. She told me she was going to bed early, although I can't imagine she'll sleep through the fireworks. You can hear them all over town. They echo off the mountains." She paused. "If you want to talk to Keira, you know where to find her. I know you're leaving soon, but if there's anything you still need to say, you should say it."

"Thanks for the tip."

"I want to thank you for your help yesterday," Mark interjected. "I don't think I ever said that. But the fact that you saw Mandy and were able to give her description to the police was very helpful. It would have been just speculation if you hadn't seen her leave my room."

"I was in the right place at the right time. I just saw Adam at the beach. He said they haven't found Mandy yet."

"No, but she appears to have left town, which makes me very happy," Mark said. "I am sorry I got all of you involved in my mess. I know I've made some mistakes along the way. I probably should have gone to the police the first time Mandy contacted me."

"Or told your son," Ruth said.

"Yes." Mark let out a sigh. "I left a message for him this morning, but he hasn't returned my call. That's not unusual. We don't have a close relationship. But I'd like to speak to him before Mandy gets it in her head to go straight to Richard."

"Just keep trying," Ruth said. "Make him hear you. You're not close because of this secret. Maybe if it comes out, you'll be able to change the nature of your relationship."

"I hope so." Mark paused as his phone buzzed. "Maybe this is him. No. Dammit."

"What's wrong?" Ruth asked.

"It's a text from Mandy."

"What does it say?" he asked, his gut tightening.

"It's not over. You are going to feel my pain unless you pay up." Mark looked up from his phone as he finished reading the text, a grim look in his gaze.

Ruth frowned. "What does that mean? You're going to feel her pain?"

"I don't know. She makes a lot of threats like that. In the past, I've always paid. Maybe I should do that now since the police haven't found her. It might calm her down."

"Oh, I don't know," Ruth said. "Are you sure that's wise?"

"Honestly? I have no idea what the right move is. Maybe I'll send her half, just to tide her over. I'll do it now."

"You send it through an app?" he asked.

"Yes."

"Good. Then you'll be able to show the police a record of your payments." He waited as Mark completed the transaction. "Was it really just fear for your son that made you pay the blackmail?" he asked curiously.

"It was my guilt, too," Mark said. "I should have gotten my wife into psychiatric care before that fire. I knew she was spinning out. But she thought she could handle it. And I thought I could handle her. We were both wrong. Valerie wasn't a bad person; she was sick. I don't believe she went to the house to kill Gretchen. The fire was an accident. But I did blame myself for it when Valerie told me her story. Before that, I really believed Gretchen had been smoking. She was a smoker, so it wasn't unbelievable. Her family didn't question it, either. We all believed in the story."

"Well, it's done," Ruth said. "All you can do is move forward, Mark. Valerie took a lot from you and Richard, and Mandy has taken her share, too. You need to be free of both of them."

"I'm finally beginning to believe that might happen," he said, as he gazed into Ruth's eyes.

Mark and Ruth were clearly falling in love with each other. Dante could see it on both their faces. They'd found each other after having spent a lifetime apart. It was touching. It also seemed a bit tragic that they'd missed so many years together.

"I think you should stay at my house tonight," Ruth said. "I don't want you alone at the lodge if Mandy is going to cause you more trouble."

"And I would never put you in the line of fire," Mark said. "I'll be fine. I think the money will ease her stress. Part of her problem is that she's broke, so it's not just about revenge. She needs the money to live. She seems incapable of staying in a job for longer than a few months. Anyway, let's not think about her anymore. Let's watch the fireworks and then I'll take you home. No arguments, Ruth. Your safety is my primary concern."

"You're sweet." Ruth turned back to Dante. "If I don't see you again, it was lovely to meet you, Dante, and I hope you throw many more strikeouts."

"Thanks. I'll still be here for a few more days, so our paths may cross again."

"I hope so, but my daughter can be very stubborn. She also isn't the best mind reader. If you want her to know how you feel, tell her. If you have something you want to ask her, then ask. That's my advice. Take it or not."

"I'll think about it." As they moved toward the beach, he got into his car and slid behind the wheel. As he started the engine, Ruth's words ran through his head. He needed to talk to Keira, but she clearly didn't want to talk to him. *How hard should he push? How much time should he give her?*

He was still looking for some answers when he got back to the inn. He shut off the engine, but he didn't get out of the car right away, conflicted as to what he wanted to do. It was early. He could go to Keira's house, or he could let her have the space she wanted.

As a car cruised slowly through the lot, he stiffened, wondering if it was the press or Mandy, but then the car parked, and an older couple got out. He relaxed as they walked toward the front door. They were just guests, not crazy paparazzi or blackmailers.

Thinking about Mandy reminded him of the text she'd sent to Mark: *It's not over. You are going to feel my pain unless you pay up.*

Was it just another threat, like the one she'd left on the wall of the inn? But it had sounded a little different—*you're going to feel my pain. What would make Mark feel that pain?*

A bad idea suddenly came to mind.

Mandy's sister, Gretchen, had died in a fire. Her pain had come from that loss. The loss of someone she loved during a fire.

As he stared at the grand inn, he wondered if Mandy would try to set a fire there. But she'd already had that chance when she'd been in Mark's room. That would have been the perfect time to do it. *Why would she do it now?* Plus, she might have figured that Mark wouldn't stay at the inn after she trashed it.

His stomach began to twist and churn as he remembered that Mandy had been to Ruth's house, too. She knew Mark and Ruth were seeing each other. *Would her next target be Ruth? Or Ruth's house?*

He quickly reversed out of the parking lot and drove across town, his breath coming faster with each passing minute. He tried calling Keira on the way. But she didn't pick up. He left a message telling her it was urgent that she call him back. Then he swore as the light in front of him turned red. He told himself to calm down. He could be following a wild idea that had no basis in fact, but he had a bad feeling, and he couldn't shake it.

CHAPTER TWENTY-SIX

KEIRA HEARD A SMALL CRASH, like someone had dropped something downstairs. She looked from the computer on her bedroom desk to the nearby clock. It was eight fifty. Fireworks would start around nine. *Why would her mom come home before the fireworks?*

She got up and walked to her door. She could hear someone moving around downstairs, but no voices. That seemed odd. *Had her mom had a fight with Mark?*

That didn't make sense. Her mom was solidly in Mark's corner even after they'd learned his secret. Her gut tightened as an odor wafted through the air. It smelled like gas. It reminded her of a terrible night only a few months after her mom's accident when her mother had turned on the gas stove to heat some water and then forgotten about it. The pan had been on fire when she'd woken up to the smell and ran into the kitchen to put out the fire. But that had been in the days when her mom's brain wasn't functioning right. She didn't have those problems anymore.

But the smell got stronger as she left her room and walked down the stairs. She could hear someone in the kitchen. She moved down the hall and threw open the kitchen door. "Mom?"

She froze in shock as she saw a red-haired woman pouring

gasoline on the floor.

The woman dropped the can and lifted the fire starter in her hand.

"Don't do it," she cried, suddenly realizing she was standing on a gas-slicked floor and the liquid had formed pools around the room.

"It's too late," the woman said.

"It's not, Mandy. You don't have to do this. You can walk away."

"How do you know my name?"

"I know all about you and your sister, the fire, the blackmail. The police know, too. It's over, Mandy."

"I didn't think anyone was here," she said, her dark eyes cold and bleak. "But maybe you're supposed to be here, just like my sister was supposed to be at that house. Mark probably doesn't care about you, though. He just wants your mother. She should be here. But you're the next best thing. Her pain will be his pain."

"No! Mark's actions have nothing to do with me or my mother."

"He likes your mom. I saw them kiss. He's moved on. He found happiness again, but I never will. He took my sister from me."

"Wasn't it his wife who did that?"

"He knew about it."

"He said his wife was mentally ill."

"That doesn't excuse her. She killed my sister, but she never paid for it. And Mark kept her secret." The woman backed toward the kitchen door leading out to the patio.

The glass was broken. That must have been how she got in.

As Mandy lifted the fire starter, Keira bolted back through the door leading into the hall. She needed to get as far away from the kitchen as she could, but she slipped in the gasoline that had spread down the hall. As she hit the wall by the stairs, an explosion ripped through the house, and a tremendous wave of intense heat sent her flying through the air. She landed hard, with heavy, dusty debris raining down on her. She tried to move, but she was pinned to the ground by something very heavy. Terror ran through her as flames leapt down the hall. She only had a minute before they would reach her, before they would hit more fuel.

Coughing from the extreme smoke and heat, she tried to squirm free. She kicked out at whatever was holding her, but nothing was moving. She wanted to scream and cry, but that would be giving up, and she couldn't do that. She had to keep fighting.

And then she felt air hit her face. There was so much smoke and fire she didn't know if the windows had burst or if the front door had opened, but she gasped, hoping for some clean air to breathe. It might be the last breath she would get to take.

"Keira?"

She heard his voice through the crack of the fire. *Was she imagining it?* "Dante?" she said, her voice thick with smoke and far too low. She yelled more loudly. "Dante. I'm here."

He came into sight, his features illuminated by the growing fire. "Are you all right?" he yelled.

"I'm trapped. I can't move. Something fell on me."

"Half the ceiling, it looks like." He started grabbing pieces of wood and plaster and tossing them to the side. But there was a portion of a large beam pinning her legs down. "Dammit," he swore, as he tried to budge the beam.

"You have to get out of here," she said. "The fire is too hot. Call 911."

"I already did, and I'm not leaving you." He grabbed the wood with both hands and pulled as hard as he could, screaming in frustration, or maybe it was pain.

"Your arm," she cried. "You'll hurt your arm."

"I don't care about my arm. I care about you."

As another small explosion rocked the house, he used his arms, his body, his power for leverage and, somehow, he was able to move the heavy beam enough for her to scramble out from under it.

"I'm free." She tried to stand up, but pain shot through her foot.

"I've got you." He swept her up in his arms, moving swiftly through the smoke and debris, until blessed fresh air hit her face.

The loud booms and flashing lights confused her until she realized the fireworks were going up over the lake. It felt surreal: the fire behind her, the explosions overhead. In the midst of it all, the fire engines arrived, and two paramedics raced over to meet them. After assuring the firefighters that no one else was in the house, they were taken to the back of the ambulance, where they were given oxygen and checked for injuries.

Her left foot was swollen, and it looked like she would need an x-ray to see if anything was broken, but that was the least of her concerns. Watching the firefighters attack the blazing fire made her suddenly aware that she and her mom were going to lose their home. Everything they owned would be gone. So many years of memories were going up in flames. But they were alive. That was all that mattered.

When the paramedic suggested that they take her to the hospital, she refused. "I don't want to leave yet," she said.

"I can take her to the ER when she's ready," Dante told the medic, as he handed back the oxygen mask.

"All right," the EMT said. "Definitely get that foot checked."

"I will," she promised. She slid off the back of the ambulance onto one foot. Dante put his arm around her and helped her hobble over to the short brick wall that ran around the edge of the property. As they sat down, he put his arm around her, squeezing her close to his body. She looked into his face, which was streaked black from the smoke. There were white specks of plaster in his brown hair, and his face was sweaty, his clothes also covered in ashes and dust. But he'd never looked better to her. "You saved my life," she said. "How did you know?"

"I didn't know, but I had a bad feeling after I ran into Mark and your mother at the beach."

"What do you mean?"

"Mark got a text from Mandy telling him he was going to feel her pain. He sent her some money after reading the text to try to calm her down until the police could find her. But as I was driving home, I thought about what she'd said, and I remembered that she'd been here at the house. I called you, but you didn't pick up."

"I had my phone on silent."

His lips tightened. "Because you were avoiding me."

"Yes, I was avoiding you and everyone else. I didn't want to go to the beach, and my friends kept calling, so I stopped answering."

"You should have gone to the beach. You should have been with your friends. They all missed you."

"You saw them?"

"Yes. I was hoping to run into you." His lips tightened. "What happened here? Did you see Mandy?"

"Yes. I thought I heard someone downstairs, and it seemed odd that my mom would come home before the fireworks show. I went into the kitchen and caught Mandy pouring gasoline on the floor. She dropped the can when she saw me. She said she didn't think anyone was in the house. But then she added that Mark was in love with my mom. If my mom lost her daughter, then she'd be in pain, and he'd feel her pain. Plus, my mom would blame him for what happened. I tried to reason with her, but she wasn't listening. When she headed toward the back door, I ran in the other direction, but I wasn't fast enough. Everything blew up around me. I guess the ceiling came down."

"You were so lucky, Keira." He leaned over and gave her a kiss.

She savored the heat of his lips, a different kind of fire than the one taking down her house. This heat was solid, comforting, and a reminder that she was alive. "You're the reason I was lucky. I don't think anyone is around. The houses nearby are all dark. The neighbors must be down at the beach. If you hadn't come by—"

He put his hand against her mouth to stop her. "I did come by. Don't think of the alternative."

"It's impossible not to. I could have died."

"But you didn't. You're okay." He brushed the hair off her face and kissed her again. "I was terrified when I pulled up and saw the fire. And then seeing you trapped under all that rubble—"

This time she was the one who put her fingers against his lips. "We both need to stop thinking about the bad stuff that didn't happen."

"You're right." His gaze narrowed as she shivered. "Are you cold?"

"Probably just a little shocked."

He wrapped both arms around her, bringing her into his chest. As he did so, she couldn't help but notice the wince of pain that ran across his face. She pulled back to give him a searching look. "You hurt your arm, didn't you?"

"No, it's fine."

"I don't believe you. I knew you shouldn't have moved that beam. It was too heavy. All the progress you've made—"

"Stop. I don't care about my arm."

"Yes, you do."

"No, I don't," he said firmly. "I care about you, Keira. I'm in love with you. I would have cut off my right arm to save you."

She stared at him in amazement, feeling too rattled to believe him.

"I'm in love with you," he repeated. "I ran into your mom earlier, and she told me that I needed to tell you how I feel, so I'm telling you."

"It's too soon for love."

"No, it's not. I love you, Keira, and if my arm never works again, I don't care, because you are more important to me than baseball."

She shook her head in bemusement. "How can that be?"

"It just is. You have to believe me. Everything snapped into place when I saw your house on fire. Baseball is not the most important thing in my life anymore; you are. I'm hoping you feel the same way, even though you haven't said anything, which is strange, because you usually talk a lot."

She smiled, overwhelmed with so many feelings she didn't know where to start. So, she began with what was most important. "I'm in love with you, too, Dante. I've been trying to fight it, telling myself this was just a fun fling. But it was more than that."

"A lot more," he agreed.

"But being in love doesn't change our problems with geography and responsibilities."

"We're going to have to find a way to work that out. I want to be with you, Keira, and I usually get what I want," he added with a small smile.

"I like your confidence, as misplaced as it might be."

"We have to try to make things work." He paused as Adam came toward them.

"Are you two all right?" Adam asked with concern.

"Yes," she said. "I just hurt my foot, but otherwise I'm okay."

"Tell me what happened."

She repeated what she'd .already told Dante, noting Adam's expression growing harsher by the minute.

"We'll find Mandy," Adam assured her when she was done. "I promise you that. I honestly thought she was out of town. I should have made sure you and your mother had protection."

"You couldn't have known Mandy would go from vandalizing a hotel room to setting our house on fire, Adam."

"Well, she won't get away with this. I'll make sure of that."

"I know you will." As Adam walked away, she turned to Dante. "I need to call my mom. I don't have my phone."

He took his phone out of his pocket, then said, "But you don't need to call her; she's here."

Her mother came running across the grass, followed by Mark. There was terror in her eyes. "Are you all right, Keira? Adam said you were in the house when it caught fire."

"I'm okay," she said quickly.

Her mother gathered her into a tight hug. "I was so worried. When I heard my house was on fire, I couldn't believe it. What happened?"

"It was Mandy." Her gaze moved from her mother to Mark. "She poured gasoline in the kitchen and then set it on fire. I confronted her, but she got away."

Mark drew in a shaky breath. "I'm so sorry, Keira. I thought she left town. I should have realized she would go after Ruth, after this house. How can I ever..." Words failed him as he gasped for breath.

"It's not your fault," she told him, seeing the pain in his face. "You didn't know. This is on Mandy, no one else."

"But you've lost your home." He gave a hopeless, helpless shake of his head as he turned toward her mother. "I never should have looked you up, Ruth. I put you and Keira in danger, and now you've lost everything."

"Not everything," her mother said, putting her hands on his arms. "Keira's alive, and so are we. I learned a long time ago that life and health is all that matters."

"You're being too generous, Ruth."

Her mom was being generous, and the reality of what they'd lost would probably hurt—a lot. But as Mark and her mother hugged each other, she could see the love between them. It felt strange, because it had been her mom and her for so long, but it also felt good. Her mom was back to normal, or at least close to normal. She could make her own decisions. She could take care of herself. Maybe it was time she recognized that.

As she looked around the area, she could see a crowd gathering behind two police cars. Her friends were among that crowd: Lizzie, Chelsea Hannah, and Jake were there along with Gianna and Zach, as well as the neighbors. She gave them a wave and a thumbs-up. They waved back with relieved but concerned smiles.

As she shivered once more, Dante put his arm back around her. "Why don't I take you to the hospital?"

At his words, her mom broke away from Mark, worry filling her gaze. "Did you just say hospital? Keira, you said you were all right."

"I think I sprained my ankle or something," she said vaguely, as the pain from that injury began to take hold in a sharper, more penetrating way. She'd been numb from shock, but no longer. "I need an x-ray."

"I'm going to take her to the hospital," Dante said. "Where do you think you two will spend the rest of the night?"

"I can go next door," her mom said. "Erin and her husband can put me and Mark up. I saw them on my way in. They said it was no problem."

"No," Mark said, with a definitive shake of his head. "I can't make anyone else a target."

"I think we should stay together," Ruth argued.

As her mom and Mark continued their conversation, Dante looked back at her. "You could stay with me at the inn. To sleep, nothing else. If that doesn't work, I'll go wherever you want to go, but I'm not letting you out of my sight."

She gave him a tired smile. "That sounds nice. Mom," she added, interrupting her mom's conversation with Mark, "Dante will take me to the hospital, and then I'll stay with him at the inn."

"All right. I guess Mark will go back to the lodge, and I'll stay with Erin," she said with an unhappy sigh.

Keira couldn't share her unhappiness. She would feel better knowing her mom was with the neighbors and not with Mark. Until Mandy was in custody, Mark was still a target, along with anyone who was with him. "We'll meet back here in the morning," she said. "I'm sure we won't be able to get in before then, if we can get in at all. Maybe there will be something left to salvage upstairs or in the garage."

"We'll figure it out." Her mother sounded stronger than she had in years. "Dante, you take care of my girl."

"I will," he promised. "You can count on that."

Dante helped her off the short wall and they made their way toward his car, which was parked across the street. She stopped to exchange hugs with all of her friends. Thankfully, they already seemed to know the story, so she didn't have to retell it. As she got into Dante's car, she took one last look at her house. The fire was just about out, but there was still a ton of smoke in the air.

"Are you okay?" Dante asked, giving her a concerned look.

"I'm angry and sad, but I'm also grateful that I'm alive. When we get to the hospital, I want you to get your arm checked out, too."

"It's going to be all right, Keira."

She really wanted to believe him, but she needed his arm to be okay, even if it made their choices more complicated. She couldn't be the reason he lost everything.

CHAPTER TWENTY-SEVEN

DANTE DIDN'T TAKE a full breath until he helped Keira into his guest room at the inn just before midnight. She'd been diagnosed with a minor fracture in her foot, which had been placed in a boot. Luckily, she hadn't needed surgery or a cast, and the pain was treatable with medication. It could have been a lot worse.

Keira got on the bed, resting her back against a pair of fluffy pillows. She stretched out her legs and let out a long sigh.

He sat on the edge of the bed next to her, seeing pain in her eyes. "Can I get you anything?"

"No, thanks. I'm okay."

"You don't look it."

"You're supposed to lie and say I look beautiful." She smiled. "Just like you look handsome with chunks of plaster in your hair and soot on your face."

He grinned. "You do look beautiful. I'm hoping that smile means the medication is taking effect."

"My foot doesn't hurt too bad, but I feel exhausted."

"The adrenaline and shock are starting to wear off. You need to sleep."

"You must be feeling the same way." Her gaze moved from his

face to his shoulder. "Are you sure the doctor said your shoulder is okay?"

"I'm sure." Hannah had come to the hospital and had the doc on duty take a look at his arm and shoulder while Keira was getting an x-ray. "If anything, I may have strained my arm, but it doesn't feel like a setback. I'll get it checked more thoroughly at the rehab center tomorrow."

"You better."

"And you don't need to worry about me." He grabbed his phone as it buzzed. "It's Adam."

"Hopefully, he has good news. Can you put it on speaker?"

"Of course. Hello? Adam?"

"Yes. Are you still with Keira?"

"She's right here. You're on speaker."

"Good. Lizzie gave me your number since Keira lost her phone in the fire. I wanted to let you know that Mandy has been taken into custody."

"That's great." He felt an intense wave of relief. "Where did you find her?"

"She made it to the north shore. She'll be transferred back here to the county jail tomorrow. We have video of her breaking into Keira's house from the neighbor's camera next door. We also have her buying gasoline earlier in the day on the north shore. The case against her will be strong. She won't get away with this."

"Thank you so much, Adam," Keira put in. "Have you spoken to my mother?"

"Yes. I spoke to her and also to Mr. Langley. Everyone is up to speed. I'm sorry about your house, Keira. Let me know what I can do to help you sort through all that."

"I will. I'll talk to my mother tomorrow and go from there. But I'm very relieved to know that Mandy is not still running loose. That's a huge relief. I didn't want to know what might come next."

"You don't need to worry anymore. I'll talk to you tomorrow."

"Goodnight," Keira said.

"Thanks, Adam," he added, then set the phone down and exchanged a smile with Keira. "Mandy is done. There's evidence to prove she was in the house and set the fire. Plus, she also tried to kill you. The list of charges against her should be long."

Shadows passed through Keira's eyes. He'd just reminded her how close she'd come to not making it out of the house alive.

"It's strange to think that someone was willing to kill me. We'd never even met before last night. She didn't know me. She didn't know my mother," Keira said, a shaky note in her voice.

He put his hand on her leg. "Mandy clearly has mental health issues. It wasn't about you. It wasn't even about Mark."

She nodded as she met his gaze. "It was about her sister, a loss she couldn't get past."

"Which doesn't excuse anything."

Her expression hardened. "You don't have to worry about me wanting to go easy on her. She destroyed our home. I want her to pay for that."

"She will."

"I know. Adam will make sure of that." Keira blew out a breath. "I don't want to talk about Mandy. I'm so happy this is over now. I know that seeing my house in the light of day will hurt a lot. There were a lot of memories in those walls and things from several generations. I don't know if our family treasures survived. Although, we did move some boxes of albums and other knick-knacks into the garage a few years ago. Maybe they made it through the fire."

"I hope they did." He could see fresh pain in her eyes and wished he could do something to make it all better, but he couldn't change what had happened.

"If they didn't, we still have our memories. And we're alive to make more memories." She lifted her chin. "We'll bounce back."

He knew she would. "You have impressed me in so many ways tonight… Actually, not just tonight, but since I met you. You're a strong woman, Keira. Brave, loyal, fiercely protective of the people you love, incredibly unselfish, and you're a fighter. You never play the victim, even when it's warranted, like tonight. You just put your head up and square your shoulders and are ready to march on."

She blinked away a tear. "That's very sweet, Dante."

"It's not sweet. It's the truth."

"Well, you need to stop being so nice. You're going to make me cry. I don't know why I'm suddenly feeling emotional."

"You're feeling emotional because you've had a rough night. You're allowed to cry. I can offer you a shoulder."

She gave him a faint smile. "I might take you up on that. But I have to say, Dante, you've impressed me, too. The way you ran into my house and refused to leave…" She shook her head. "You could have been seriously hurt or worse. But you stayed with me."

"There was no way I was going to leave you."

He took her hand in his as she gazed back at him with her beautiful brown eyes. She was feeling emotional, and, damn, if he wasn't feeling the same way. He was trying to focus on the fact that they were both alive, but he was still acutely aware of how close he'd come to losing her.

"You should have left," she said. "But you're stubborn and very confident."

"I can't argue with that," he said lightly. "Sometimes it comes in handy."

"It did tonight. And I really hope your arm is okay."

"I told you not to worry about that. I'm fine. And I want you to feel better, so tell me what I can do for you?"

Her smile slowly lifted her lips. "Hold me?"

"I can do that." He took off her shoe and the awkward boot, careful not to jar her foot, which had been wrapped in a bandage. Then he kicked off his own shoes and turned off the light, finally stretching out next to her. He pulled her into his arms so she could rest her head on his chest.

As the dark quiet enveloped them, he realized how much time he'd spent thinking about where he needed to be, but he hadn't realized until just this moment that the only place he needed to be was right where he was: next to Keira. He had to find a way to make that happen after tonight.

Dante woke up to the sun streaming through the curtains. He was shocked that it was almost ten. Keira shifted away from him as her eyes fluttered open.

She gave him a sleepy smile. "Hey."

"Hey," he echoed, as he stole a kiss from her soft mouth. "How did you sleep?"

"Surprisingly well. What about you?"

"Best night's sleep I've had in a while. I like sleeping with you."

"Even if all we did was sleep?" she teased.

"Yes. Because I still got to hold you. How's your foot?"

"It aches a little, but nothing I can't tolerate."

"Tough girl."

"Not really."

"Don't deny it. I've seen how strong you are." He pulled her back to him, needing to have his arms around her, needing to kiss her again. But his phone started buzzing, and he was concerned it could be important news about the fire or Mandy, so he cut the kiss short and took the call. "Hello?"

"It's Lizzie. I hope I didn't wake you."

"No. We're up."

"Good. Because I'd love to bring you some breakfast. When is a good time?"

"Any time," he said. "Maybe twenty or thirty minutes."

"Perfect. I'll see you soon."

He set down the phone. "Lizzie is bringing us food."

"That's wonderful. I'm hungry," Keira added, as she sat up. "But I must look like a mess."

"An adorable mess." Her long brown hair was tangled with ashy dust throughout, her face was still smudged, and her clothes smelled like smoke. Or maybe that was his clothes. "We probably should have showered last night."

"I was too exhausted. But I need to pull myself together. There's a lot to do today."

"I'm available to help with whatever you need. In fact, I'm going to call the clinic and cancel my morning session."

She frowned. "You shouldn't do that."

"I want to go with you to your house."

"I appreciate that, but I want you to get your arm checked out."

"I'll keep the afternoon session," he said. "Do you want help getting into the shower? Or getting your clothes off?"

Her eyes sparked with amusement. "I think I can manage that myself and since we only have a short time until Lizzie arrives, I'll be quick, and then you can go after me."

"Together would be faster."

"I don't think so, Dante," she said with a laugh. She leaned forward and gave him a kiss. "Another time."

"Fine. There's a robe on the back of the door if you don't want to put those clothes back on."

"I don't. I should ask Lizzie to bring me some clothes. Can you text her while I'm in the shower? Just tell her to bring me anything."

"Sure."

She slid off the bed and then limped into the bathroom.

He sent Lizzie a text, then got up and pulled the covers over the bed. He took a quick look in the mirror on the wall, realizing he looked as bad as Keira had. He didn't know if he had time to take a shower before their breakfast arrived, but he could at least change his clothes. As he finished putting on a pair of clean jeans and a T-shirt, his phone began to buzz. The GM's admin was texting him about his plans to join the team and if he needed help with his flights or transportation.

That answer was a little more difficult to answer now than it had been yesterday.

He couldn't leave Saturday. There was too much to say and do before then. Keira was homeless now. Her life was in shambles. He wanted to be there for her. He also wanted to figure out how they could take their love for each other and turn it into a relationship. Because the one thing he'd realized last night was that living without her wasn't an option.

He'd always been a man who shied away from commitment, especially to anything or anyone who might take him away from baseball. But he'd committed to her last night when he'd risked his arm and his life to save her. In doing so, he'd gotten a clarity he'd never had before.

He looked up as Keira came out of the bathroom in a white terry-cloth robe. Her hair was still damp, her cheeks pink from the moist heat of the shower, but her gaze was as bright as ever. She really was very good at bouncing back from adversity. "No longer a mess, but still beautiful," he said, walking over to give her a kiss.

"Thank you. It's your turn."

A knock came at the door. "I'll take a shower after breakfast. I'm starving."

He opened the door and Lizzie rolled in a small table, filled with covered dishes. She put it by the window and then threw her arms around Keira.

As the two women hugged for a long minute, he could see the love between them. Keira might be an only child, but her friends were as close as sisters.

"I am so glad you're all right," Lizzie said as they broke apart. "I brought you some clothes." She walked over to the table and pulled off the tote bag that was hanging from the handle. "This will get you through today, but you can come down and pick out whatever else you need for the next few days."

"That's so nice, Lizzie. Thanks. I have clothes at the shop I can wear, so I shouldn't need too much."

"I'm happy to share my closet with you. Now, tell me how you're feeling and what is going on with your foot?"

"A small fracture. It should heal quickly, and it doesn't hurt that much unless I put all my weight on it. The doctor gave me a walking boot. Hopefully, I won't have to wear it on Saturday. At the very least, I am hoping to skip it for the walk down the aisle and the photos. I may need it for the reception."

"No one cares about that, least of all, Hannah. We're just extremely thankful that you're..." Lizzie's mouth shook. "I don't even want to say it."

"Don't say it," Keira said. "Dante and I have made a pact to not think about what didn't happen, and we should make the same promise to each other."

"It will be difficult, but I'll try." Lizzie turned her gaze toward him, gratitude in her eyes. "Thank you for saving Keira. I still don't know all the details, but Adam said you saved her life."

"The firefighters were right behind me," he said.

"Don't listen to him," Keira said. "Dante did save me. He was amazing."

He cleared his throat and changed the subject. "So, what did you bring us for breakfast?"

"I got a little carried away," Lizzie said with a laugh.

"You?" Keira joked. "Shocker."

Lizzie smiled. "I know. I can't help myself. Anyway, I brought you a ton of food: a veggie omelet, lemon-ricotta pancakes, waffles with blueberries, fruit, and a hash-brown scramble. I know it's going to be a difficult day for you, Keira, having to see your house and figure out your next move, so I wanted to make sure you had a good breakfast. Also, whatever I can do to help, I'm available."

"I appreciate that," Keira said. "But you didn't need to bring so much food. There are only two of us, and I still have to fit into my bridesmaid's dress."

"Oh, you'll be fine." Lizzie dismissed Keira's comment with a wave of her hand. "I'll let you two eat. But I am only a phone call away, and I want to help, so put me to work."

"I will probably take you up on that, but I'm still trying to pull myself together," Keira answered. "Once I see the house again and talk to my mother, we'll come up with a plan."

"Okay. Enjoy."

As Lizzie left, they pulled two chairs up to the table and sat down. They shared everything, not bothering to fill their own plates, just digging in with their forks to eat whatever took their fancy. Everything really was different with Keira. It was so easy, so comfortable, and so right. They could talk or not talk. The silence was effortless as the conversation. They were connected in a way that he'd never felt before. *How had he ever thought he could just say goodbye and leave?* That idea seemed ludicrous now.

When they were finally finished, Keira sat back, putting a hand on her stomach. "I'm stuffed. That was delicious."

"Lizzie outdid herself. Your friends really care about you, Keira."

"I'm very lucky."

"And very loved." He was struck again by how much Keira had in this town, her mom, her friends, her businesses—her whole life. *How could he ask her to give any of it up?* "Being in love is the easy part, isn't it?" he muttered.

Her eyes widened at his words and a gleam of wariness entered her gaze. "Yes, I guess it is."

"I meant what I said last night, Keira. I am in love with you."

"But…" she queried.

"I don't want you to sacrifice anything for me."

"I don't want you to sacrifice anything for me," she returned.

"Where does that leave us?"

She gave a helpless shrug. "I'm not sure. There's so much to think about. I need to talk to my mom and see the house and catch my breath. I need time, Dante."

"I understand. A lot has happened in the last twenty-four hours."

"It has. And I think you were right. Being in love is the easy part."

He hated the note of despair in her voice. "But neither of us has ever picked the easy way, have we? We're fighters. We like challenges—the bigger, the better."

She gave him a faint smile. "These challenges are a little bigger than I like."

"The bigger the obstacle, the sweeter the victory."

"You don't accept less than what you want, do you?"

"Not without a fight." He paused. "I know you're emotionally spent, Keira. I don't need anything from you right now. Just let me be there for you. Let me support you."

"That sounds really nice. I just need a minute, Dante, to get myself together. Although, we may not have that many minutes before you leave—"

He cut her off with a shake of his head. "We're not going to worry about anything that isn't happening within the next few hours. I'm going to grab a quick shower and then we'll go see your house and meet up with your mom. That's all we need to think about at the moment."

As he got up, she said, "Dante?"

He looked back at her, seeing the spark of light in her eyes. "What?"

"I just want you to know that I can fight, too. And I want to fight."

Relief flooded through him. "Then we'll see where we end up. With the two of us fighting together, I don't see how we can lose."

* * *

Keira thought she was ready to fight, but when Dante pulled up in front of the smoking remains of the burned structure that had once been her home, she felt overwhelmed by the battles ahead of her. Her relationship, her home, her life—there was a lot to consider. But for this first step, she was very glad she was not doing this alone.

She got out of the car and stood on the sidewalk, her insides churning. She felt sick at the sight of the destruction, and a wave of anger ran through her. Dante put his arm around her shoulders.

"Breathe," he said quietly.

She forced herself to do just that, because it was the only thing that kept her from screaming in pain and sorrow. And she was afraid that after the screams would come the tears, and she needed to put off that cry because her mom and Mark were walking across the grass from the house next door. She had to be strong for her mother. And focusing on that was what kept her upright. That and the fact that Dante's solid presence gave her added strength.

She felt mixed emotions as she looked at Mark. It wasn't his fault, but she still wished he'd come clean about Mandy earlier.

Maybe they could have stopped things from getting this far. But they couldn't go back in time and blaming Mark wouldn't make things better. In fact, it would just make things more difficult for her mom.

"Keira," her mom said, her gaze running down her body and coming to rest on the boot on her foot. "How bad is it?"

"I told you last night it's a minor fracture."

"You always downplay your injuries. Dante? Is she telling me the truth?"

"She's not lying, but I think the pain is a little worse than she'll admit."

She frowned at him. "Whose side are you on?"

He smiled. "Yours. Always yours."

She turned back to her mother. "I'll be okay, Mom. What's going on around here?"

"I spoke to the fire marshal. His crew left about an hour ago," her mom replied. "He said we can go inside, but he warned me that it's not good and we won't be able to go up the stairs."

"Really? I was hoping the upstairs might have survived."

Her mom gave her a sad look. "I don't think it did, honey."

"Okay. Well, let's do this." She stepped away from Dante and slipped her arm through her mom's and they walked up to the house together, leaving Mark and Dante outside. They needed to do this on their own.

As soon as they entered, they came to an abrupt stop. She didn't know what she'd been expecting, but the reality of the devastation was worse than she'd imagined. The ceiling had fallen through in several places. The steps were completely impassable, and the smell of gas and smoke was still thick in the air.

As her gaze moved down the hall, she could see the spot where she'd been trapped. That could have been where she died. That realization sped up her heart. She'd never been so close to losing her life. But she wasn't going to share that with her mother.

"This is awful," her mom said, her voice shaky.

She turned to face her mom. "It is awful, but we can rebuild. It won't be the same house, but it will be a new one. And you'll get to decorate it just the way you want. We've been talking about a kitchen remodel for years. Now, we'll have a new kitchen—a new everything."

Her mom gave her a weak smile. "You have always been such an optimist, Keira. When things get really dark is when you get the sunniest."

"Like you said last night, we're still alive, and we have each other. That's what matters. There might be some things to salvage in the garage."

"That's our best hope."

"Do you want to check it now?"

"In a minute. Mark and I talked most of the night."

"I thought he was going back to the Sunset Lodge."

"I didn't let him. I didn't want him to be alone. And when we found out Mandy was in custody, it didn't make sense for him to go back to the motel. Erin and Peter were fine with him staying. Anyway, Mark is going to buy the house a couple of streets over. I'm thinking that I might stay there with him while this house is being rebuilt. You could stay there, too. It has three bedrooms. Or you could get an apartment if that's too awkward, but it's what I'd like to do."

She stared at her mom, seeing strength and confidence in the woman in front of her. "You really are okay now, aren't you?"

They both knew she wasn't talking about the fire.

"I've been trying to tell you that for a while," her mom said. "I don't want you to stay in Whisper Lake for me. I only want you to stay here if that's what you want. Is it, Keira?"

"I don't know. I have a lot here."

"But you don't have Dante."

"No. He can't stay, Mom. He's not like Justin or Zach. They could move their businesses here, but Dante's career doesn't happen in Whisper Lake."

Her mom gave her a compassionate look. "I understand. But yours could happen somewhere else. Has he asked you to go with him?"

"No. But he told me he loves me. He wants to find a way to make things work."

A smile lit up her mom's eyes. "I thought he might love you. How do you feel?"

"I love him, too. It's crazy. It's too fast, isn't it?"

"Not if it's right. Sometimes you just know."

"That's how I feel. I just know he's the one." She drew in a breath. "I'm thinking that it's time for me to make some changes, not just because I want to be with Dante, but because I've been drifting and spreading myself too thin for a long time. I thought I could do everything well, and it turns out I can't. I need to make some hard choices."

"Like what?"

"Put Brenda in charge of the realty business. Make Connie a full-time manager at the boutique. They're both more than capable. The money can continue to come in to help support your needs and mine. However, what no one else can do but me is the design work. It's what I love the most. I've been so stuck the last few years —not because of you."

"A little because of me," her mother said.

"Maybe a bit, but also just because I couldn't choose a lane. Now I feel like I can, like I have to."

"I feel that way, too. I've been restless the past year, Keira. I knew I needed more, but I didn't know more what, and I didn't know how to get it. Mark has reminded me of who I used to be, and I want to be that person again. I want to be independent and free and busy. I want to take care of people. I don't want them to take care of me." She paused. "Maybe we both needed this house to burn down in order to get unstuck."

She smiled at that thought. "It was a drastic event, but it does force some big decisions."

"I know you haven't asked for my advice, but I'm going to say one thing. Don't let Dante go, Keira. Not without trying to make it work. You owe it to yourself to find out if it can."

"I think you're right."

"So, what are you going to do?"

"I'll let you know after I talk to Dante."

"All right. I can live with that." Her mom opened her arms. "Give me a hug."

She hugged her mom for a long minute, so many emotions of love and gratitude filling them both up. And then, a little teary-eyed, they left the house that was no longer their home. But there were brighter skies ahead, good changes, new people. It was an end, but also a beginning.

After they left the house, she asked Dante to drive down to the lake. She directed him to a quiet cove that was one of her favorite places. They parked on the side of the road and then walked down to the beach. Thankfully, it wasn't far, and with her walking boot, she was able to maneuver without too much pain.

There were only a few people about—a man walking his dog and a woman and two little children digging in the sand by the shoreline. Otherwise, they were alone.

She led Dante over to an outcropping of flat rocks where they sat down and looked at the water. "It's so peaceful here," she said, breathing in the clean lake air, relieved to be away from the smell of the fire. "Whenever I get worked up, I come here. It always relaxes me."

"I'm glad. You haven't said much since we left the house. Was it difficult to go inside?"

"Yes, but it made it easier to leave. There wasn't anything there to salvage except the few boxes in the garage that might have escaped."

"I'm sorry."

"Me, too. But my mom and I had a good conversation."

"You were gone a while," he murmured. "What's she thinking?"

"She has it all figured out. Mark is going to buy the home I showed him a few days ago. It's about three blocks away from our house. My mom will move in with him while she rebuilds. I don't know that she'll ever move back in, or maybe they both will. It seems like they might have something special."

"He does seem like he really cares about her, Keira."

"I know. It's going to take me time to forgive him for not being honest earlier, but I think I'll get there. If he treats her well, then I'll be happy for them."

"That's fair. What about you? Will you move back in when it's rebuilt?"

"No. I don't think I'll ever live there again." She gazed into his beautiful blue eyes. "I'm okay with that."

Surprise and wariness moved through his gaze. "It's early to make that final of a decision."

"I don't think so. I got a lot of clarity when I walked into the destruction. With everyone gone, it was easy to say goodbye to the past."

"Where do you think you'll live?"

"Well, I have some ideas I wanted to run by you."

"I'm listening."

"I need to back up a little. On Tuesday, before all the craziness happened, a woman came into my shop. She's the stylist for the actress Jessica Stillman. Jessica, apparently, fell in love with Chelsea's gown, and she has a couple of events she might want to hire me for. Her stylist asked me to go to LA next week to meet with her. It could be a really lucrative contract."

"That's great. Seriously great. You said yes, didn't you?"

"I told her I'd call her."

"Why would you hesitate?"

"Because I've gotten used to hesitating," she admitted. "To saying no to things that might disrupt my life and my mom's life. But now I can see that I've been using my mom as an excuse. I can't keep doing that. She's better, and I'm happy about that. I just have to accept it and look forward. So, I think I'll go to LA."

"You should definitely do that. Maybe Los Angeles is where your future is."

"I don't want to live in LA. I don't think I need to. I might have to make some trips there, but I can design from anywhere." She licked her suddenly dry lips. "Even from Miami."

His gaze lit up. "You'd come to Miami with me?"

"If you want me to."

"Of course I want you to go with me, Keira. But I don't want you to sacrifice anything for me."

"I don't want to do that, either. I want to be a little selfish, Dante."

"You deserve to be selfish. You've been taking care of your mom for years. It's your time, Keira. Look, I've been thinking, too. I'm up for a new contract at the end of this season. If we need to be somewhere that's better for you—LA, New York, anywhere—I can make a move to a team in a location that works for both of us."

She was surprised by his words. "Really? You'd do that?"

"In a second. Since I got injured, I've been terrified that I'd have to figure out a life without baseball, and I couldn't see one. Baseball became my happy place after my mom died, and I didn't think that happy place could be anywhere else, but I was wrong. Last night, when I held you in my arms while you slept, I felt happier than I've ever felt before. I can live anywhere, and I can do anything, as long as you're with me."

Her eyes teared up at his words. "That's the nicest thing anyone has ever said to me."

"I mean every word, Keira."

"Being with you, Dante, has also given me some of my happiest moments. I think you're my happy place, too."

"Then let's keep the happy train going." He gently swept a tear off her cheek. "I found something real with you, Keira. I can't let you go."

"I'm not going to let you go, either. I've never been to Miami, but it sounds like a fun city. I bet you have a fancy apartment."

He gave her a grin. "I do. I also have a boat."

"Seriously? You never mentioned that, not even when we were on Adam's boat, although you did seem very comfortable on it."

"It didn't come up."

"Because you didn't bring it up. You didn't want to brag. I've always thought you were down-to-earth for being a superstar."

"Speaking of celebrity, I can't promise that photographers won't be following us around at times or that there won't be more made-up stories about us."

"I don't care about that. The world can think what they want. As long as you and I are honest with each other, I'm good."

He shook his head in bemusement. "I'm so used to being around people who care very much what the world thinks. You're one of a kind."

"So are you."

"This is going to be good, Keira. You and me. I want a forever deal, by the way, nothing short-term. I don't commit to much, but when I do, I give it everything I have."

"So do I. And I want to give you everything that I have." Her heart ached with love. "Can we start on forever now?"

"Absolutely." He wrapped his arms around her, and she opened her mouth to his hot, sexy kiss.

EPILOGUE

THE DRESSING ROOM at the church was filled with beautiful women, but the prettiest one of all was the red-haired bride with the pale skin and the smattering of freckles on her face and shoulders. Keira smiled at Hannah as they gazed at each other in the mirror. Hannah's off-the-shoulder dress clung to her bust and fell in a soft drape of silk and lace to the ground.

"We look amazing," Hannah said.

"I agree." Her bridesmaid's dress was a bold blue that was short and sexy and could definitely be worn again, as long as she made sure none of the four other bridesmaids were wearing the same dress at the same time.

"Let's get a photo with everyone," Hannah said, holding up the phone in her hand. "A selfie. Everyone squeeze in."

"Isn't there a photographer around here somewhere?" Gianna asked.

"I want one that's just us, as we are," Hannah replied as the other women crowded around, and she took the group photo. Then she turned around to face them. "You are all my best friends and having you here with me today makes it so much more special. I was never sure I'd actually get married, but here I am, marrying a guy I spent a lot of time hating."

"Sometimes you can't get out of your own way," she teased.

"Look who's talking," Hannah said pointedly.

"True, but I'm working on that." She cleared her throat as her gaze swept the group. "I told Hannah this last night, and she insisted I tell you all today, so since we have a few minutes, I'm just going to say it now. I'm in love with Dante."

"Oh, we all knew that." Lizzie rolled her eyes.

"Okay, maybe you did. But you probably don't know that I'm leaving Whisper Lake." She held up a hand at the sight of their distressed expressions. "Don't say anything yet. Let me finish. This is good news. I'm moving to Miami with Dante, but it's not just for love. The move is also going to mark the launch of my design business. I'm turning over my interests here to my managers, and I'm going to give my design dream one more shot."

"That's great," Gianna said.

"I think it will be great. And I may not be starting from zero. I got a call from Jessica Stillman's stylist, and I'm going to meet with Jessica next week. She loved your dress, Chelsea, and she has three events she may want me to dress her for."

Chelsea clapped her hands. "Yay. I'm so happy. And she would be lucky to get you."

"It's not a done deal. She still has to like what I design, but if she does, it could be very lucrative."

"Wow," Chloe said. "That is a huge change. I'm going to miss you, Keira."

"I'm going to miss all of you." She blinked back a tear. "And I cannot start crying yet."

"None of us can," Gianna said with a sniff. "I'm really happy for you, Keira, even if my face is saying something different."

"I'll be back to visit. My mom is here."

"And you're sure about this move?" Chloe asked. "You haven't known Dante very long to move across the country for him."

"I'm not doing it for him; I'm doing it for me. I've met someone I'm crazy about, and I don't want to let geography get in the way. Dante said his contract is up at the end of this year. He'll try to move close to wherever I need to be."

"That's amazing," Lizzie said. "Can he do that?"

"He says he can. We'll see how things go." She paused. "You've all been telling me for a while now that I'm spreading myself too thin, and you were all right. I couldn't seem to pick a lane, make a decision, but meeting Dante and having my home burn to the ground really kicked me out of my rut."

Hannah gave her a dry smile as she shook her head. "Not the way any of us wanted it to go."

"It's how it went. I'm really happy, which seems bizarre considering how much I just lost. But I'm in love, and I'm going after my dream again. It turns out that's all I need. Being in Miami, with no other distractions, will also help me give the design business the focus it needs."

"I think Dante will be a big distraction," Hannah said with a laugh. "But, yeah, maybe in between all the hot sex, you can design some kick-ass dresses."

She laughed. "I will find the time."

"We should do a girl's trip to Miami," Lizzie said. "Just because we're all getting married, having babies, and making big changes doesn't mean we have to lose each other."

"I'm in," Hannah said. "And I'm happy for you, Keira. Remember when the four of us used to play our imaginary games in your backyard?"

"Yes. You were the nurse or the doctor."

"I was the mom or the cook," Chloe said.

"I was the artist," Gianna put in. "And you were always making clothes and playing fashion show, Keira. We're all doing what we were meant to do."

"Really?" Lizzie asked, surprise in her gaze. "You all knew what you were going to do when you were kids?"

"We did," she said. "It just took me longer to get back to that dream."

"Because you took care of your mom," Gianna said. "And look at your mother now. She has a boyfriend. She's healthy. You got her back to that point."

"She got herself back, too." She blinked back more tears. "I'm going to miss you all so much. I would love to have you visit any time. Dante showed me photos of his apartment, and it's spectacular. He also has a boat. I had no idea he had so much money."

Lizzie laughed. "He's a professional baseball player. What did you think?"

"I guess I just didn't think about it."

"Probably why he likes you so much," Chelsea said dryly. "You saw the real him. Trust me, as a celebrity, that isn't always easy to find."

"I know. I'm lucky. But I don't care about his money or celebrity. Dante gets me. He pushes me in the ways I need to be pushed, and he believes in me. And we laugh a lot. Now I'm going to stop talking." She opened her arms. "Group hug."

She opened her arms up and they ran into each other's arms. She loved these women with all her heart, but she loved Dante even more.

When they broke apart, she said, "I'm going to find my plus one."

Hannah laughed. "I'm taking credit for getting you two together. That first date was only because of me."

"All right, I'll give you the credit," she said with a grin. "I'll be back in a few minutes."

"I'm going to check on Leo," Chloe said. "It will just take a second."

"Don't worry. I'm not going down the aisle without both of you," Hannah said.

"I'm really happy for you," Chloe said, as they walked down the back hall of the church.

She gave Chloe a sharp look, hearing sadness in her voice. Then she stopped walking. "We'll still see each other. I'll be back."

"I know. Don't mind me. Weddings are just hard…" Chloe cleared her throat. "I always think about Kevin, how I thought we'd be together forever, but now we're divorced, and I'm raising a kid by myself. I never saw that in my future. Not that I don't love being a mom, because I do."

"You just didn't want to be a single parent."

"I did not."

"I'm sorry." She hesitated. "Are you going to be sitting with Adam at the reception?"

Chloe shook her head and gave her a pointed look. "No. And you all need to stop trying to put us together. We're just friends."

"It seems like it has been more than that."

"No. It hasn't. Adam is a great guy. He has been very supportive, but we're not in love. There will be someone else for him."

"And someone else for you."

"Maybe. We'll see. I'm not in a hurry. I have my hands full with one very demanding male, so I'm going to focus on Leo. I better find him now. He's sitting with Gianna's mom, but I want to make sure he's not too much for her." Chloe paused. "I'm glad you found Dante, Keira. I have a good feeling about you two."

"So do I. I never thought I'd find the right guy by sitting down at the wrong table, but I did."

Chloe laughed. "I might have to try that sometime. Come on. We don't have much time."

Dante got to the church parking lot about fifteen minutes before Hannah was due to walk down the aisle. As he got out of the car, he grabbed his suit coat from the backseat and shrugged it on. There was a crowd of people still streaming into the church, but it was one beautiful brunette slowly hobbling her way down the steps who caught his eye. She'd gone without her walking boot so as not to ruin Hannah's photos, another unselfish gesture that was pure Keira.

He hurried across the lot. When he reached her, he threw his arms around her, because even though he'd seen her two hours earlier, it felt much longer than that.

She gave him a bright smile as she lingered in his embrace. "You look very handsome."

"And you look spectacular. I like your dress." His gaze moved down the clingy dress, appreciating the way it clung to her body. "I can't wait to take it off you."

She gave him a playful punch on the arm. "That will be hours from now. Anyway, wait until you see Hannah's wedding gown. It's the show-stopper."

"I'm looking forward to that."

"I'm so glad you were able to stay for the wedding. This will be our last chance to hang out together with all my friends for a long time."

"We'll keep in touch with them, Keira, I promise." He knew it would be difficult for her to give up so much of her life, and he intended to make it as easy as he could.

"I know we will. I'm actually more worried about missing you at the moment. It's going to be hard not to see you for two weeks."

"It will feel like forever," he agreed. Keira would head to Los Angeles on Monday and then return to Whisper Lake to organize her life and get her managers up to speed. After that, she would fly down to Miami. He couldn't wait for them to be together in Miami, but he was also excited to see her take her first steps toward a full-time design career. "The time will go fast, and you'll be busy in LA with Jessica Stillman."

"I am eager to hear what Jessica wants. It will be fun to work with someone new. Hopefully, she'll like my design drafts and will want to sign a contract."

"I'm sure she'll love you. How could she not?"

"You're prejudiced."

"I might be," he admitted. "But I know how talented you are. Jessica would be lucky to have someone as dedicated as you are to creating the perfect dress."

"Thanks for the vote of confidence. By the way, my mom and Mark are saving you a seat. They're in a great mood, because Mark just officially bought the house around the corner."

"That's exciting." He'd heard there was an offer but not that it had been accepted.

"It is. They're both thrilled. My mom gets to stay in the neighborhood, and she'll be close enough to walk over and watch the rebuild. Until that house is out of escrow, they'll live in the cabin that my friend owns."

"Our cabin?"

"Well, not technically ours," she said with a laugh. "Although, we did make some memories there."

"Some smoking hot memories. When is the cabin going up for sale?"

"About a month. There are still a few things to be done, but my mom can oversee those as well. She's actually excited to have more work to do. I'm excited to have less."

"The perfect trade-off. Maybe I should buy the cabin."

Surprise filled her beautiful brown eyes. "Why would you want to do that?"

"Because I love it. Because it always felt like ours, and we'll need a place to stay when we come back to visit, which will be often."

"There's still my house. I'm not sure what we'll do with that once it's rebuilt."

"True. We can think about it."

"I like that you want to buy a place here, though."

He pulled her closer to him. "I want you to be happy, Keira. I know you're making sacrifices for me."

"I'm really not, Dante. We need to be together, and I'm more flexible than you."

"For now," he agreed. "But the future can be anything we make it."

"As long as the future is us together, I'm good."

At her words, he thought he might just be the luckiest guy in the world. "Me, too."

"It's funny that we met because Hannah insisted that I needed a plus one for the wedding. That's the only reason I went on that date. I sat down at the wrong table, but I met the right guy. And now you're here—my plus one. How different would our lives be if we never met?"

"I don't even want to think about it. I love you, Keira."

"I love you, too. Now, I better go get Hannah married."

"I'll be waiting for you when you're done. I'll always be waiting." She gazed into his eyes with so much love, his heart ached. The loneliness he'd grown up in and lived with for most of his life was gone now. Keira was filling all the empty spaces. "My mom would have loved you," he murmured. "I wish you could have met each other."

"Me, too. I want to keep hearing about her. I want to keep hearing about everything."

"That's good. Because when you're around, I can't seem to shut up."

She gave him a loving kiss filled with the promise of happily ever after. Then she took his hand, and they walked up the steps and into the church.

One day, there would be another wedding, and Keira would be in a white gown, and he'd be standing in the front waiting for her. He'd never thought he would make a good husband or a family man but meeting her had changed that. Now, it was all he really wanted. And he didn't intend to strike out.

# # #

ABOUT THE AUTHOR

Barbara Freethy is a #1 New York Times Bestselling Author of 70 novels ranging from contemporary romance to romantic suspense and women's fiction. With over 13 million copies sold, twenty-five of Barbara's books have appeared on the New York Times and USA Today Bestseller Lists, including SUMMER SECRETS which hit #1 on the New York Times!

Known for her emotional and compelling stories of love, family, mystery and romance, Barbara enjoys writing about ordinary people caught up in extraordinary adventures. Library Journal says, "Freethy has a gift for creating unforgettable characters."

For additional information, please visit Barbara's website at www.barbarafreethy.com.

Made in the USA
Middletown, DE
21 July 2021